MERMAID
IN
CHELSEA
CREEK

www.mcsweeneys.net

The McSweeney's McMullens will publish great new books—and new editions
of out-of-print classics—for individuals and families of all kinds.

McSweeney's is a privately held company with wildly fluctuating resources.
McSweeney's McMullens and colophon are copyright © 2012 McSweeney's & McMullens.

Printed in China by Shanghai Offset.

ISBN: 978-1-938073-36-6

First printing 2013

MERMAID
IN
CHELSEA
CREEK

Michelle Tea

S

For Dashiell

Chelsea was a city where people landed. People from other countries, people running from wars and poverty, stealing away on boats that cut through the ocean into a whole new world, or on planes, relief shaking their bodies as they rattled into the sky. People had been coming to Chelsea since before Sophie Swankowski was born, since before her mother was born. Sophie's family came from a tiny village in Poland that nobody had ever heard of and that nobody knows of still. When they came to Chelsea, a city with trolley cars and brick houses and grand trees, they brought with them smoked sausages and doughy pierogi stuffed with soft cheese, flowered scarves for the women's heads and necklaces made from cloth and marbles. They brought with them strong magic, the magic special to their Polish village, just as all the other immigrants brought with them the magic of their abandoned lands—Russian magic and French magic, Irish magic and Puerto Rican magic, Dominican magic and Cambodian magic, Vietnamese magic, Bosnian magic, Cuban magic, up and up through the years, always a new people spilling into the small city, always with a new magic. The fading magic was carried in the bones of the grandmothers and the great-great-aunts, the

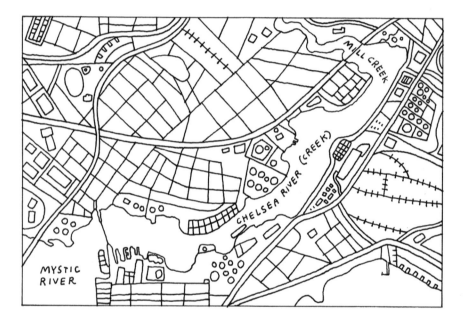

old, strange women with the funny smells that scared the children born new into Chelsea, women who ate foods that worried those children, unusual foods they didn't sell at the supermarket, where they sold *everything*, all of it lined up in bright boxes. The old women ate food that made their breath smell like a long-ago time, and the children were afraid of what was back there, as they scuttled out from the smothering hugs, out to the brick and cement, the telephone poles and electrical wires, the roaring buses and the graffitied everything, busted playgrounds, a city with so much wear and tear on it, so many people with so little money coming to it for so long, the threadbare buildings and dollar stores, the railroad tracks where men slept in the tall grass, the sub shops and pizza places and the corner stores selling scratchers and cigarettes, the corner bars with no windows and men inside heaped and immobile as the cracked stools they sat upon. The children ran out into the streets and the old women thought quietly about how a place could have no magic, how their grandchildren would grow up magicless and never even know it. And the old women would shed a tear and lament the old countries they'd abandoned, longing for a land where the magic came up into their bones just from standing on its earth.

. . .

ALL OF THE magics were different, but then all of them were exactly the same. And the stories brought from the many places were all different, but then, they were all the same. And the oldest story, the silliest and most dangerous story, the saddest and most hopeful story, was the story of the girl who would bring the magic, the girl who would come to save them all.

"Save us from what?" snapped the adult children, impatient with these old women and the hocus-pocus they'd never been able to shake, even with their electricity and televisions, their blenders and flushing toilets and the million plastic gadgets they could never have imagined in their village. And the old women told them about how a girl would come and she would be a magic girl, she would twist the world we think we know and knot it into a bow, she would stop time and peer into your heart, she would take on your troubles—and yours, and yours—and they would pass through her and into the earth. The old women told them about how the girl would eat salt to stay pure and unharmed, to keep her magic sharp and crystal, and about how you would know the girl as a baby who craved salt, who ate it like sugar, enough to poison a normal child to death.

The magicless adults who had been born into this new land, into Chelsea, felt sad for the old women, who had sacrificed so much to come to this new land and seemed so disappointed in it that all they could do was make up fairy tales to comfort themselves. And the old women began to die away as old women do, their aged and magic bones buried in new earth, and no one remained to tell their stories but their stories somehow remained, a low whisper that blew off the dirty harbor, that echoed with your footsteps as you passed quickly beneath an overpass, that drifted like an aroma from a kitchen window, something familiar but strange, gone before you could grasp it. They were present at slumber parties, when girls gathered like witches at midnight, the room dark and vibrating with giddy excitement and mysterious thrill, when ghosts were talked of and pranks were played, the stories crackled in the air like static electricity, passing between the girls like sparks from fingertips: a story of a girl who could let all the sadness of the world pass right through her, and everyone would be happier for it, depressions would lift and cruelties would fade and broken people would be healed by this girl who ate salt—just stupid salt, the stuff on the kitchen table. But the old women had known that salt was a crystal, made by the earth itself, full of deep magic. Salt made everything pure, and the girl who would come and swallow the world's troubles, bringing back a golden time, would eat great piles of salt, common table salt and magical salt from the bottom of the ocean, salt pulled from the waters of the sea and salt dug out from mines and caves.

And all across the city, that city and so many cities just like it, all around the earth, there was a sense of waiting, of biding time—though if you asked them, anyone, what they thought they were waiting for, nobody would know what you were talking about.

Chapter 1

A mermaid in the creek. Through the haze of grease that formed a scum on the water, iridescent where the sun skimmed the surface, Sophie saw its body—unreal, but unmistakable. Breasts naked under the muck, hair swirling wet and weighty around her—and, yes, a tail, scaled like a fish. The mermaid had pale, stringy bits dangling from that great, muscular tail, and as she kicked beneath the waters Sophie could see the scales shift and the scabby tendrils drifting like the fringe of a jellyfish. The mermaid was graceful in her design but ragged in her condition, and as she tumbled below the waters, arcing above a shopping cart that had been left for decades to rust, her eyes searched the land above and her gaze met Sophie's with a force that filled the girl with powerful anger and sadness. The shock woke her from her vision with a terrible jolt. All in all, Sophie had been passed out for forty-five seconds, but the dream state had the illusion of lasting much longer.

Coming to on the stiff, dirty weeds that lined the bank of the creek, Sophie could feel her body humming. It buzzed with the gentle buzz that accompanied the pass-out game, but the pleasantness of it was sickened a bit by the bolt of dark feelings that had cut her phantasm off so abruptly. She felt it roiling in her guts like that time she'd eaten a bad slice of pizza downtown, how it had made her sweat and retch as if the pizza had become a wild beast, fighting its way back out of her. Suddenly, Sophie craved salt. In the dry cave of her mouth, down her throat, which felt strange and thick, into her tumbling tummy, she craved a bag of pretzels, the rocky salt collected at the bottom, tipped straight back into her mouth— the reward, she thought, for polishing off the snack. She longed for the greasy Tupperware salt shaker in its place on the stove, dumped onto her tongue, a wet pile she could suck on like a candy, slowly dissolving. Without thought, just animal instinct, Sophie rolled onto her side, her nose angling toward a dense tang in the air, the oceany salt of the dirty creek. Faster than her best friend could cry out in disgust, Sophie tugged her still-shimmering body to the edge of the water and plunged her face into it, mouth open, inhaling the dirty creek into her, the perfect, necessary salt of it obliterating the darker flavors of things she'd rather not think about. The sharpest taste, salt; she felt it travel through her like a delicious knife, the shock of it cutting through her, making her want *more more more*. She sucked at the creek hungrily, like a wild animal digging into its kill; beneath her, along the sandy, littered floor, something tumbled forward, dark and fluid.

Behind her, Ella screamed, startling a flock of pigeons into the sky.

Sophie felt a hand grip her long and tangled hair, jerking her out from the muck. Something hot grazed her cheek, singeing it: Ella's cigarette. Sophie swatted at the burn with her creek-wet hands, unconsciously slurping at the water that sluiced from her soaked bangs into her salt-thirsty mouth. *More.*

"Ow!" she snapped, her face a chaos of wet, slurping and swatting and swearing. "You burned me with your cigarette!"

Ella looked briefly at the smoldering butt between her fingers, and threw it into the creek with a hot fizz. "That," she said, "is probably the *least* gross thing that has ever been thrown in that creek. Do you know what's in there? Piss! Puke! Like, rusting, germy bacteria—there are probably whole new *diseases* in there that you just drank. There are *dead animals* in there. People drown *cats* in there. Dogs come here to *die*. My uncle gets paid to dump shit in here your grandmother won't allow at the dump. That's *toxic waste*. Are you trying to *die*?" Unable to adequately express her rage, Ella kicked her sneaker into the earth, sending an empty soda can pinging off Sophie's knee. Sophie stared at her friend.

"*Seriously*. What. The fuck. Was that."

Sophie thought about it. As she thought, a taste arranged itself on her tongue. The luscious bite of the brine gone, she tasted—well, tastes she'd never tasted before, and probably wasn't supposed to taste in the first place. Like sucking on the spoke of a rusty wheel, or the gelatinous plastic of a bag of drowned kittens. Grit crunched beneath her teeth, releasing a chemical that made her gums back away from her teeth.

She spit away a shard of glass that had cut into the roof of her mouth, startling at the phlegmy blood that spattered on the dead grass. Ella shrieked and lit a brand new cigarette. For the first time ever, Sophie wished that she smoked. Even that burnt stink would be better than this. She thought of the times her mother had waved a hand across her face, saying *Brush your teeth, it smells like something died in your mouth*— well, now something had, a whole bunch of terrible something.

"Was that a cry for help? Are you, like, suicidal or fake-suicidal or however that works and you want me to, like, notice and tell your mother?" Ella released a balloon of pungent smoke into the air and Sophie tried not to gasp after it, desperate. The tingle had totally left her body, the sweet feelings of the pass-out game were gone. She was gross with creek water and horrified at what she'd done.

"I... I don't know," Sophie stuttered. Ella pulled a wide cloth headband from her brow. Her hair, sleek and black as a clean creek at midnight, spilled across her face, stray tendrils sticking to the strawberry gloss on her lips. She threw the headband at Sophie.

"Wipe yourself off," Ella ordered. "Then throw it in the creek. I don't ever want to *think* about that headband again." She shuddered and took a long pull from her cigarette.

"Really," Sophie said, bunching her unkempt bangs in the cloth and wringing out the water. "I just, I was having this dream, and it was a, a mermaid, and then I needed to drink the water, I—it's so crazy, I don't know why I did that!" Overwhelmed, Sophie weakly flung the headband toward the water and watched it flutter soggily to the stiff, dead grass, landing beside the jelly blob of a used condom. Both girls averted their eyes.

"Well, I've never heard of that," Ella said resentfully. "I've never heard of passing out and then getting, like, *possessed*."

"I know, me neither," Sophie agreed.

Sophie couldn't count how many times she'd played the pass-out game with Ella, her best and only friend. They played it in their houses when no one was home—rarely at Ella's, with her impossibly large and ever-expanding family. They played it in the public bathrooms that no one ever used at the back of the mall, locked in the handi-capped stall. They played it behind the dumpsters in the mall parking lot, they played it on the railroad tracks, each girl taking a turn, the one spotting the other, watching her tip her head over, Ella's long, perfect hair sweeping forward like a silk curtain; Sophie's scrunched in snarls like underbrush tangled with briars and thistle. The huffing and the puffing, the head coming back, hands squeezing the sides of the throat, breath held deep in the lungs, and then... up, up and away. How their bodies would tenderly collapse, one girl catching the other, the enchanted one drifting away into a dream like a backward fairy ring, into a place where time stalled and chugged and stalled again, so that when she came to, her body ringing with tingles, it felt as though a year had passed instead of scarcely a minute.

Sophie and Ella used to do all kinds of things. Sophie, a storyteller, would create a strange and wonderful tale and Ella would draw pictures with markers and together they would make a book. At the Salvation

Army in the city square they would hunt through the dingy toy bin in search of naked and unloved Barbies, talking the clerk down from a dollar to fifty cents, and bring the doll home, where they would scrub her and untangle her synthetic locks and restore her to her proper Barbie beauty. They would play board games and watch the rerun television shows of other eras—*The Brady Bunch*, *I Love Lucy*—long into the night. But lately Ella had deemed most all activities either gay or retarded, choosing instead to practice smoking in a stylish manner and playing pass-out. Sophie could feel a new energy around her friend, as if a part of her that had been shut off was plugged in and humming, emitting a forcefield. She seemed tougher, colder, both more in your face and farther away. She seemed, Sophie realized as she watched her friend watch her through the haze of smoke that hung, clotted in the humid air, like she just didn't like her anymore. She tried to see herself through her friend's eyes. Her grubby clothes, her bleeding mouth, the hair she couldn't be bothered to brush. Where Ella wore smudges of color on her face, Sophie wore dirt. Shame rose in her like mercury up a thermometer, and she shook the thought away. What did *she* think of Ella? Ella, whose mean streak once was such a guilty pleasure, the witty way she eviscerated dumb boys and dumber teachers, mimicking her fussy aunts, lacerating

any man on the street foolish enough to make a kissy-kissy noise at her—the streak had widened, become a harsh swath, and it was aiming itself right at Sophie. Sophie felt something twitch inside her, as if she could flex a magic muscle and find herself inside her friend's thoughts, inside her heart. She felt close to Ella in a way that felt wrong, and dangerous. *Crazy.*

Ella flinched. "Stop *looking* at me like that! You are getting more and more loco, Sophie. It's getting weird, okay? You got to get it together, 'cause I can't handle crazy shit like this." She shook her head firmly, tucking her hair behind her ears.

"It cuts off oxygen to your brain, passing yourself out," Sophie said quickly, deflecting the blame from her, her increasing strangeness, her inability to *get it together*, and onto the game. "It messes with the chemicals in your blood, it's like we're giving ourselves seizures."

"No it's *not*," Ella said. "Nerd. Where did you hear that?"

"The internet."

"Nerd. Were you googling 'passing out'?"

"Yeah, basically. I mean, why do you think everything happens? It's 'cause we're messing with ourselves. You know there's a girl who passed out and never came back? She's in a coma."

"Liar," Ella quipped, lighting a new cigarette off the butt of the old.

"You're chain-smoking."

"So. You just drank *the creek*. If we are in a cancer race I'd say you just *leaped* ahead, *biiiiitch*." Ella had a way of saying *biiiiitch* that made Sophie crack up. And Sophie had a way of cracking up that made Ella crack up. The pair had spent so much time goading one another into hysterics, much to the annoyance of the world around them, which hardly ever thought they were funny. The burst of laughter that erupted out of them was such a relief to Sophie that she reached out to grab her friend by her newly shaved leg. Like a hammer had tapped the dip in her knee, Ella kicked out defensively, sending a spray of dirt over Sophie, to stick muddily to the wetness of her t-shirt.

"Don't *touch* me, okay?" Ella snapped, backing away. "You *know*, Sophie, don't you touch me, I don't know what you got now." Ella rubbed her legs together like twin sticks seeking fire, trying to chafe away whatever contaminant she imagined Sophie had left on her.

Sophie's laughter stopped short, and she drew her hands back, stuffed them beneath her, her butt in terry-cloth shorts pressing her palms to the dirt. There were things about having a body that were extra hard on her friend. Sophie didn't get why it had to be that way, but that's how it was. It was like the world was filled with microscopic particles of filth and grime that no one but Ella could see. To Ella, bacteria, the seeds of catastrophe, the seeds of disease, lurked on toilet seats, on forks and spoons, in the air that breezed across her body. She had made a certain peace about living in a world filled with contaminants, and considered it an accomplishment that she was able to brave such filthy places as the creek bed and the mall bathroom, though if not for the blissed-out promise of the pass-out game, she'd never be able to stand it. Ella imagined her skin like a length of sponge, thirsty to soak things into her. She took lots of baths and lots of showers, and was very particular about the food she ate. Sometimes she would just get it in her head that a piece of vegetable was contaminated, or start tripping out about what the animal on her plate might have eaten in life—had it eaten poison? Bugs? Had it eaten the poop of other animals? By eating it, wouldn't Ella be eating poison and bugs and the poop of other animals? She would push her plate away, refusing to eat. No one could convince her otherwise.

Sophie wondered if something was wrong with *her* for not paying more attention to all the germs and bacteria out there, but she really couldn't get herself to care about that. The world seemed fine, and evil bacteria, though she knew it existed, just wasn't comprehendible. Doctors had cures for most everything, anyway. What she didn't understand was how Ella could smoke cigarettes, but to Ella cigarettes were different. Having grown up in a house of smokers, cigarettes were the atmosphere. Though they created their own problems, they were in a different category from bacteria, germs, and filth. But most importantly, smoking made the wild tangle of fear inside her smoother. She didn't know how it worked, but it did. And it made her feel fearless to do it—tough, invincible, immortal. A nice way to feel when you're a girl convinced in her heart that she is bound to encounter an invisible pearl of E. coli, a splash of Ebola, a flea full of plague. Leaning against the back of a warehouse by the train tracks, a pilfered cigarette in her hand, Ella could relax into the notion that at the very least she *looked* hard, together, really *Chelsea*. Even if on the inside she was all bunched up with fear.

"I'm going home," Ella said, frantic, crouching low to examine her leg as if Sophie's gentle touch had left a bruise, drawn blood. "You don't even know what I am going to have to do to deal with this. You have no freaking idea." Ella's voice rang out angrily. "And snap out of it! You're bugging me out. It's like you're more brain damaged than ever."

The insult stung Sophie, as it was intended to. Had her friend suggested she was newly brain damaged? Well, after sipping from the toxic creek, how could she be blamed? But *more than ever*? Had Ella *always* thought Sophie was brain damaged? She thought about the cruel way Ella could speak of others—fucking *retarded*—and imagined the words meant for her, felt tears spring to her eyes and plop down her face. She sucked the droplets into her mouth, grateful for the comfort of a salt that was safe, clean, her very own.

. . .

ELLA RAGED TOWARD the torn chain-link fence that did a poor job keeping the kids who lived in the nearby housing projects away from the water. The ripped-away metal was eaten through with rust; no one paid attention to this part of the city. It was possible no one paid attention to the city at all. It was that kind of place—far from the New England of sailboats and lobsters, checkered tablecloths on picnic tables, lighthouses, wooden toboggans to sled down a hill in winter, frozen, snow-dusted ponds for ice-skating. Chelsea was none of that. It was flocks of dirty pigeons and dented old cars; fish sticks with freezer burn and fast-food drive-throughs; scuffed, neglected parks, trash-strewn train tracks and a putrid creek. It made sense that Sophie and Ella enjoyed the pass-out game as much as they did; the world of the dream state was so much nicer, prettier, and more magical than the city they spent their days in.

"You're being a jerk!" Sophie shouted weakly at Ella's back as she ducked gingerly through the fence, shrinking away from the gangrenous prongs of rusted metal, and was gone. When she got home, Ella would lock herself in the bathroom and scrub both legs with hot water, using every single cleansing product in the room. Shampoo, face wash, soaps, foot scrub. From underneath the bathroom sink she'd lift a bottle of tile cleaner, hands shaking and a pit in her stomach, absolutely compelled to use it in spite of knowing it was awful stuff, too much for her skin, too crazy to need it so badly. The grainy powder wore at her skin, creating a sickly pink froth. When she was done each leg would gape a raw, red wound in its center, slick and painful to observe, both radiating a patchy redness like a terrible sun. Her mother, looming nervously outside the bathroom the whole time, would try to catch Ella when she opened the door, but Ella would shake her mother off and bolt to her bedroom, to lie in her bed and cry, her sputtering fan aimed at her calves, which stung and emanated heat. Ella would know she'd made herself look ugly and wounded and she would be too full of secrecy and shame to wear shorts for a week. She'd weep with embarrassment; weep at a week of summer beachtime spent in a pair of jeans that would bring sweat down the back of her legs, stinging into her abraded skin. She'd weep with confusion, knowing that what she had done made no sense. But most of all she'd know in her heart that the scrubbing had made no difference, that the poison of the creek was still all over her, and at that, she'd weep and weep and weep.

Chapter 2

Sophie pulled a key from a length of rawhide she wore around her neck, tucked into her t-shirt, and let herself into her home. She was surprised to find her mother in the kitchen, the light blue smock Andrea wore to her job at the clinic stuck to her body in the heat. Damp patches spread out from her arms, her fair neck was reddened from the walk home in the sun, and her hair was disheveled upon her head, bits of blondish-brownish-reddish hair bursting in a humid frizz of curls. Andrea held in her hand a chipped dish of iceberg lettuce, a hastily chopped tomato, and a pool of glistening dressing. She shoveled the food into her mouth in rushed, hungry gulps. The freckles sprinkled across Andrea's cheeks always made Sophie imagine her mother as a girl, even though grown-ups had freckles, too. There was just something about it that made Sophie flash to faded photos from long before she was born, the colors in them suggesting the world itself had a slightly different palate, the yellows mustardier, the greens pinier, her mother's pale skin deeper, as if perpetually tan. Photos of Andrea in skirts and dresses and bathing suits, four, ten, thirteen years old, a shy smile pulling her freckled cheeks up toward her eyes.

"What are you doing here?" Sophie demanded, instantly regretting her tone. She sounded pissed, or challenging, or some other unfriendly way of sounding, and the tone would not be lost on her mother.

"I live here," Andrea snapped back. "I pay the rent here and buy the food here. I thought I would take some of the food I bought and eat it here in this kitchen I'm renting. If that's all right with you?" She scooped dressing onto the last pulpy bit of tomato and forked it into her mouth, tossing the dish in the sink with a clatter. She turned to her daughter and regarded her with a squint. "Come here," she ordered. Sophie stepped toward her. First her mother grabbed her hands and brought them to her nose for a sniff, her nose seeking the smell of smoke—cigarettes or worse. What she got was a burst of something ugly, like swill left in the August heat too long, with the tang of something metallic.

"Ugh," Andrea gasped, waving at the air with her hand. "You smell like something died! Why are you all wet?"

Sophie twisted away from her mother. "I got hit with a water balloon. Some little brats on Tudor Street, I think they used dishwater or something."

The lie came easy, as they tended to. Sophie had ceased feeling bad about all the little fibs she fed Andrea. If her mother would just calm down, she thought, she'd be able to be honest. But her mother was perpetually tense, high-strung, and so suspicious of Sophie that she made Sophie suspicious of herself. And so she'd become used to giving her mother the least alarming story she could muster, regardless of it was true.

"Were you with Ella today?" Andrea interrogated. Andrea always brought up Ella when she was unhappy with Sophie—with her appearance, her smell, her attitude.

"Yes."

"Were you smoking with her?"

"No! I hate smoking! I don't smoke, I've never even tried it!" It was true. To Sophie, cigarettes smelled like acrid, burning hate. She couldn't comprehend wanting to suck the stuff into your body. She hated being around Ella's toxic clouds and was perpetually navigating their wind-borne procession while they were hanging out.

"Were you smoking pot or doing other things? God forbid?"

"No, Ma! And Ella doesn't do drugs, either! She only smokes cigarettes."

Mother and daughter stared each other down. Sophie was at a disadvantage here. When Andrea had first asked her daughter if Ella smoked, Sophie had lied. But Andrea then brought a bag of trash out the clinic's back door and spotted the shifty, lanky Ella sucking down a cigarette in the shoddy park across the way. Thusly proven a liar, Andrea reserved the right to never believe another word her daughter said.

But another thing kept Sophie vulnerable to her mother's suspicion—she felt guilty. She knew the pass-out game wasn't pot or pills or any other drug—nothing that sat with a stink on her skin or gave her bloodshot eyes—but her mother wouldn't like her doing it, and would maybe even lump it with pot and pills, vices worse than cigarettes, even. Sophie had never tried a drug, but she bet the pass-out game made her as high and hallucinatory as any of them. She cast her eyes down at the busted linoleum floor so that her mother wouldn't read the conflict in her face, but she had.

"Well, you're up to something," Andrea said finally. "Making out with boys?"

"No!"

"You'd better not be." The way Andrea grouped making out with boys with cigarettes, pot, and pills confirmed to Sophie a suspicion of her own: that kissing boys was something fairly gross that nonetheless made you feel temporarily magical. If there were boys around worth kissing she might've braved it, but the boys of Chelsea were in much the same state of disrepair as the city itself.

"Laurie LeClair came in today," Andrea said abruptly, and Sophie was glad to feel her mother's judgment move away from her and onto another.

"Really?" she asked. "What for?"

Laurie LeClair was a local legend. A few years ahead of Sophie at Our Lady of the Assumption, the girl had been unremarkable until she hit eighth grade. It was then that her transformation began, sudden and flamboyant. Her hair, formerly a mousy brown, was stripped to a nearly reflective platinum blonde. Her eyes, small and blue, became smaller and bluer as she circled them with an inch of muddy liner. The jewelry she layered onto her Catholic school uniform looked like it could double as weapons. Her face bloomed with streaks of harsh color, as did her throat, the skin there marked with what looked like bruises. Many girls had seen Sister Margaret, the principal, looming over Laurie in the ladies' room, her hands planted on her polyester hips, the porcelain sink running with motley rivers of washed-away makeup as Laurie scrubbed her face with a handful of rough, brown paper towels. Laurie's jewelry was confiscated, and if the nun could have confiscated the hair from Laurie's head she would have. It sat there, fried flat to her skull, the darkness at the crown growing in faster than Laurie could bleach it away. A rumor went around that she even had tattoos—lousy homemade ones her boyfriend gave her with a needle and ink. The rumor said that he stabbed his name into her skin, or his initials, or their initials side by side, like a declaration of love carved in wet cement. A rumor said it was on her butt, or high, high up on the back of her thigh, or on the inside of her thigh, a place so tender Sophie winced at the thought. But before any of these rumors could be proven true or false, Laurie was gone. She'd gotten "in trouble." Sophie wondered what such trouble could be. Did she cheat on a test, or steal something from the school? Did she write on the bathroom walls, or get caught shoplifting at the mall? Did she call Sister Margaret a bitch, or did she get in a fistfight with another student? No. "Trouble," Sophie learned, was a word for "pregnant."

Removed from the school, Laurie LeClair's legend swelled. Instead of ceasing, the rumors grew more lurid. Laurie had lots of boyfriends, and let them all tattoo their initials onto her; her legs a kaleidoscope alphabet, inky letters bleeding into each other beneath her skin. It was said that from far away she looked like she was wearing dark lace stockings. Laurie had a drug habit—it was cocaine, no, heroin, no, it was cocaine and heroin and she gave it to herself with needles, jabbing the crook of her elbow or scraping it along her arms or pricking the web of skin between her toes. Sophie felt degraded just hearing these tales. What had begun as a curiosity became something darker. The glee her classmates expressed in sharing the gossip brought up suspicion and scorn in Sophie—just why did everyone want so badly for Laurie LeClair to be such a mess?

But some of the tales were true. Sophie knew this because her mother worked at the clinic. The private business of every body who walked through the sliding doors made its way to her, and Andrea was not a tight-lipped woman. Like her classmates, Sophie's mother took a perverse delight in the teenager's situation. She was there when Laurie waddled in, in the throes of childbirth, fluid trickling down her bare legs, angering the cabbie whose taxi had dumped her at the curb. Laurie came in alone and left with a baby girl.

"Do you know what she named her?" Andrea sneered. "Alize!"

"What does that mean?" Sophie asked.

Andrea snorted at her daughter's innocence, not quite sure if it was feigned or genuine. "It's a beverage. An alcoholic one. Very cheap, like a wine cooler."

"Well," Sophie considered, "people name their babies Brandy. That's alcohol, right?"

"Yes, and people name their babies Rose, and Lily, but you wouldn't want to be named Crabgrass, would you? You're just being difficult." And Sophie was. She didn't know why the urge to defend Laurie LeClair had risen up so strongly, but it had, coexisting with a baser interest in what had happened to the girl now.

There was the time Laurie had come in with her face smashed in the places her boyfriend's fist had landed. A doctor's examination had uncovered more bruises, and as usual the girl's neck was all marked up with hickies. When Andrea told her about it, Sophie had gasped in concern, but Andrea had only shaken her head coldly.

"Some girls like that," she said with a simple shrug, a comment that Sophie puzzled over for weeks. Some girls liked to be beaten up? That couldn't be true. And even if it was, it had to mean that likes and hates had gotten so tangled up inside them that it became a sort of sickness, not a true *like*, not the way Sophie liked reading books or sleeping late into the morning or feeling the pastel dreamscapes of the pass-out game. Sophie felt a worry for Laurie LeClair but, having no place to go with it, shelved it where all her other useless worries were stored. Occasionally Andrea would return with more stories of the girl's sad life—a stomach pumping for alcohol poisoning, a cockroach trapped in the cave of her baby's ear. Sophie's stomach lurched as the horrible stories took her on their ride. Who knew a chilly cockroach would seek out warmth in the nook of a baby's ear? Sophie wished she didn't.

It was sometimes hard not to share these horrid tales with her classmates, knowing the rush of instant friendliness and importance it would grant her, but she told only Ella, whose promise not to tell was solid. Scornful, cranky Ella looked down upon almost everyone in that school but Sophie, keeping her distance from the swarm of chattering students and their ill intentions. She couldn't afford to get too close: if they ever found out about her germ thing, and her germ-related food thing, it would be her they'd gossip about when rumors of Laurie ran dry. She trusted only Sophie, whose unwillingness to betray Laurie LeClair, a girl neither of them actually knew, confirmed that her trust was sound.

. . .

"SHE ALMOST KILLED her baby." Andrea was rustling for her keys as she said this, patting her smock pockets and glancing around, as if the news she had delivered was banal, and perhaps to Andrea it was. Life at the Chelsea Clinic brought with it a constant stream of tragedy—gunshots and stabbings, malevolent infections, illness spiraled out of control. Sometimes Sophie wondered if her mother's hardness was how she coped with having to witness so much sadness all day long.

"What do you mean?" Sophie gasped. "What happened, what did she do?"

"Hypernatremia. Salt poisoning."

"She poisoned her baby's salt?"

"She poisoned her baby *with* salt. You can't give a baby salt. They can't handle it—it makes their kidneys stop."

"Well, well, was it a mistake? Did the baby get into the salt?"

Andrea gave her daughter a look that expressed disappointment with her mental faculties. "A baby isn't going to eat salt. Salt tastes terrible."

"I love salt," Sophie protested. Andrea's look turned steely, and she turned away.

"Normal babies don't think salt tastes good. Babies—"

"I did. I *loved* salt. I remember eating it right from the shaker, that same Tupperware shaker—"

"No you didn't, and if you were stupid enough to try I would have slapped it out of your hand. Salt can kill small children, infants and toddlers especially. It's a great way for a mother to kill her kid and then act like it was a big accident, like the kid just 'got into' too much salt. It happens all the time, especially here." Andrea stopped and watched her daughter, waiting for her inevitable questions to come.

"What do you mean, here?"

"I mean in Chelsea. We have a lot of hypernatremia. A lot of babies die from salt. Every so often there's a rash of salt killings." She paused. "You've never heard about this?"

Sophie wondered at a place that would fill her head with outlandish fantasies about a teenaged girl's tattoos, yet neglect to fill her in on an epidemic of crazed mothers murdering their babies with table salt. But under her confusion was a ribbon of something familiar. "Ma," she said, annoyed. "I feel like you're messing with me."

Andrea jingled her house keys in her hands. "It's because of all the immigrants," her mother said, the distaste in her voice suggesting she'd forgotten that her own mother and father had been immigrants themselves. "They come here from the old countries with all sorts of crazy old wives' tales, make-believe stories they think are true, and then they do stupid things because of it. Things like poisoning their babies with salt." Andrea's anger at this deadly foolishness was clear.

"But why?" Sophie asked, though she felt in her mind that she already knew, in some sleepy-stubborn part of her brain, the part that kidnaps your dreams and won't give you anything but the slightest thread to latch onto. Maybe someone had told this to Sophie when she was very small—her Polish-from-Poland Nana, perhaps, or Papa, before he had disappeared.

"There is a myth, a very old myth, about a girl who'd be the most special girl in the whole world, the most important girl ever born. Like the second coming or something. She'd save the world, I don't know, and she'd have the ability to eat huge amounts of salt, even as a baby. It wouldn't hurt her. That's how you'd know she was the one. So every so often there's an outbreak of people dosing their baby girls with salt to see if they can take it. The babies usually die. It's like believing in a comic book, Sophie," Andrea said sternly, as if Sophie had been arguing her, not standing mutely, as she was. "It's like believing your baby is Superman so you throw her off a roof to see if she'll fly. They ought to be put into jail for life," she muttered.

"So that's what Laurie LeClair did? She gave her baby salt to see if she was the... the super salt girl or something?"

"Yep. She should know better. She's not fresh off the boat. I can't believe how strong these stories are. The city needs to do a public service announcement, telling people it's a lie; that they could go to jail."

"Can they?"

"Sure! They should! That's murder!"

"But if she wasn't trying to kill the baby, just seeing if it was special—"

"Sophie. You don't abuse your children to see if a fairy tale is true. You don't endanger your children, no matter what your beliefs are.

There was that little girl in Boston who died because her parents were religious wackos who didn't believe in doctors, they thought they could just pray and God would save her." Andrea shook her head. "I even believe in God, and I know that's wrong. God helps those who help themselves, that's what God does. But some fairy tale? It's criminal. Criminal. As far as I'm concerned it's murder, whatever the intention."

Sophie wondered about Laurie LeClair, and if she was on so many drugs that she thought her baby was some supernatural being. It gave her a sadness that sat in her bones. She didn't understand why a person's life had to be so bad. It didn't seem fair. She tried to imagine what it would be like to be Laurie LeClair, with drugs in her body and a boyfriend who hit her, marks on her skin that wouldn't ever go away and a baby she thought could maybe be impossibly special. At first she couldn't imagine it and then, terribly, she could. As if Laurie LeClair's life came into her like an indrawn breath, Sophie was filled with the feeling of it, a hot, dense sensation like a wall of rotting refuse, claustrophobic, lightless. It filled her lungs, a feeling of despair no amount of dreaming or hoping could crack, and then there was—the smallest pinprick of something airy breaking through the wild and spiraling pain, a bit of brightness so foreign to this world that it seemed insane, and it was, it was insane, the idea to feed salt to her baby girl. It twirled like a dust mote on a thin shaft of light, and as hard as it was to look at it, it was easier than looking at everything else, the deep, stuck, never-ever-ever feelings of that heavy, impenetrable wall of hurt.

Sophie didn't know she had fallen backward into the fridge until a magnet stuck there jabbed her in the ear, and another wave came upon her. To feel so small, to feel so small and ugly that a cockroach seemed big, seemed better than you, more functioning, more intelligent. Sophie swung her head, her dirty-blond hair swinging about her, and she hollered. She didn't want to feel Laurie LeClair. Andrea was at her side, pulling her up from where she had slid, down to the linoleum, her head striking the fridge as she struggled against the assailing emotions, dislodging bills and coupons from their magnets, sending them skittering across the floor.

"Sophie! Sophie! Sophie!" Her mother shook her shoulders, filled with her own raw panic at her daughter's sudden seizure. She considered slapping her across the face but couldn't bring herself to strike her. "Sophie! Sophie! Sophie!" she cried. "Sophie!"

And inside the dank cavern of Laurie LeClair's reality, Sophie Swankowski's name was lowered down to her, a rope to haul her self back into her self. *Sophie*, she thought, *I'm Sophie, I'm Sophie, I'm Sophie, I'm Sophie.* Slowly, too slowly, as if it were a living thing that had sunken its claws and was loathe to let go, the sensation began to retract, until Sophie was not Laurie LeClair but was only her self, sweating in her hot kitchen, her hair in fresh tangles, her face flushed with the effort of her return, her mother's hands upon her, her body ringing with a need for salt. Her mother, filled with rage and fear and love, each emotion taking its turn upon her face like a great wheel had been spun, and both waited to learn which it would land upon. It landed on the cusp of fury and devotion. With a shake more forceful than necessary Andrea gave her daughter a final jolt, then pulled her to her in a ferocious embrace.

"What?" she cried. "What? What was that?"

Sophie pushed her mother off her with unexpected strength, diving for the stove, splattered with bacon grease and congealed cots of Hamburger Helper sauce, she tore the plastic cover off the salt shaker and poured her mouth full of crystals, letting them tumble down the back of her throat. The claws of Laurie LeClair's life had left her punctured, and she could feel the salt falling into those torn places and filling them up. She was barely aware of the sounds she was making as she ate at the pile on her tongue, choking and animal. Andrea smacked the shaker from her hand and rudely shoved her fingers into her daughter's mouth, wiping away the thick mound of salt and flicking it to the floor with a cry of alarm and disgust.

"Stop it!" Andrea hollered, and this time the will was there, her hand, gritty with salt, came down across Sophie's cheek, swiping her mouth, leaving a trail of salty paste she licked at without thinking. "Stop it!" Andrea repeated in horror, wiping the salt away with one hand while smearing it in the girl's hair with the other. They looked at one another in fear and revulsion, and Sophie thought, her mouth still thick with salt, maybe Ella was right, maybe she *was* brain damaged, maybe she had hurt herself playing pass-out, and the thought scared her so terribly she burst into tears, still traumatized on the inside by her visit to the psyche of Laure LeClair, still haunted by the mermaid of her vision, the creature's sadness sharp as a sword, but an *ancient* sword, sheathed in the musty, dusty leather of an animal that had been extinct so long no one even knew it had ever existed. Oh, no. Something was awfully, awfully wrong with her. With her entire body atremble, she clutched out at her mother, grabbing onto her arms with almost the same force that her mother gripped her shoulders. "I pass myself out!" she blurted, a terrified confession, afraid of what she'd done to her mind and afraid of her mother's wrath, ashamed at her foolhardiness with her body, guilty at betraying the secret pleasure she shared with her friend, that so many of the girls shared with each other. Andrea looked at her quizzically, then with understanding, and the wheel of emotion was spun again, this time coming down on the cusp of rage and fear.

Chapter 3

Dr. Chen was a small woman with pale skin and dark hair that shot out in little points across her forehead. Her eyes burned bright beneath eyebrows that rose and dipped like roller coasters on her smooth forehead, and she was very smiley. Sophie had been going to see her ever since she was a baby, and Andrea had worked in the same building as her for the past five years. "They think she's a saint," she'd often express to Sophie, recounting a particularly crazy day at the clinic. Who were "they"? A baby bitten by a rat, a man whose liver was soaked through with alcohol, a diabetic woman with a body too heavy for her own muscles to move. It didn't matter how awful their conditions were, what revulsion they might inspire, Dr. Chen cared for each of them with palpable tenderness, touching them gently, smiling in a way that edged their terror away. When she listened to a patient talk about the way his body was failing, a sensation of grace rose up, the feeling of demise halted, the doctor's office a magical room where the sad laws of entropy and decay were paused, just for a moment, just long enough for a person to catch his breath and receive a bit of mercy.

"Well," said the doctor, flashing her quick and shining eyes from Sophie to Andrea and back to Sophie again. "You really shouldn't be hyperventilating. Passing yourself out. But you knew that, right?" Slender fingers darted out to ruffle Sophie's unruly tangles.

Sophie nodded sheepishly. She felt more embarrassed than anything. The time she'd spent in the purgatory of the waiting room had dulled her terror, numbing her out with its abrasive atmosphere: fluorescent lights, a too-loud television bolted to the wall, the sick old man in the corner moaning steadily, a trio of hyperactive kids dashing in shrieking arcs. Her own mother grumbling bitter grumbles about having to miss work so that she could bring her careless daughter to her very place of employment.

"You do not know what it is like to be here and not be getting paid," she hissed to Sophie, slapping an ancient copy of *Better Homes and Gardens* shut on her lap. She glanced furtively at intake, where her arch nemesis, a coworker named Dorothy, was resentfully pushing papers. "She better not call me over for anything. I am not on the clock."

Sophie sunk down in the busted waiting-room seat, ashamed at the drama she'd stirred. She felt profoundly tired; all she wanted to do was collapse into her bed with the sheets so cool, sheets worn so soft they felt thin as Kleenex in places, her lovely bed filled with all her smells. She wanted to tuck herself in and drift away in the dusk, fading like the summer sky outside her window. She wanted real dreams, dreams with senseless plots and absurd juxtapositions, normal dreams that didn't leave you haunted by new emotions. Dreams that occurred at night, as they should, unfurling through the darkest hours. She wanted to wake up fresh, this dumbest of days behind her, becoming history, just one of the millions of days lived and forgotten. But first she'd have to see Dr. Chen.

. . .

"I KNOW I shouldn't do it," Sophie mumbled. Maybe if she sounded really down on herself everyone would leave her alone.

"Now, now." Dr. Chen shook her head, her smile an easy thing on her face. "So many of the kids do it, you shouldn't feel bad about it. It's natural to be curious. It is quite a sensation."

Sophie and Andrea both started at the doctor's sly admission, Andrea in scorn and Sophie in surprise.

"You mean... you did it, too? When you were my age?"

"Yes, I did," Dr. Chen affirmed. "I did all sorts of foolish things. The important thing is—I stopped before I hurt myself. And you must promise me that you will stop now, too."

"Okay." Sophie nodded. She just couldn't imagine calm, sophisticated Dr. Chen, so cool and crisp with her bright white coat and perfect hair, clutching her throat and rolling on the ground. She nearly blushed at the thought, and Dr. Chen caught her.

"It is silly to think of, isn't it? But most girls do such things. Andrea?"

Sophie sucked in a lungful of air at the suggestion. As strange as it was to visualize Dr. Chen, it was simply impossible to conjure an image of her own uptight mom, her almost-always-angry mom, her scornful-at-most-everything mom, letting go with the gasping huff-and-puff, allowing herself to float away. She honked out a rude little laugh.

But, when Andrea was thirteen years old she had spent six months fascinated with this dream state her body could create. She didn't know if she was more insulted at Dr. Chen outing her before her daughter, or at Sophie's smug assertion that Andrea could never have done something so reckless, so childish, could never have been a child at all, that she had come onto the earth full-grown, the stressed-out single mother of a back-talking nerd.

"Dr. Chen," she began, her tone pissed.

"Andrea." The doctor held out her hand. "I mean only to bring you and your daughter together here. The truth is, Sophie, this is a dangerous game to play, and you should not do it again—but sometimes it seems to me that every adolescent girl is playing it."

"And if every adolescent were smoking pot, would you suggest I remain calm about that, too?" Andrea challenged.

"There are a lot of similarities." Dr. Chen rubbed her chin, ignoring the question. "They both kill brain cells, get you high, trigger a false euphoria."

"What would produce a real euphoria?" Sophie asked.

"Sophie!" Andrea snapped. "Don't act smart."

"It's a valid question." The doctor nodded. "Real euphoria. Falling in love, those sort of feelings trigger euphoria. But then, often the love that triggers the euphoria isn't 'real' love, if by real we mean requited, or lasting." She sighed. "Runners, people who train for marathons, often experience euphoria, as do people whose bodies are enduring the first stages of starvation. Dieters, fasters, anorexics." The doctor seemed confounded by her own thought process. "Perhaps all euphoria is false. Or, what we understand from euphoria is false. Because it makes us feel happy, we think we *are* happy, even if something terrible is happening to us. It's purely chemical."

"Dr. Chen. Is Sophie okay?" Andrea was brimming with impatience.

The philosophical, chatty kindness she shared with her patients seemed sweet enough from a distance, but annoying firsthand.

"Sophie's going to be fine!" Dr. Chen crowed, clapping the girl on her leg and standing up from her chair. She stretched her body into the air with a yawn and a groan. "Sophie, be suspicious of anything that gives you a quick rush of good feelings. True good feelings should be earned."

"But my brain's okay?" Sophie asked earnestly.

"Better than average brain." The woman winked. "Keep asking questions, even if they drive everyone crazy. Especially if they drive everyone crazy." She winked again, this time at Andrea. "Now, who do we have out there today? Victor Perez, is that who I saw carrying on in the corner? Victor Perez is the most arthritic man in the whole world," she told Sophie.

"Really?"

"To hear him tell it, yes. So I have got to come up with the most powerful arthritis remedy in the whole world." She shook her head and wrapped her hand around the doorknob. "It's a tough job, I tell you. Andrea, I hope you take the rest of the day off, spend some time with Sophie here. And Sophie, I'll see you for your checkup before you start high school in the fall. Where are you off to, hmm? One of those preppy schools in Boston?"

Dr. Chen could not have known of the tender spot she'd hit with her small talk. Sophie was dying to go to a one of the preparatory high schools across the big green bridge that arched into the city. There she would learn things that were real and true, things like art and psychology, and about all the different kinds of people in the world. Her classmates would have sophisticated hairdos, and her teachers would spend their days off feeding homeless people and protesting wars. Sophie had heard of these schools, but Andrea had shot her down. "Designer schools," she had snapped. "They're no better than the public high school. You're just paying for the name."

"It's better for getting into college," Sophie had suggested, her voice cracking a bit. It was the first time she'd brought up such a possibility. College. If her fantasies about the prep school were vivid, the story Sophie had told herself about college life were positively wondrous, full of rolling lawns she would lounge upon with her clever, witty, new best friends, girls with shining ponytails and smart skirts. They would share with one another their latest thrilling opinions; they would gossip, have crushes, be moved by poetry and pass among them a contagious interest in the world they'd just become a part of. Around them would rise Gothic buildings containing dusty books that explained the secrets histories of everything. College. But Andrea had only replied, "There's got to be room in this world for the ditchdigger." Sophie didn't know any ditchdiggers, unless her mother meant the men in giant yellow construction trucks who broke up chunks of concrete when a road needed repair. Is that what she was supposed to do with her life? She was confused. But when Andrea ended the conversation with a quick jab, "You should have been born a Kennedy," Sophie finally understood what was being said: Andrea didn't have the money, and Sophie didn't get it.

"She's going here, to Chelsea High, just like her mother," Andrea told the doctor, phony pride stringing her voice tight across her throat.

Dr. Chen nodded. "I went here, too. Wherever you go, there you are."

Sophie watched her mother and Dr. Chen watch one another. Dr. Chen's coolness felt open, friendly, as if there wasn't any reason, ever, to *not* be in a totally awesome mood. Her hair lay on her head perfect as a doll's wig. Sophie couldn't imagine anything ever mussing the sleek bob, especially not Dr. Chen, whose strides and motions had a fluid grace.

Andrea, on the other hand, seemed like she had burst through a wall to get where she stood. The heat affected her, keeping her flushed, keeping the fine curls at her temples wet and flat against her skin. She shone. The bobby pins she used to keep her hair in line looked jammed into the mass of curls haphazardly. Her dark eyes bounced in her face. They held a certain edgy sparkle, always in motion. Andrea exuded a strange combination of urgency and exhaustion, as if she'd been saving babies from a burning building all day. And it wasn't because of Sophie's seizure. Sophie's mother was always like this.

As the doctor twisted her wrist to swing wide the door to her office, an ethereal whistling sound became audible; a high-pitched, mysterious ringing growing louder, fuller, melodious, and ending with a violent smack on the doctor's curtained window. The glass shook with the impact, and everyone jumped.

"Oh, dear," murmured Dr. Chen. She moved swiftly toward the window and, pushing aside the yellow curtains that filled the room with lemony warmth, flung open the glass. Immediately there was a fluttering, and something feathered and gray filled the space—a pigeon, soot colored and stocky, with the strangest contraption affixed to its tail feathers. Perched on the windowsill, it tucked its wings tight to its plump side, and fixed an eager, orange eye on the doctor.

"Oh, no," Andrea grumbled. "They've got to net this building. These things are going to make sick people sicker." Andrea switched into work mode and stepped toward the bird, making to shoo it away, but it only waddled sideways, ducking her flapping hand.

"No, no." Dr. Chen smiled. She laid out her fingers like an elegant invitation and the bird accepted, daintily wrapping its skinny feet around the doctor. Andrea gasped. It was as if Dr. Chen was brazenly picking her nose, or scratching her bum, or plugging her thumb into her ear and smearing fresh wax onto her desk. Surely, she had lost her mind. The doctor gazed at the animal with a sort of reluctant admiration, possibly pride. She brought her arm up so that the others could witness the bird's full form, including the strange cluster of tubes fixed to its backside with threads of glinting copper wire.

"This is Livia," Dr. Chen introduced.

"You *know* that pigeon?" Andrea asked.

"This pigeon is a friend of mine. I guess you would call her my pet, though she's a bit more independent than a dog or a cat. She lives in a dovecote on my roof."

"What's wrong with her?" Sophie peered at the object stuck awkwardly to the tail feathers.

"Nothing is wrong with her." The doctor stroked the bird's iridescent neck the way one would pet a docile cat. Andrea flinched as she watched the doctor's sterile fingers rub the greasy feathers. "This is bamboo." She touched the carved tubes lightly. "Bamboo whistles. When she flies, it makes the sweetest sound. Perhaps you heard it right before she smashed into the window. Silly bird," she murmured, pecking the pigeon's smooth gray head and leaving a bit of red lipstick on the feathers there. "You're too smart to fly into a window! What was that about?" As if in answer, the pigeon shook itself all over, lifting from the doctor's hand and taking to the air, there in the cramped office. Andrea cried out and backed away from the commotion of feathers, but Sophie remained still, even as the bird clumsily advanced and then settled on her head. She could feel the bird's sharp claws tapping her scalp, sliding into her hair. She stayed very, very still.

"Oh my god," Sophie said, feeling like a strange statue in a park, a girl with an animal perched on her head. She thought briefly of Ella. If her friend could see her now, she very likely would end the friendship for good, judging Sophie contaminated beyond repair.

"Dr. Chen!" Andrea scolded. "Please, get your bird off my daughter!" But Andrea made no move to brush the bird away. Its status as the doctor's special pet had elevated it above the common pigeons trolling for scraps in dumpsters around the city. It wasn't wild—it

belonged to Dr. Chen. Andrea felt it would be rude to swat it. But what kind of pet was a pigeon? A grimy one, she imagined. Still out there flying around in the muck, tucking germs into its dingy feathers. "Please!" she snapped again.

Sophie rather liked the bird settling on her head, though she feared its droppings. Its claws brought a roll of goose bumps down her neck, and her hair felt alive beneath its movements. The doctor shook her head at the scene and snapped her fingers at the pigeon. With a push off that stung Sophie, Livia jumped back into the air, flapping onto the doctor's outstretched hand. Dr. Chen walked the animal to the window, stretching her fingers like a bridge for the bird to waddle across.

"Go home," she said firmly. And the pigeon did. With all the world before it, its take off was powerful and smooth. It glided into the sky, pulling air through the whistles on its tail, leaving a flute of sound in its wake. "Listen to that," the doctor said, smiling, and Sophie rushed to the window to see her new friend disappear, straining her ears to hear the last of the music as it faded. Like the thin, fragile tone of a finger on a ring of glass. Like the subtle vibrations of something gently, artfully struck. Andrea followed her daughter to the window, inspecting the girl's head for fleas and bird poop. She found nothing but kept digging. Sophie allowed it. Her mother's scratchy fingernails reminded her of the bird, its comforting heaviness and skittering claws.

"Did you do that?" Sophie marveled. "Give it that whistle?"

The doctor nodded. "I learned from my father. It is a very old art, mostly forgotten. Once, long ago, whole flocks of pigeons were whistled. They would fly together and it would be an orchestra in the air, like heaven was announcing itself to the world. Imagine! A sky full of such sound!" The doctor sighed wistfully, blowing her own light whistle through her lipsticked mouth. "But not all pigeons like the whistles. Some find it terrible." She scrunched her face. "Would you want a tuba rigged up to your butt? I would not!"

Sophie considered it. She wouldn't want to have to lug something around on her body, but she would like to leave a trail of invisible beauty behind her as she moved through the world. She would like to stir the air and feel her passing change it. "I don't know..." she said thoughtfully.

"Livia likes it very much. She's proud to have the whistle. I watch her swoop off from the roof—she finds new ways to tumble and soar that bring different sounds to her tail. She is a true artist."

"How do you know?"

"You know." The doctor nodded. "Do you have a pet?"

"A cat."

"And you know what your cat likes, and what she does not like?"

Sophie thought. "She likes being petted, and then she hates it, and bites. But I know right when she starts to hate it. I can just tell."

"Cats are the meanest." Dr. Chen shuddered, as if Sophie had revealed that her pet was a dragon. "When they are done with your affections they slice you up!"

Andrea, finished with her inspection, smoothed her daughter's hair down, and addressed the doctor with a grim look. "Dr. Chen, I'm going to have to report this. It is *so* unsanitary! I can't believe you allow *pigeons* in here, in a *hospital*. On my daughter! I don't care if they're your pets."

"Okay, Andrea," the doctor said amicably. "Do what you must. I promise you that Livia is a clean bird, though, and that Sophie is fine."

And with that Dr. Chen cracked her office door, swinging it wide on its hinges. In rushed the cacophony of the rooms beyond: the dinging elevators, the braying of a mother trying to control her kids, the steady typing of the intake workers, the whooshing of the glass doors sliding open and closed, open and closed. The television communicated its bad news to a slumped audience too consumed with their own bad news to pay attention. Wheelchairs spun by, beefy orderlies wheeling gurneys, a nurse pushing a med cart. Their motion spawned a breeze that fluttered the posters on the doctor's wall, graphic posters in blood red and liver purple, illustrating the body's many systems. The yellow curtains hung still before the now-closed window. Dr. Chen waited patiently for Sophie and Andrea to exit. They seemed stunned by the hectic activity beyond the room. "I know." She nodded. "It's a lot to return to. If I had my way, I'd spend all my time on my roof with the birds."

"You have more?" Sophie asked, intrigued. Dr. Chen nodded.

"A whole bunch." She smiled. And she took the first step, out of the office and into the clinic, breaking a certain spell.

. . .

"YOU'RE STILL PUNISHED." Andrea's mouth was a grim line on her face; her face was a resolution on her body.

"That's not fair," Sophie declared, remembering her mother's guilty grimace when the doctor suggested that she, too, had played the pass-out game once upon a time. "That's hypocritical."

"Don't think you're so smart just because you learned a new word," Andrea snapped. "You're still punished."

Sophie was insulted. "*Hypocritical* is not a new word," she said. "I've known *hypocritical* for, like, a long time." She folded her arms and leaned back against the plasticky car seat. It was so warm from being parked in the sun of the clinic parking lot that it felt like hot melting taffy beneath her thighs. She pulled the visor down to knock the sun away. She'd thought summer was going to be so great because there'd be no school, no nuns. She'd forgotten it just meant more and more Mom.

"Maybe I did it once," Andrea relented. "Maybe twice. But I wasn't doing it all the time, and I didn't give myself a seizure."

"Dr. Chen said it didn't hurt me!"

"That woman needs her head examined." Andrea shook her head. "She barely looked at you, and then she lets some germy *pigeon* run all over you! I am so reporting her. I don't care if her bedside manner is great. There's something wrong with her." She flicked her eyes up and down her daughter, searching for remnants of the earlier strange behavior. "What was it then, huh?" She shook her head. "You're grounded. I want you where I can keep an eye on you."

"You're not home, Ma," Sophie said, with *duh* in her voice. "You won't be keeping an eye on me. You won't even be there."

Andrea chewed her lip. It was true. She glanced sideways at her daughter. This was how it happened. The mothers were away at work because the fathers were away god knows where and before you knew it the girls turned wild and you had a Laurie LeClair on your hands, all shot up and smacked up and knocked up. Andrea herself had paid the price of her own young wildness—was still paying the price, arguing with her daughter on a hot summer's day. She wasn't going to let history repeat itself. She had to get her daughter under control.

"I'll send you to be with your grandmother," she threatened.

"No way," Sophie cackled. "You hate Nana more than you hate me."

Andrea's gasp nearly flung her hands from the wheel. "Is that what you think? That I hate you?"

"Well, you don't act like you like me," Sophie said in a voice that started out sounding tough but weakened as the heaviness of what she was saying hit her. Did her mother really not like her? Were mothers even *allowed* to not like their daughters? Was there a special agency Sophie could file a report about this? What would happen? Were there orphanages and foster homes for the children of perfectly capable, functional mothers who just took a strong dislike to their offspring? Sophie felt her eyes fill with a painful mist, like she'd been gassed with something toxic. *Don't let her see you cry*, she ordered herself.

"Sophie, you don't understand how tough this world is. You think you do, I know you really think you do, but you just don't. You think you can rattle off some smart-ass remarks and that'll get you whatever you want? You think some fancy school is going to give you some big-shot life?" She shook her head. "That's just what I'm going to do. That is just what you need. A summer at your grandmother's. I don't feel... *great* about it, but you've really left me no choice." Andrea paused and chewed her lip. She shook her head again and sighed. "There's really no place else for you to go."

Sophie's blood chilled as she realized her bluff was up. Why did she have to run her mouth like that? Why could she never resist picking a fight with her mom? A simple grounding issued by a working single mom would have been a cinch to sneak out on. She could have been running around the city and been back home sulking on the couch by the time Andrea returned from the clinic. She could have smuggled Ella inside to watch television, releasing her between programs to smoke her cigarettes in the alley next door, stashing her in a closet when her mother came home for lunch, freeing her when the coast was clear. The subterfuge could have even been fun. *No fun now, not with Nana*, Sophie thought, the grief settling in. Sophie was about to spend the remainder of the long, hot summer hanging out at the town dump.

Chapter 4

"**W**ell, I guess that's, like, the end of our friend-ship, then," Ella said coldly. Her voice tunneled through the telephone wires, entered Sophie's ear, and bore into her heart.

"Ella, come on. I'll shower, for god's sake. I'm not going to be rolling around in trash! I'll probably just be, like, sitting in the trailer with my nana. Watching soaps, eating cookies. You could come, too. You'd love my nana. She just likes to hang out talking shit and chain smoking those grody, long-ass cigarettes." Sophie paused, searching for a way to bribe her friend into joining her. "I bet she'd even give you cigarettes. She has really bad judgment."

"And why is your mom making you stay with her?"

"To punish me for playing pass-out."

"I can't believe you cracked so easily," Ella said. "I'm disappointed in you, Swankowski. I thought you were stronger."

"Sophiiiiiiiiieeeeeeee!" Andrea hollered from the front door. "I said noon, it's past noon! Don't make me late!"

"I gotta go," Sophie spoke into the phone. "You're crazy if you think I want to be hanging out at the town dump. It's going to be the most boring summer of my life."

"Well, I'll remember you while I'm tanning on the wall at Revere Beach," Ella said breezily. "Until your memory fades, of course. And then I'll forget all about you."

"You're being a bad best friend," said Sophie, and hung up the phone. The thought of Ella holding a dead line in her nicotine-stinky fingers was satisfying for a minute, until it was replaced by the image of Ella lounging on the wide expanse of concrete that lurched above the ocean at Revere Beach. Wearing a risqué bikini, the mirrored lenses of her sunglasses reflecting sunshine and blue sky, smoking and looking way older and more worldly than her thirteen years. Adventures would come her way—new, cooler friends; boys in cars. Ella would speed through New England eating neon Italian ices and prancing in the scuffed pumps she had found for a dollar at the Salvation Army. Sophie was hot with jealousy, like a sunburn on her heart. Who would be there to help Ella when a splash of the polluted ocean splattered her coconut-oiled skin? When a dirty seabird as big as a dog came waddling her way, a mess of filthy feathers? Ella needed her, Sophie assured herself. No one but Sophie really knew how sick her friend was. It was a dark sort of comfort, but since she needed Ella just as fiercely, she let herself have it.

. . .

THROUGH THE CAR window Sophie watched Chelsea smear by. Clusters of kids, boys mostly, radiating agitation, leaning against buildings, on stoops, kicking debris through lots. Old ladies from other lands made their way gingerly down cracked sidewalks, picking their way with canes, shuffling in their rubbery shoes. Women too young to have bruise-colored pillows beneath their eyes pushed baby strollers. The green of trees blurred the sky. Sophie loved passing over the train tracks, the snake of wood and metal undulating toward Boston. Andrea drove quietly, steering the car toward the outskirts of Chelsea, past the giant, tarp-covered pile of rock salt heaped by the rusty bridge that crossed into East Boston. Past the water where scrappy boats bobbed in the muck. Past the warehouses where produce was hauled in, loaded onto trucks, and shipped back into the world. So many parts of the city were mysteries to Sophie. Her routes were simple: to and from school, Ella's, the creek and the mall. The store Andrea sent her to for groceries was blocks and blocks away, taking her past gangs of awful, harassing boys, and so she went instead to Hennie's, the ancient, dusty Polish grocer Andrea hated. Her mother had claimed to see mice and other vermin scurry into the darkest corners when the door creaked open, leaking sunlight into the dim, wooden store. Hennie's accent was thick as the dust that lay on the shelves, on the foods from other eras, things no one would ever come looking for—surely the people who ate such strange pickled meats and potted fish had passed on, and their offspring were shopping at the other, fluorescently lit grocer, its aisles stuffed with Doritos and bright cartons of sweetened juice and cereals with cartoon characters waving from the boxes.

But Hennie sold the basics, too: milk, Pepsi, cigarettes, meat, and Andrea never suspected that the ground beef she fried up for Hamburger Helper came from Hennie's shadowed deli case. Hennie herself was large and hunched, with a babushka knotted beneath her chin—a scarf that held back her gray hair, just a curl or two scrambling out onto her broad, wrinkled forehead. The most striking thing about Hennie was her eyes, a blue so pale they seemed to flash silver in the poorly lit shop. Cataracts, Sophie had thought, but no, they were simply the old woman's eyes, lit from within like a lamp. In spite of the fact that Hennie's shop brought to mind a Grimm's Fairy Tale crime scene, despite Hennie resembling the sort of elderly witch that snuffed out small children, pickling their limbs in great jars of brine and then selling them from her dusty shelves, Sophie wasn't scared of her. And she wasn't grossed out, even when a faint scuttling noise seemed to confirm her mom's accusation of pests and vermin. Sophie was vaguely fascinated, as if stepping into Hennie's grocery was akin to entering the great hushed hall of an art museum, or a scientific laboratory from another time. It was truly like no place she had ever seen, with bins of candies from other worlds and centuries, shelves of colored glass bottles holding liquids, and a flicker in the faint lighting that suggested lanterns or candles.

"Hello? Hello? Hello?" Andrea's harpy tone cut through Sophie's reverie, and she snapped to attention as her mother pulled the car awkwardly up a long gravel drive. Sophie became aware of a smell in the air, like rot and dust, something earthy and chalky at once. The dump spread out before them, splayed wide to either side and clambering up a hill, where some of the more fanciful garbage—plastic deer, pink flamingos, a giant ceramic dog's head—had been whimsically arranged, creating a cartoony sculpture garden.

"Did you hear a word I was saying?" Andrea demanded. "Are you having another seizure? What is going on with you?"

Sophie was embarrassed at spacing out to thoughts of Hennie and her odd, old-world grocery store. She couldn't tell her mother that she'd been thinking about how the way Hennie wore her chiffon scarves pulled over her head reminded her of how her nana wore similar bits of chiffon bowed around her skinny neck, but to much different effect. "Just bummed that I can't be at the beach with Ella," she sighed instead, and it wasn't much of a lie. The day was warm and bright, with not a single cloud to shade the sun's brilliance. She could easily imagine the scene just one city over—music leaking from the windows of cars cruising the strip, slices of pizza as big as your head, boys with tiny gold crucifixes glinting on their bare chests—all of it wrapped in the dank, briny stink of the ocean that banged up against the wall. The delighted screams of kids bobbing in the scummy surf. Gulls shrieking as they picked through the trash washed up on the rubble where the concrete wall broke away to sand. Ella making

Sophie pick which boy she'd kiss if she absolutely had to, and *eeewing* at her selection. She'd been looking forward to summer for an entire year. Sophie's pout was true.

Andrea snorted at her daughter's regret, finding it not even worth her comment. "Be good to your grandmother. Don't give her a hard time. Do what she says and be helpful."

"What's she gonna make me do?" Sophie whined.

"I don't know," Andrea said strictly. "But you'll do it. Whatever it is. I don't care if you're shoveling shit or digging a ditch, you help your grandmother."

"Is she going to pay me?" Sophie begged. Maybe a summer job wouldn't be so bad. She could save up and when her mother finally tired of this stupid punishment she'd have tons of dough for pizza and Cokes at the beach.

"Don't ask her for anything!" Andrea snapped. "In fact, I think the less you interact with each other, the better."

Andrea brought the car to a halt at the entrance, where a man sat slumped and asleep in a cramped booth. Not only his clothes, torn and worn, but the very skin of his body seemed scavenged from the junkyard. Like a slumbering trashland spirit he snored, smeared in soot and crusted in grime, the soles of his holey boots glistening with gummy slime.

"Ew," Sophie spat, and Andrea could not even scold her for it. She bit her lip and leaned her head gingerly out the car window.

"Ronald? Ronald?" she called.

Ronald? Sophie thought of Ronald McDonald, and placed the man as the mascot clown of this crazy land. Ronald's snores were louder than Andrea's calls. She leaned her elbow on the horn, filling the air with abrasive sound. Ronald jerked on his stool and began to slide off. He was saved by a giant hole in the rear of his dungarees, which had caught onto the stool and held him in place.

"Whaddaya need?" he yelped. "Whaddaya dumpin? Whaddaya got in there?" Ronald squinted like a man who'd lost his glasses. When he squinted his eyes disappeared into the dirty folds of his puffy face.

"Ronald, it's Andrea. Is my mother around?"

"Andrea! Andrea, Andrea, Andrea!" the man chanted and chuckled, delighted.

"Is he drunk, or retarded?" Sophie asked.

"Sophie!" Andrea's hand flew out like a startled bird and whacked her daughter in the leg. "That's just rude." She returned her attention to the man in the booth, who swayed now, still anchored to his seat by the hole in his pants. Her voice turned oddly tender. "Ronald, I'm looking for Kishka." The man's head

advanced, like a turtle coming out from its shell. His eyes remained slit but he seemed to be peering in Sophie's direction, so she gave a halfhearted wave. Ronald waved back. "Ronald, is my mother here?" Ronald nodded, flipping his grubby hand deeper into the dump. "Could you walk Sophie over to her? You know Sophie?" Andrea looked searchingly at the man. "My daughter? Sophie?"

The man leaned, and then leaned further. His grimy face came so close that Sophie could smell him—curbside swill with a shot of whisky. A fume of dirt and booze baked in the midday sun. "Sophie?" he spoke, and when his eyes connected with her it was like a film peeled off them, just for a second—a terrible second. It jolted Sophie and she leaned over her mother and hit the power-window button on the door, sending a pane of glass up between them and the man.

"Ma!" Sophie yelped. "Do you *hate* me? I'm your *daughter*, you're really going to send me off with this guy?" Andrea was always a little neglectful, but sending her off to be murdered by this junkyard goblin was a new level of carelessness.

"Ronald won't hurt you," Andrea said quietly. "I'll be surprised if he can even walk you over there without falling over."

Sophie shook her head. She couldn't wait to tell Ella about this. There was no way Ella would be able to stay mad at her when she learned how heinous and cruel her punishment was, that her own mother was leaving her in the care of an inebriated lunatic at the city dump. She hauled herself out of the car and slammed the door, glaring at her mother as she backed away. She imagined the car overheating, spurting great cones of steam into the air. She imagined all four tires popped and sagged, the vehicle lumbering to a stop on warped rims. She wished vengeful destruction onto her mother's car, stopped just short of howling these curses at the woman as she backed the car back down the gravel slope, the air-freshening tree bouncing cheerfully from the rearview mirror.

As her mother faced her through the windshield the glaring sunlight seemed to bounce between them like a bolt of lightning, and Sophie felt herself invaded with a complicated feeling—there was fear and regret, jealousy and revulsion, hardened love and spinning bewilderment. And Sophie realized those were just the feelings she herself inspired. Intertwined with all these pulses was another low hum—heartbreak.

The sensations took up all the space in Sophie's rib cage; she could feel it inflate her lungs and speed her heart. She tilted like Ronald had, drunk from this hot shot of emotion. It wasn't Sophie's feelings toward her mother she was feeling, it was her mother's own feelings toward Sophie. She felt the truth of it as clearly as a voice in the air. It wasn't that she was reading her mother's mind, she was reading her heart. *Mom.* She knew what her mother smelled like, knew what she felt like to hug, knew what she sounded like. This was a new sense, but it was every bit her mother, was like *wearing* her mother somehow, but on the inside. It was fascinating and terrible, heartbreaking and tremendous.

In the moment it happened Andrea felt her emotions pull away from her, then quickly snap back like a great rubber band of feeling.

Rattled, she braked the car, took a deep breath in confusion, then continued backing away from her daughter. She pulled away from the dump shaken by that single moment—a millisecond really—when the frantic, constant feelings of her interior had been *gone*. Just not there. A flash of pure peace had flickered through her, only to be submerged by the tsunami of emotion that rolled back in. Normal. Andrea felt normal again, all churned up inside with worry and fear for her daughter, worry and fear of her daughter, not to mention the rocky, sad emotions that flared up at the sight of Ronald—poor, broken Ronald and his hijacked mind.

Andrea glanced at herself in the rearview mirror—was she still herself? Freckles and wrinkles, her eyes small and sharp, a brow with a good arch, her damn uncontrollable hair held back with a fortress of bobby pins. After so many years of watching her daughter, now when Andrea looked at herself she saw the image of her offspring, too: the reverse of looking at Sophie and seeing her own uncanny reflection, which also happened. They were of one another. Sophie's wild hair would curl stronger with age, and her cheeks were freckled—not the blizzard scattered across Andrea's cheeks, more like the faintest markings on a bird's egg. These were some of the things Andrea had given her.

The car receded into the distance until it was nothing but a dented-up bit of metal reflecting sunlight on the road back to town. At the mouth of the dump, Sophie steadied herself, shaken by what she'd felt, and then that thirst for salt rose up in her, a craving that cranked her mouth open, had her scavenging the air for a mist of salt off the nearby harbor. She took her breaths deeply, hoping to steady herself, and her tongue rolled around digging for that, that… what did salt taste like? She licked her lips, savoring where her own sweat had dried above her mouth, and her mind teemed with thoughts.

Her mother kept ugly feelings for her in her heart. So it was true. It was a shattering understanding, but an odd comfort as well. To feel suspicious, even paranoid, and then to scold yourself for your suspicions and paranoia—that was the crazy-making carnival ride Sophie had been purchasing tickets for. *My mother hates me, how horrible—no, your mother doesn't hate you, you're insane—how horrible you are.* Now Sophie knew that she wasn't crazy, that her mom was bad vibing her, deeply. But there was something else, some other feeling nestled in there, so hard to extract from the tangle. Respect? Awe? Awe seemed too grand—Sophie blushed at the idea, why would her mother be in awe of her? But, no, *awe.* And, the fear she had picked up had a different flavor to it, the sort of fear one might experience upon encountering a tiger, wild and bristling, gorgeous and striped, ready to take you into its mouth full of teeth. *Why me?* Sophie marveled. *Why all that?*

Sophie looked down at herself. Still softened with baby fat, in a t-shirt marred with sweat from the sticky car and its busted air conditioning. Cut-off jeans in a dirty fringe around her thighs and an old pair of Vans jammed onto her feet. Even her blonde hair had a negative modifier—*dirty* blonde, the shade was called. Her cheeks were plump and her eyes, too, appeared plump—chocolatey brown, heavily fringed, somehow both rounded and tilted. Sophie liked her eyes the best, but they were not powerful enough to redeem the mediocrity of the rest of her. In school she did okay—slightly better in English and social studies than in math and science, but not too good or too bad at any of it. No real hobbies or talents to brag about, just an enjoyment of the pass-out game and the company of her slightly wilder, annoyingly unpredictable best friend Ella. But still. Sophie rummaged through herself and came up with a ghost of the feeling that shot off her mother, that swirl of respect and awe and reverence and thought, *That's for me.* She straightened her shoulders and turned toward Ronald. He began walking toward her, dragging the stool by the seat of his pants.

"Ronald," she said. "The stool?" She nodded at the furniture. Ronald was oblivious; the stool seemed to be actually helping him. As his lumbering form swayed, the stool caught him. He tilted backward and the stool's wooden legs dug into the earth as his rear end came to rest on its seat. It was like Ronald was a new creature, evolved to accommodate his devolution. As he dragged himself closer to Sophie she caught another strong whiff of him. The alcohol wasn't just coming out on Ronald's breath—though it was, a flag furling and unfurling from his mouth. Beneath the sour punch of his breath was another odor, the smell of it leaching from his pores. Ronald was pickled. Sophie remembered the way he had begun to peer at her, a strange flicker of clarity in his eyes, and felt the start of something turning inside her. With a full-body jerk she wrenched herself away from it. No. Nope. No freaking way. She was not going to experience the inner realms of Ronald, the drunken city dump mascot. She faced him coldly. How had her mother, usually so bitchy, dealt with him with such patience? How did her grandmother handle him? What would Ella do? Throw a rock at him and run, probably. If the rock seemed clean enough.

"Point, Ronald," Sophie demanded. "Where is my grandmother? Take your finger and point." Ronald's face turned up toward the sky. His swollen eyes pasted themselves shut against the sun and he leaned back heavily against his stool. He was like a sundial, orienting himself. Or perhaps he had passed out. Ronald's hair was dark and needed washing, badly. Whole locks were held together with a dusky, oily grime. Maybe he had some streaks of gray, or maybe that was just debris, plaster and dust. Chunks of rubble were caught in his tangles. His dark skin was even darker, reddened from his time outdoors. A mist of sweat coated his body, Sophie watched it shimmer on his arms and her thirst for salt galloped inside her. *No! Eeew, gross, gross, the grossest!* Worse than the rancid debris of the city creek was Ronald's dirty, sweaty arm, and yet—so salty. Sophie bit her tongue so that it filled her mouth with water. She felt monstrous as a vampire yearning for blood. The water in her mouth helped not at all. The craving inside Sophie wasn't thirst at all—it was the opposite of thirst.

Ronald, oblivious, righted himself upon his crooked stool and popped his eyes open. For the first time she watched the man focus—on her. A smile ate his face, revealing rows of perfect, white teeth beneath his lips. They surprised Sophie; everything about Ronald seemed ruined; she'd expected a jack-o'-lantern's grill, jagged and discolored as a ripped chain-link fence.

"I know you." Ronald nodded his head, happy the way a child is happy, happy at nothing, making no sense. "I know you, do you know me?"

"Yeah, you're Ronald. I'd like for you to tell me where my grandmother is."

"You don't know me." Ronald shook his head, his words long and mushed by his slow-motion tongue. "That's not allowed." Then his arm lifted, and he pointed down the hill. Away from the office her grandmother kept in an Airstream trailer beneath the only shade trees on the property. Away from where the trash grew into mountain ranges on the horizon. Sophie followed the point of his dirty finger, his nails green and fungal, toward a squat, lopsided building, a shed ringed with hulking metal barrels.

"Angel," Ronald coughed the word wetly, like something that had blocking his air passages. "She's with Angel."

"Great," Sophie clipped. "Thank you." The man began to tremble back into motion; his feet, jammed sockless into a beaten pair of sneakers, shuffled. The stool's legs sunk deeper into the soft earth. Ronald was running in place. "Nice to see you," he croaked. Sophie left him there, began the trek down the hill, her Vans kicking up puffs of dust that coated her bare, sweaty legs. The dump would make her gross, she thought sadly. Her nose would become accustomed to the amazing variety of foul stinks the breeze carried this way and that. The odor of swill decomposing in the sun would become as familiar to her as mown grass. She'd expect her skin to be gritty and smudged. Her hair would clump like Ronald's into dreadlocks of grease. Just great. She comforted herself by the thought that at least no one worth caring about would see her. At least this wasn't school, where an overslept morning could send you, disheveled, into the world of catty classmates, the world of boys Sophie just did *not* want to think were cute—she did not, they were jerks, most of them, serious jerks, could win medals in an international jerk competition, the cream of the jerk crop right there at Our Lady of the Assumption School in Chelsea, Massachusetts—but, they *were* cute. Several of them were cute. That she thought so made Sophie as mad at herself as at them, the losers. Tripping people as they passed on their way to the pencil sharpener. Sending mortified girls dashing into the bathrooms on false claims of period stains bleeding through their uniforms. Greeting everyone with the salutation, *Hey, faggot!* Sending phony love notes to students whose loneliness sat on their skin plain as acne. She hated them. But their cuteness was undeniable. She felt a relief at never having to see any of them during this, her punishment summer spent at the dump. She would submit to the grime, become like a feral cat wandering the heaps of trash.

Chapter 5

Sophie saw her grandmother only a smattering of times each year, usually on holidays. Her home was dim and the furniture was old, bought new many years ago, when she had lived there with Sophie's grandfather, before he disappeared. No one liked to talk about Papa Carl's disappearance—it brought up in Andrea a sadness Sophie couldn't bear to witness. It made the world seem topsy-turvy to watch her mother, so strong and harsh, be shoved to the brink of tears so abruptly, her adultness suddenly full of wobble, as if it could tip over and a little-girl Andrea would tumble out. Sophie didn't like her mom's bad moods but at least they were consistent, and she'd learned how to maneuver around them. To see this tender, wounded streak exposed paralyzed her, filled her with a strange mixture of love and fear, and the urge to hug her mother and run quickly away. Clearly her mother had loved her father. That Kishka had loved him too was harder to see, as the man's name brought out of her grandmother a bitter rage that made her cigarette smoke hotter, that made the muscles in her skinny neck tense so that she'd loosen the breezy scarf kept knotted there, sometimes taking it off and wrapping it around her hand, like a boxer taping his fingers together before a fight.

Well, he was a man after all, Kishka would say, and Sophie couldn't tell if this was Kishka's understanding, her dark acceptance—it is a man's prerogative, after all, to leave as he wishes—or, if it was the old woman's regret at a mistake—she'd believed Carl was special but it turned out he was a man after all, a thing that leaves. Either way it made Sophie shift with discomfort, and so she didn't mention her grandfather, whom she'd met many times but so long ago she had no memory of him, only photos pasted into yellowy photo albums, baby Sophie sitting on the lap of a faceless man. Faceless because someone—Kishka in her rage or Andrea in her grief—had cut out the offending image, leaving a perfect, round hole, a gap where the gluey page of the album striped through. Sophie found them creepy, and imagined an envelope somewhere containing a confetti of her grandfather's

tiny heads. He'd disappeared, and then they had disappeared him. Sophie hated all of it. She hated that anyone could disappear. She wondered what it meant, but never did she imagine boarding a bus, running away, hopping a train. She thought of a slow shimmer that vanished her.

Kishka's apartment was frozen in the era of Carl's vanishing. Nothing new had entered, nothing old was discarded. The place held the stillness of a museum. Andrea doubted her mother even

slept there anymore, choosing instead to sleep inside the cluttered Airstream trailer that tilted on the side of a hill at the dump. Sophie had glimpsed the Airstream's interior during the Fourth of July barbecues Kishka threw for her workers; the tight space was a havoc. A giant television sucked a bounty of channels from a satellite dish perched in a nearby tree. Great glass ashtrays overflowed with lipsticked cigarette butts. Mess scattered the capsule, including a couch so heaped with sheets and pillows it gave the impression of a bed. A desk held piles of papers, and more paper poked from the slammed drawers of file cabinets, as if trying to crawl from their habitats. Air conditioning chugged from a hulking machine jammed into a window. Sophie wasn't permitted more than the briefest peek inside.

"See?" Her grandmother would flap open the door, then shut it before Sophie's eyes had the chance to adjust to the dimness. "Just a hangout for an old lady. Nothing fun in there for a little girl."

Sophie always hated the cookouts at the dump, but as it was a holiday, Sophie and Andrea's presence was insisted upon. The glare of the sun was unrelenting and carcinogenic; the stink of charcoal and lighter fluid barely masked the putrid stink of the summertime trash. Her grandmother's employees were self-conscious and obligated, the occasional city official dropped by, beaming their fake personalities onto everyone. If she had been allowed to roam the grounds perhaps it would have been interesting, but the dump was off-limits to little Sophie. Again and again she would stray toward the heaps of fascinating junk-stuck muck, only to be called back by Andrea, her mother's voice raw with annoyance and repetition. Well, not today. Now that Sophie wanted nothing to do with the putrid piles, it would almost certainly be required of her to touch it. Why was life so mean?

As she approached the crooked, wooden building Ronald had pointed toward, Sophie became aware of a steady, powerful rumble. If she'd lived in a different part of the country perhaps she would have stopped and braced herself for the rolls of an earthquake, but Massachusetts didn't get earthquakes. They got blizzards in the winter, a sheet of frozen white that canceled school and turned the rules of the road upside down—the streets teeming with sleds, and the cars, buried under mounds of snow, now things to climb upon and slide down. They got hurricanes sometimes, winds that could blow you down, that beat the trees until their branches snapped, until their trunks tumbled into the street, the giant snarled mat of their roots upended, dripping dirt. But no earthquakes, no volcanoes, nothing that could explain this jumbling, rumbling sound—so loud Sophie could feel it like the bass of very loud hip-hop blaring from the supersonic car speakers of a Bellingham Square lowrider. It grew louder as she neared the building and its ringed fortress of tall, round buckets. The vibrations climbed her bones. As she came upon the barrels, she saw that they were shaking, and was stopped by the tremble of what they held inside. Jewels? Jewels. Jewels! Like a cracked geode, each rust-scabbed, dingy barrel was brimming with rough sparkle. Millions of pebble-sized chunks glittered blindingly in the sun. One barrel contained bright green jewels, the corners smoothed to touch. The next, deep blue jewels, like droplets of some Caribbean lagoon. More barrels held cold, dark green jewels, the hard color of the Atlantic at winter. She picked up a handful, half expecting to see angry waves trapped inside, like bugs stuck in amber.

There were red jewels—rubies?—and so many barrels full of crystal clear jewels, each cut into different sizes, that the abundance of sparkle hurt Sophie's eyes and caused her to gasp in excitement. Diamonds? She plunged her hands into a bin, slid them deeper and deeper, until she was up to her elbows in diamonds! They felt cool against her skin. She lifted her hands and let them rain from her cupped palms, falling between her fingers, a chunky waterfall. A neighboring barrel of milky white jewels stopped her. What would this be? She wracked her brain for a gem that looked like this, solid and white and smooth, like the bumpy, antique lamp her mother kept by her bedside; *milk glass* she called it. Milk glass. Glass.

As quickly as Sophie had been sucked into the rich fantasy of junkyard treasure, so quickly did her imagination spit her back out. Glass. She felt about as intelligent as Ronald, whom she had left up the hill with a stool stuck to his pants. Of course there were not bins and bins of precious jewels being stored at her grandmother's dump! What a lunatic, to think so for even a moment! Was she a child, after all? Sophie burned with private embarrassment, and was glad to be alone. Certainly in all her wonder, she would have blurted something about the diamonds and rubies and emeralds that were now, clearly, the rubble of beer bottles, the smashings of jars, and the glass of shattered car windows tumbled edgeless and smooth.

Sophie crept deeper into the space behind the barrels, observing rows of smaller buckets filled with jagged glass shards ordered by color, waiting to be tumbled. Shelves made from scrap wood held bottles that looked tremendously old; words and designs rose from their surfaces. Sophie ran her hand over one, feeling the word *elixir* roll beneath her fingers. She divined an order to the mess, a system: which barrels held finished products and which were next to be tumbled, empty shelves waiting for more raw bottles to come in, and shelves holding bottles too precious—antique?—to crush and crumble into ornamental debris.

Once she accepted that the shining nuggets were nothing but unexceptional bits of broken glass, Sophie's wonderment returned. Nothing was precious here, but all of it was pretty. Buckets and buckets of regular, everyday glass somehow bashed into dazzle. The more she thought about it, the more she liked it. There was something about a piece of smashed windshield tricking you into thinking it was a priceless diamond that conjured a sort of respect for the glass. She was proud of it, as if it were a living thing that had pulled off a clever feat. It still felt nice to plunge her hand into the cool bin of beads, felt just as cool on the sun-hot skin of her arms as when she'd mistaken them for jewels. Sophie felt relaxed among the glass. They were all equals here.

She found a bucket containing chunks of multicolored, rounded beads that looked like a giant bin of candy. Her mouth watered. She'd forgotten to eat breakfast, and her hunger for salt lingered. Would her grandmother feed her? She had never seen the woman eat, only smoke. Even at the Fourth of July cookouts Kishka would sit with a cocktail in a plastic tumbler, knocking the melting ice against the sides, and take drags off her dramatically long cigarettes. Kishka liked charring marshmallows over the burnt grill, but after she blew out their tiny fires and plucked the blackened crackling of the skin she threw the rest of the candy away, half-melted and sticky in the grass, to be scarfed up by a junkyard dog.

The rumbling sound faded as Sophie plucked her way through the barrels and bins. The vibrations had settled in her bones and now felt natural. She climbed atop an overturned bucket to reach a row of shelves stocked with those charming, antiquated bottles that had been spared from pulverization. The height of the bucket increased her view of where she was—Angel's place, whoever that was. She could see Ronald up the hill, his head plopped onto his chest, unconscious on his stool in the brutal sun. The glare of the day on the great heaps of trash was too much to look at. It burned a wall of light onto Sophie's eyes, she had to blink it away to see again. When she could, she noticed the pigeons. A wide flock of them, assembled on the roof of the crooked building, staring at her with their small, orange eyes. Sophie felt that she'd been caught, but doing what, and by whom? A gang of scabby birds? *Rats with wings,* her mom called them, throwing handfuls of uncooked rice into the gutter outside their house as if someone had just been married, but no. Supposedly the rice expanded in the greedy birds' stomach until their insides exploded.

"Really?" Sophie had asked, skeptical, disapproving that her mother was wasting perfectly good food this way.

"You do what you can," her mother said, resolutely, upending the plastic bag, shaking out the final grains. Sophie never even saw the birds come for the rice. They stayed high above, their scabby claws clutching electrical wires, and the rice grew grimy in the street below, carried away by insects and rain.

Once she noticed the pigeons, Sophie could hear their *coo*, a breathy whistle beneath the steady locomotion of the rumbling sound. The roof was dotted with wide glass bowls of rainwater, and some of the birds bathed in them, their wings stretched surprisingly wide, creating an upwards splash with their scrawny bird legs. Sophie, already in a state of enchantment from the heaps of crystalline glass, found her senses unexpectedly pleased by the pigeons. Their coos were delicate and steady, like a room of devotees chanting *Om*. The architecture of the wing was magnificent, wide and strong at the base, a flying muscle, tapered at the tip. The perfect stripes of the feathers, lightest gray to charcoal, the iridescence of their heads, the fuchsia and green of it matching the gleams of certain glass in the barrels below. Sophie watched the pigeons bathe like a hunter who'd stumbled upon a nymph in an old myth. She moved carefully, as if her activity would startle them into the sky, but they had been watching her for longer than she'd been watching them. As they kept up their murmured coos and shifted their plump bodies, Sophie spied an appendage, bulky and odd, jutting from the rear of one bird. She squinted in the sun.

"Livia?" she asked. The bird wobbled, settled into itself, its body a nest of feathers, the unmistakable bamboo flute wired to her backside. "Livia!" Sophie felt excited to know the bird—perhaps she should catch it and return it to Dr. Chen! The bird seemed to have liked her, maybe it would come to her easily, as it had walked onto the fingers of its master. Sophie like the idea of being special to an animal, even a useless, dirty one like a pigeon. It was special to have a creature so instinctive seek you out. It must mean there was something good about her, she decided, something subtle that animals, with their refined sense of goodness and danger, could detect. She started to call to Livia again, but noticed another protrusion on the backside of yet another bird. It was the same bamboo whistle the doctor had affixed to her pet. As the flock continued to rustle, Sophie realized that many of the birds had them, hollow whistles that looked like miniature organ pipes bound to their tail feathers. If any of them were Livia it was impossible to say, but certainly they all belonged to Dr. Chen. Did the woman know her pets spent their time lounging at the city dump? Would she care? Sophie stood still, her hand resting on a fat brown jug from another time, her eyes on these mysterious birds. And suddenly, the tremendous, backbeat rumbling stopped, and in its place rushed a silence that made Sophie's ears pop, a roar of nothing. The birds, finally acting like normal pigeons, took off as if a shot had been fired, gracefully swooping in perfect formation. In the deafening quiet Sophie could hear them pulling music through their flutes, a sound like ribbons would make if ribbons could sing as they fluttered, something high and sweet and liquid whistling through the air, twirling through the clap and smack of wings. The rickety door of the crooked building creaked open, and out stormed her grandmother, with Angel, the glass artist, scuffing behind her.

"I'm telling you, I am hearing it *in* my dreams, and it's giving me nightmares!" Sophie's grandmother was waggling her hands above her head. "I feel like it's my own goddamn head in the tumbler, getting rolled around like a rock. And then I wake up and all I hear is *thu-thunk, thu-thunk, thu-thunk,* and try going back to sleep with that racket! My trailer is *vibrating* with it, Angel."

Kishka's silver hair still held the stain of long-ago blond upon it, a yellowy tint. Her scratchy, chiffony scarf was knotted around her neck, the ends of the bow fluffing in the breeze of her agitated motions. Behind her stood Angel. Sophie, frozen still on the upended bucket, investigated Angel. Boy, or girl? The tumbler's work pants were baggy and coated with dust and grit. A flannel shirt with its arms ripped off to accommodate the heat. Angel's arms were folded across Angel's chest. Sophie looked for breasts, felt like a creep, looked away. She hadn't noticed any. Angel's arms were muscled, but skinny, too. Was that a scribble of hair poking out under the arms? Was that even a clue? A knit cap was pulled over the person's head, with choppy black hair poking out from underneath. The hair was long for a guy and short for a girl, at least in Chelsea. Angel's face was broad and smooth.

"I'm sorry, Mrs. Swankowski, we have a landscaper in Boston who just placed an order, and I'm expecting a design firm in here later this week to clear out most of the finished glass. It's certainly bringing in the money—"

"Listen, buster." Kishka shook her knuckly fist. "You think I'm worried about *money?* I make my dollars off *garbage.* The only thing this rotten town produces! I'm fine. But you better find a way to quiet that machine or else *you're* out of a job."

Sophie watched this person named Angel get a little bit smaller, and nod at her grandmother. She wondered if she could do that *thing* she did, the thing she just did to her mom by accident, the thing she stopped herself from doing to Ronald, when she sort of *pushed* herself into another person, and could suddenly feel them so sharply. Was she pushing herself into them, or was she bringing them into herself? Or was she a little bit crazy, had she made herself broken and strange playing the pass-out game? Sophie could feel the pull inside herself, and gave herself over to it. Maybe it was a creepy, sneaky thing to do, like reading someone's diary but worse, snooping in their most private spaces. Surely this was creepier than just scanning Angel's body, looking for breasts or no breasts. Sophie braced herself against the shelf, clutched at the worn, splintery wood, lodged her hip against it, and she sent herself out into Angel. Never had she done such a thing of her own volition; the other times had been involuntary, it had come upon her like a seizure, but Sophie saw now that she could control it, and was a shocked at the speed and the ease with which some part of her sped toward Angel. She felt that first shimmer of entering a person's sphere, a new flavor almost, one she'd never tasted, a certain shift of mood, she was about to feel what it felt like to be Angel, she opened further with cautious excitement, and that seeking, speeding part of herself smashed against what felt like darkness made solid. The collision was abrupt, like running into a sheet of glass you hadn't known was there. Its shatter knocked Sophie from her perch, tumbled her into a bin of shining beads, sending the blobs of color rolling across the dirt. Sophie's eyes locked with Angel's as she tumbled, the two of them linked somehow, and as her body hit the ground two thoughts rose inside of her: *Angel is a girl, and she knows I tried to do that.*

Chapter 6

It was only a moment that Sophie was out, but the dream she had in the dark space of her mind felt eternal. She was clutched in the talons of a giant bird, its claws like a cage around her body, its dark feathers batting and disorienting her. Sophie tried to steady herself on the claws but her hand slid off them; she tried to grip the creature's scaly legs but they were so terrible to touch she drew back her hand and gagged. She couldn't breathe with the evil smell of the beast, and began to thrash and kick at the claws, bringing a shriek from the bird as it looped its long neck down and locked its terrible eyes on Sophie. A great razored beak stuck with blood and fur and skin; bulging eyes with ruptured red blood vessels streaking like lightning across the yellowy whites; a knotted chiffon scarf around its neck. It opened the knife of its beak to scream.

"Oh my dear, dear granddaughter! My little bumblebee! My tiny birdie-girl!"

. . .

SOPHIE WAS AWAKE, gasping air back into her body, the air her fall had knocked from her lungs. She was tangled in the bony limbs of her grandmother. Kishka's feathers fluttered into her face, ticking her eyes—no, it was her scarf, the scarf her grandmother always kept knotted around her neck. Scratchy-soft, spritzed with perfume. Kishka's smell was a deep, green smell, the smell of a lime petrified to stone. It was a hard, heavy smell, something dug from a cave. Kishka smelled of emeralds, if emeralds had a smell. The initial lightness of the perfume was pleasant, but as you inhaled more deeply it grew darker, leaden, til you feared the fumes of it in your lungs. Sophie pushed herself away from her grandmother, and breathed deeply.

"What?" Kishka cried, insulted. "A grandmother can't give her hurt granddaughter some care? I'm just seeing if my little tweety bird is okay," Kishka watched the girl stand up, unsteady, like a colt just dropped from her mom. Sophie felt dizzy. She was afraid to look at Kishka and see a set of wild, yellowed eyes beneath her regular grandmother eyes—squinty eyes, always peering through a veil of cigarette smoke or against the fierce summer sun. She jumped as her grandmother's bony hands came clutching at her chin—*claws*, Sophie thought, she and her mom always laughed at Kishka's claw-hands, but it wasn't funny now, how did Sophie ever think it was funny, nothing was funny about a grandmother that was also a shrieking bird-monster clutching at your face with her talons. Sophie jerked away but Kishka's grip grew tighter, her fingers sinking into the girl's skin and then releasing. All the while Sophie kept her eyes closed, afraid to look, even though the scene of the vicious bird clawing at her face was no better.

"Oh, dear." Kishka pulled her hand away from Sophie's chin, and Sophie opened her eyes. Kishka's fingernails were pointy and ragged, with blotches of chipped-away nail polish here and there but the splash of red on the jagged tip of her thumb wasn't polish at all. Sophie stared at her grandmother, dizzy and horrified, as she licked the girl's blood from her claws. "You hurt yourself," she said, nodding at the scrape, beading with blood. She slid her jagged nails into the knot of her scarf and freed it, quickly daubed at the cut on Sophie's face. Sophie jumped back at the touch, but Kishka's hands were like an iron vise upon her.

"What is *wrong* with you?" her grandmother spat. "I'm trying to fix you up from your tumble and you're acting like I'm trying to kill you! You bang your head or something?" Kishka opened her mouth and her tongue slid out to moisten the scarf. Sophie shut her eyes again but too late, too late, the sight of her grandmother's tongue, thin and pale as a worm, forked like a snake and rising from a coil at the back of her throat, made her feel sick.

"There, there." Kishka patted the wound gently with the moistened scarf, cleaning the red smears off Sophie's chin. The old woman glanced at Angel. "Well, children hate getting a spit bath from an adult, but it's my right as a grandmother, isn't it?" She knotted the scarf back around her neck and pulled Sophie in for a hug.

"My little Humpty Dumpty took a real tumble, didn't you? Did you bang your noggin?" She released Sophie, held her at arms length, her hands on her shoulders. Kishka smiled, a smile Sophie had seen all her life. *Had* she bonked her noggin?

She placed her hands gingerly on the top of her head, on her shoulders and knees, on her face. No part of her body felt hurt, but some strange place inside her felt deeply bruised.

The thought of the bird, of her grandmother's tongue, sent a pukey feeling straight through her. It had been like a vision from the pass-out game, only terrible. Sophie worried that she had brought that dream space too close, and now her body was falling into it on its own.

"You only tumbled from a little bucket, for goodness sake," Kishka said. "I think you just gave yourself a scare. You gave us a scare, too! When did your lazy mother drop you off? Oh, here—Angel, this is my granddaughter, Sophie. She got her mother mad at her and now she's going to be staying here at the dump all summer. Sophie, this is Angel. He runs the glass recycling until I tear it down and fire him. Which is any minute."

Sophie looked at Angel, and Angel winked at her. It was a quick wink, so quick wondered if she'd really seen it. As she reached to shake Sophie's hand, Angel winked again, slower, if a wink can be slowed. "Great to meet you." Angel's voice was gruff, but female. Sophie peered at her. What was this strange day when everyone was something else? Angel pushed a bit of hair behind her cap with—well, could hands be male or female? Sophie was starting to feel dumb.

She knew Angel was a girl, but her nana seemed to think Angel was a guy, and Angel somehow knew that Sophie knew she was a girl, and appeared to enjoy putting one over on her boss. Sophie relaxed, relieved to be included in the joke, if that's what it was.

"No egg on your head?" Kishka reached out and ruffled Sophie's curls, her fingers getting stuck in a snarl. "Well, what the—doesn't that mother of yours comb your hair? It's a rat's nest!"

"I'm fine, Nana," Sophie finally spoke. She helped pull her grandmother's fingers from her hair. Just regular-old fingers, bony and old. Sophie's hair tangled easily; if she didn't brush it each morning the snarls formed in sleep would continue to weave together throughout the day. She pulled a rubber band from her pocket and pulled the mess of it quickly into a bun. "Mom's really busy," Sophie explained. "She had to get to work."

"There's no excuse for walking around looking like a homeless person," Kishka insisted. "I can be mad at you about it, or I can be mad at your mother. Which would you rather?"

Sophie realized as her grandmother stared at her quietly that she expected an answer.

"My... mother?" she said.

"I thought so. Smart girl." She went again to ruffle Sophie's hair, thought better of it, then reached into her housedress for a pack of cigarettes. "Anyway, I was just telling Angel here that his tumbler is too loud; it makes it impossible for me to take my naps, and I'm an old woman—old women need naps."

"I can get a smaller tumbler, but everything will take a lot longer. And it'll cost a few hundred dollars."

"You're not getting a penny out of me, mister. Figure it out! And, I'm going to leave my granddaughter here with you. You like this part of the dump, don't you, dear? It's pretty?"

"Yeah," Sophie said, gazing back at the sparkling drums of glass. "It's really pretty."

"Well, Angel will let you help him. And if anything"—Kishka took a drag from her cigarette, let the smoke leach from her body, thoughtfully—"*weird* happens, Sophia, you come and tell me *right away*." Kishka glared at the tumbler. "And someone will be on his way back to Puerto Rico so fast his head will spin." Kishka scuffed away from the glass recycling area, her plasticky sandals kicking dust up her legs, a haze of smoke drifting around her. "I'll be in my trailer, *trying* to nap, if anyone needs me!"

"I wouldn't want to wake her up," Sophie said when her grandmother was out of sight.

"I *don't* want to," Angel said. "The machine's just noisy, and we have a lot of orders, and I think all that lady does is sleep."

"No, I didn't mean you did," Sophie said quickly. It felt sort of awful to have been left there with Angel. Sophie didn't like being around strangers. It made her self-conscious even when she wasn't reeling from a bunch of weird experiences—or *hallucinations*. "It's more like, my grandmother's kind of scary! I don't ever want her mad at me."

Angel smiled and shrugged. Her easy calm was foreign to Sophie, who was only ever around high-strung, sort of stressed-out people. It made her even more compelled to jabber nervously. "She seems to like you well enough." Angel cocked an eyebrow and waited for a comment from Sophie, but Sophie was scattered and nervous.

"So, you're from Puerto Rico?" she asked. "My best friend Ella is from Puerto Rico, too. Her parents are, she's from here."

"I'm actually not Puerto Rican," Angel said. "I'm Mexican. But I'm not from Mexico, I'm from here. And my parents are from here, too. My family has been here a while." She scratched her head beneath her knit hat. "And, I'm not a guy. But you knew that."

"Why don't you tell my grand-mother?" Sophie asked.

Angel wrinkled her face. "She'd just act weird about it. And, the less your grandmother knows about me, the better."

Sophie felt a pull to know something, something more about Angel. What it felt to be a girl like she was, tough like a boy, so casual about it. She felt that part of herself pull outward; then, remembering the smack of impact, she drew it back in. Sophie busied herself playing with a bin of beads. Angel looked at her curiously.

"You okay?" she asked. "From your—fall, or whatever that was?"

"Yeah." Sophie nodded.

"You want to talk about it?" she asked.

Talk about it? What was there to talk about, if it was just a tumble? Angel's eyes were wide and steady. Did she know that Sophie had seen something? The girl shook her head quickly. Her head felt fine. She wished it didn't. If it was throbbing, if it was cut or bumpy she could maybe explain to herself the terrible things she'd seen. But she was fine. Maybe she was going cuckoo.

"You want to see the tumbler?"

Sophie nodded.

Angel led her into the crooked building. Up close, Sophie could see that it was nailed together in the same ramshackle style as the shelving outside. The wood was the same, planks that looked like driftwood, uneven and rough, with gaps for sun and rain to fall through. A giant blue tarp lay bunched by the machine.

"To keep it safe from the elements." Angel kicked it with her boot.

The tumbler wasn't as big as she thought it would be—a roll of steel with a confusion of entries and exits.

"It's so loud it feels like an earthquake," Sophie said. "I thought it would be bigger."

"It's the glass. It's very loud. It sounds nice to me, though. If you listen closely you can hear each piece singing as it tumbles, I swear."

"Really?" Sophie was skeptical. "Maybe the machine is making your ears ring or something."

Angel laughed. "No, no, it's the glass. You'll hear it too, after you've been here a while."

That just made Sophie more certain the tumbler was ruining Angel's eardrums. She leaned against the machine, scanning the dirt floor for shards of glass, which there were a lot of. The whole place was a mixture of sparkle and grit, sort of magical in an ordinary way, and for the first time Sophie considered that maybe her punishment wouldn't be so punishing after all.

Angel taught her how to clean the mucky glass that the garbage trucks rumbled in, each of them wearing thick gloves like they were doing important, dangerous work. She showed Sophie the bins for brown glass and green, for white glass and clear glass. She told her to keep an eye out for things that looked special, might be antique. Once the glass was sorted, Angel showed her how to smash it, which was really great fun. They wore goggles to keep the sharp dust from their eyes. They poured the rubble into the tumbler, and turned it on gingerly, half-expecting to hear Kishka scream at the sound of the churn. But the churn was too loud to hear anything; Angel had to motion Sophie to follow her outside the shack, waving at her with her fat, goofy gloves.

By the outdoor shelves where Sophie had fallen, Angel pulled off her gloves and tugged the goggles from her face, knocking her wool hat to the dirt in the process. Her dark hair sprang free, long bangs flopping into her face. Sophie thought it made her look more like a girl, all the hair, and then swiftly changed her mind, deciding she looked more like a boy, like one of the shaggy-headed jerks riding through Chelsea on their dirt bikes, looking for girls to torment with whistles and kissy sounds and awful comments. Angel looked like them, only nice, which meant Angel didn't really look like them, either. Sophie figured that Angel just looked like Angel, and decided not to think about it anymore.

"Good job, kid." Angel clapped Sophie on the back, collecting her too-big goggles and gloves. The goggles stuck in the snarl of her hair and for a terrible moment she imagined she'd need Angel's help to get free. She hated the thought of Angel touching her snarls. Why *didn't* she brush her hair more? Sophie resolved to groom herself better. She had a *job* now; she wasn't just rolling on creek beds with Ella. She couldn't wait to tell her friend about her excellent day, about Angel and the glass and the tumbler.

"I have something for you," Angel said, reaching deep into the pocket of her work pants. What she retrieved sat round in her hand, spanning her palm. It was a piece of glass, a blue so faint it was like the thought of blue, the very beginning of the color. Caught inside its frosted center was a scalloped seashell, white with a stripe of rose at the bottom base, like the last glow of an excellent sunset before it sank into the sky.

"Wow," Sophie breathed. "How did you make this?"

"I didn't," Angle said. "I didn't tumble it, either. It's sea glass. It came like that right out of the ocean."

Sophie inspected it, turning it over in her palm. She pressed her fingers against its smooth edges, feeling for a ghost of the sharpness that had long been worn away by the sea. "But how did it happen?" she asked. "Like, was it glass someone made with seashells and then it got dumped in the ocean and rolled around?"

Angel shrugged. "I don't know. I guess that could have happened, but it's really old. It's very mysterious. I did do this"—she pointed to a hole at the tip—"so you could, like, wear it as a necklace."

Sophie thrilled at the thought. "Yes!" she said. "That's so cool."

"But you can't let your grandmother see it, okay? She thinks half the things that come into this place are worth something, and they're not, but she'll take it and put it in her trailer and that's the last you'll see of it. Keep it low."

"Okay." Sophie nodded solemnly. She pulled her house key out from her t-shirt and strung the sea glass onto the rope. "I think it needs a really nice chain," she said wistfully. "But I'll wear it on this for now so I don't lose it."

"Right on." Angel gave her a salute. "See you tomorrow. Get some sleep. Your bones are going to be sore after all the work we did today."

Chapter 7

"**S**o, how did it go?" Andrea asked cautiously, with a lilt of cheer in her voice that was mostly fake. Sophie had been so volatile, Andrea imagined her daughter had spent the day bored out of her gourd amongst heaps of garbage, feeding a festering hate. She peeked over at the girl and returned her eyes to the road. Washington Ave. glided by, a strip of grocery stores and barber shops, restaurants selling pupusas and plantains, or pizza and subs, or chow mein and chicken wings. Sophie's belly rumbled.

"It was fine. I tumbled glass. What's for dinner?"

Andrea sighed at the thought of cooking anything for anyone, even herself. The air conditioning at the clinic was broken, cooling the building in fits and starts all day, making work even harder and more annoying. If it were next week, closer to payday, she'd stop and pick them up a pizza, but it wasn't next week, and the dollars folded into her wallet were a thin bundle. "I'm having cereal," she said.

"You are free to fix yourself whatever you like."

"But I worked," Sophie whined. She held her hands up to show her mother, but they were creaseless and clean. She'd forgotten about the gloves. "I worked so hard I had to wear *gloves*," she said. She brought her hands to her hair and dug around her scalp. "Look," she said, finding a pebble of glass caught in a web of snarl. "Glass in my hair, even." She laid the red orb on the dashboard, where it caught the dimming sun and glowed like a coal.

"We both worked," Andrea said, "so we'll each make our own supper. If I could pluck an asthmatic child from my hair to illustrate, I would."

Sophie laughed, and Andrea almost laughed, and the mood between them felt lighter than it had in days. Andrea was relieved that she wasn't retrieving the same angry, stubborn girl she'd dropped at the dump. All day she'd mused upon that strange feeling she'd had pulling away in her car, a wonderful emptiness. She longed to feel that feeling again, but found it hard to explain even to herself. She'd have thought that feeling nothing would feel like death—something scary—but it had felt light and wonderful. And when her emotions poured back into her each feeling felt louder than before, more noticeable, as if she'd become numb to them without realizing. What were these feelings she felt toward her daughter? She felt ashamed at many of them. *Fear? Awe?* She brushed it away. Those were old feelings; she didn't need to feel like that anymore.

Sophie understood in a new way how tired her mom must be after eight hours in the sweaty clinic. She didn't think that Andrea had worked as *hard* as she had, lifting buckets and smashing glass, but still, work was tiring. "Okay," she said. "I'll have cereal. It's too hot for real food, anyway." The bolt of ugly feelings she'd felt from her mother seemed very far away, buried beneath the adventure of the dump. In the pleasant quiet of their drive home, Sophie almost pulled the sea glass from beneath her shirt to show her mother. Her hands touched the cord, but stayed there, fiddling. She dropped her hands to her lap. The glass lay cool and heavy on her sternum. It was from the ocean; there was no telling what part of the world it had come from, how many years it had taken it to wash up in Chelsea, currents and sand grinding its edges. It felt incredibly precious, too precious for anyone to see or touch. They arrived at their home without Sophie mentioning it. Andrea pulled two bowls from the cupboard, and Sophie heaved a gallon of milk from the fridge.

. . .

SOPHIE LOOKED AROUND for a place to talk with Ella on the phone. Their house was only so big, and the phone was a cheap piece of plastic, growing staticky when you walked it too far from its base. Sophie wished she had her own phone, a *cell phone*, and that she had a real room to take it into, a proper bedroom with privacy, not the glorified walk-in closet attached to her mother's bedroom. She looked in on

Andrea, already passed out on the couch, a milky cereal bowl before her on the coffee table. The television was blaring some news program, and the loud hum of the fan spun coolness onto her mother. This was the most privacy she was going to get. Sophie figured it was enough.

On the other end of the phone Sophie could hear the cacophony of Ella's home. People hollered in dueling languages for the girl. Sophie could hear Ella's younger siblings calling for her, excited and important to be delivering news of a phone call; older voices, her mother and her aunts, were a steady roar of talk. Sophie could imagine them circling the dinner table, eating cookies and drinking coffees. She felt a pang of loneliness at her own empty house, her tired mother already asleep with the sun still shining, creepy television newscaster voices intoning darkly through the apartment. Sophie wished Ella would invite her over, but knew it wouldn't happen.

"Hello?" Ella was breathless at having run through the house.

"Hi!" Sophie said. "What's up?"

"Nothing, just a million people over here as usual, a girl can't get any space. I'm dying to get *out* of here."

"Are you having a nic fit?" Sophie asked. Never having smoked, Sophie didn't know what a *nic fit* felt like, just that her friend claimed to have them, and once she started having one it was all she thought about, all she talked about, until she smoked a cigarette. Sophie thought nic fits were strange and boring.

"No way, my house is so smoky with everyone over here, I just had a cigarette right in my bedroom and no one even knew!" Ella sounded proud, having found away to make the chaos of her home work for her. "I got *burned* at the beach today. It was hot, huh?"

Sophie had forgotten about the beach. She was surprised to feel not a single pluck of envy at having missed something. "How was it?"

"How do you think it was? Awesome. There were so many cute guys. One gave me the rest of his pizza—he was *soooo* wicked cute."

"What's his name?"

"Junior. Which is crazy, right, 'cause I'm a junior, like my mother's name is Ella, and *he's* a junior, 'cause he's named after his dad, like his real name is Tony or something. But I was like, Junior! That's got to *mean* something."

Sophie paused, waiting for Ella to bust up into laughter. Was she joking? She sounded like an airhead.

Listening to herself talking to Sophie, Ella could hear how dumb she sounded, but she couldn't help herself. There was something exhilarating about giving herself over to such talk and feelings. The boy's attentions had electrified her, his steady dark eyes and his husky voice as he traded his pizza for a cigarette. She could feel another girl rising inside her, dumber in some ways and smarter in others, haughty and confident, a flirt. She supposed she'd flirted with the boy, and it had *worked*—he'd seemed both flirtier and shyer when he'd left, after smoking his cigarette down to the filter and tossing the butt into the frothy waves. Ella's body buzzed from the interaction like a hive of yellow jackets swarmed through her, beating their tiny wings. The rash her last scrubbing spell had left upon her was minor, no one noticed it, she could pretend it was gone and that the girl who'd done it was gone, too, that she was through with all that, and she wouldn't let such craziness overtake her again.

"Okay." Sophie laughed. She sounded almost nervous. "Well, ah, I was at the dump all day."

Ella had forgotten to stay mad at her friend for telling their secret and getting herself punished. She'd missed her at the beach, at first, but then, later, when the boys showed up, she'd been grateful Sophie wasn't around. How could Ella have tried on this new personality in front of Sophie, who knew her so well? Sophie who knew she was a nerd, scared of most everything, had never exchanged a germy kiss with anyone. Sophie would have kicked her with her foot and crossed her eyes at her, and the boy would have decided they both were freaks, and he would have been right. Ella felt guilty to be glad about her friend's punishment, but she was. "That sucks," she said unconvincingly. "What, did you, like, hang around in trash all day? What even happens there?" Ella shuddered at the thought, feeling the incoming crave of another nic fit.

"There's a glass recycling place, and this person Angel operates it, and she's, like, a girl, but she looks like a boy, she's really cool. And she gave me this amazing, like, jewel—not a jewel, it's glass with a seashell in it, and there's all this tumbled glass and it's so beautiful."

Ella found it hard to concentrate on her friend's breathless report. Her sister and her cousin were chasing each other in and out of her bedroom, and she could hear a new thread of gossip being shared in the kitchen, the voices rising tantalizingly higher with outrage at someone's scandalous behavior. And beneath the hum of her house, Ella thought *Junior Junior Junior Junior*, feeling the sear of the boy's presence strong as her sunburn. She tried to focus. What had Sophie said, something about a girl that looks like a boy?

"What, are you working with a lesbian? Watch out she doesn't make a grab for you, Sophie!"

"Don't be a jerk." Sophie felt protective of Angel. "I don't know if she's a lesbian."

"Girls who look like boys are *leeeesbians*, trust me. My Auntie Bertie looks just like a boy, and she is a total les and she likes to make a grab at the girls, so you be careful!" Ella laughed. "A lesbian! The dump sounds more exciting than I thought it would be."

"It is," Sophie said. She couldn't tell if Ella was being mean about Angel or not, but she decided to not talk any more about it. "Anyway, I'm so bored. My mother fell asleep in front of the television again."

"*Whooo*," Ella made a noise. "That woman likes to snooze. I wish these people over here would take a nap. Can you hear how loud it is?" Sophie could.

"I wish we could meet up," Sophie said, suddenly longing for her friend.

"We could sneak out," Ella said. "Later?"

Sophie bit her lip. She was already in so much trouble, banished to the dump all summer. She was conflicted over how she should behave as a result of this punishment. Should she be contrite and rule abiding to show her mother—what? That she was sorry? She wasn't sorry, exactly. She didn't think her punishment fit her crime. And if she was already punished for the duration of the summer, why should she behave? Sophie realized that if she *didn't* sneak out to see Ella she could forget about having a best friend. Ella would never, ever, ever come to the city dump, and look how different she already was, after just a single day at the beach without her? If Sophie let go of her, Ella would wind up—what? Sophie pictured an even tanner Ella, her dark skin oily and coconut, her long hair teased out Chelsea-style, cigarettes stuck into the hairsprayed mess of it like barrettes. Ella would wind up vapid, uninteresting, and pregnant. Pregnant? Sophie felt like it was a betrayal of her best friend to even think such a thought, but the thought was there—Ella pregnant, by the end of the summer.

"Let's meet at the creek," Sophie said. "Where we met last time."

Ella didn't like the thought of that place, with its condoms and filthy water and the memory of her friend's face-plant in the muck. But she could think of no where else to go. Street corners were patrolled by cops and cluttered with kids. Parks were locked, and too easy to get busted sneaking into them. The creek was pretty perfect. Ella wished they could just go back to the beach, and sit on the wall in the dark, straining their eyes to see where the black sky met the black ocean on the black, black horizon. Maybe Junior would be drawn back, too, looking for her. She tried to shake the boy out of her head, stay the Ella she was for Sophie, not the Ella she was that day at the beach. "Okay," Ella said. "I'll meet you there once the sun goes down."

Chapter 8

The trick to doing something you're totally not supposed to do is acting like it's the most natural thing in the world, like you have every right to be doing it, whatever it is. Sophie pushed her feet into her Vans and passed her mother, asleep on the couch. Her heart pulsed at the sight of Andrea in her work clothes, her head at an odd angle on the couch. It had to be uncomfortable. The woman had to be truly exhausted to have fallen asleep in such an awkward pose, oblivious to the blare of the TV. Sophie thought of turning it down, but then maybe the noise was keeping her mother asleep. What was it about the way Andrea looked, her sleeping mouth open, drool wetting the corners? She looked vulnerable. It gave Sophie a strange, sad feeling. She clicked the door closed gently before she left, praying that her mother wouldn't stir awake at the sound.

Ella's strategy was different. The coffee-drinking, gossiping relatives clustered around her kitchen table would stay there long into the night. As distracted as they might be with their lively conversation, they were never too distracted not to know the exact whereabouts of every child in the house. Ella stationed herself with a magazine on the hall floor outside the bathroom. Tia Lucy came by first.

"What are you doing, sitting on the floor by the bathroom?"

Ella slapped shut her magazine with a sigh. "It's so *loud* in here," she groaned. "I can't even read a stupid magazine. I keep reading the same sentence again and again."

Tia Lucy clucked her tongue in sympathy. "I hate that," she said. "You should go over to my house, it's empty. I got lemonade in the fridge, help yourself. You're too big to play with the kids and too little to sit with us old ladies." Tia Lucy laughed as she slid into the bathroom. What a joker. Tia Lucy was hardly an old lady at all. She had long hair she wore in an intricate combination of braid and bun at the back of her head, the better to see the earrings swaying from her ears. Her eyes were lined in blue and she reminded Ella of a bird. Not a dirty Chelsea pigeon but a beautiful, quick bird from a tropical island.

Tia Shirley came next. "What are you doing, reading in the dark? Turn a light on! You're going to ruin your eyes!"

Ella slapped shut her magazine with a sigh. "The lightbulb burned out. And I can't read in my room because Tracy and Junior are playing in there, and I can't read in the living room because Tio Matty and my father are watching something, and I can't read in the kitchen because you all are so *loud*."

Tia Shirley put her hand on her heart and worried her brow, as if a terrible dilemma was before them. "Ella! There has to be a place for you, too! Why don't you go to my house? Your Tio is sleeping and you can stay on my back porch with the light and read your magazine. Go—I'll tell your mother."

"Okay, I probably will," Ella said.

Sitting on the floor in the hallway, Ella received invitations from two more of her aunts to go and read her magazine at their home. So when she stood at the door, her hand twisting the knob, and hollered into the kitchen, "Okay, I'm going to your house to read my magazine, be back in a couple hours!" the women at the table cried back, "Okay, be careful!" in unison, and Ella walked out the door and headed toward the creek.

. . .

THE SKY OVER Chelsea was extra dark; occasionally the landscape would shift enough for the moon to peek through, illuminating the mass of clouds suffocating its light, and then the cloud cover would spread itself again, and the sky would return to blackness. The glow of the streetlights seemed puny, throwing dim yellow halos around the bulbs but casting hardly any light to the ground. By the time she reached the hole in the chain link, Sophie was going on instinct and memory—beyond the tear in the fence, a shapeless chunk of cement; a bit further, a toppled shopping cart. For a second the clouds shifted, and the moonlight caught on an empty bottle and shone through it to illuminate the path that wound through the tall weeds to the scabby little creek. Sophie headed out on it, wishing that she could smell the water but sort of grateful, she supposed, that she couldn't, it was so thin and dirty. They were so close to the ocean in Revere, so close to the harbor on the East Boston border, but Sophie and Ella needed the privacy of the creek, their own body of water.

Ella lived closer to the creek and was there already, halfway through a cigarette. When she hugged her, Sophie could feel the day's sun radiating off her skin. Ella smelled like the tanning oil that stuck stubbornly to her arms, and like the scented lotion she slathered on top of it. Her hair smelled like shampoo and her cigarette smelled slightly of strawberry from the gloss on her mouth. Ella smelled like a girl. Sophie couldn't imagine what she herself smelled like. She lifted her arm and huffed her armpit.

"Nice," Ella commented wryly. "Classy."

"I think I have to start wearing deodorant," Sophie mused. "Now that I have a job and stuff."

"Wait, so that's your actual *job*?" Ella asked. "Like, you're getting paid?"

Sophie hedged. "No, I'm not getting paid. But I'm working."

Ella snorted a last bit of smoke from her nose, like a dragon, and flung her butt in the creek. "That's not a job, Soph. That's slavery. There are child labor laws. I bet you could call social services on your mom and they would take you away like that." Ella snapped her fingers. "Think of it—single mom sends her daughter to the *city dump* to work, underage, without pay, for her wicked grandmother."

"It sounds so bad when you say it like that," Sophie agreed. "But it just feels like being grounded, you know?"

"No, Sophie. Really. Think about it. This could be your lucky break. Social services could take you and place you with, like, some family in the country or something. Or out where the ocean is really pretty, you know, where it's clean. You could have a dog, and your own room, and food, and I bet the people would be, like, so nice, just really nice people who want to save teenage girls from working at the dump."

Sophie joined the fantasy. "Or a family in Cambridge," she said dreamily. Ella wrinkled her nose.

"Cambridge is busted," she said. "That's where Ben Affleck is from."

"Not that part," Sophie insisted. "The good part of Cambridge, where Harvard is. Maybe I could get adopted by Harvard professors. They'd have a whole room of books, like a library. And real art on the walls, and I'd have my own room and have a pet, even. A dog."

"A smart dog," Ella offered. "Not some dumb fucking dog."

"Yeah," Sophie said. She imagined herself curled up in a sunny room with a smart dog gazing at her lovingly while she read a really difficult book that she totally understood.

"Or you'd just get thrown in with some pervert and wind up molested," Ella said.

"Or with one of those couples that live off their foster kid checks," Sophie concurred. "Like, in a house with fifteen other foster kids. Really awful kids who'd torture cats. Like, put firecrackers up their butts or something." Sophie shuddered. "People do that, you know."

"Foster-kid hoarders are creepy." Ella nodded grimly. "You're better off where you are." Ella pulled a green hair elastic from where it sat on her wrist like a bracelet, and pulled her hair into a shiny loop atop her head. "Let's get to it," she said. "I want to go first. I didn't even get to pass myself out last time."

Sophie looked uneasily at her friend. "I don't know, Ella," she said. "I've been having some weird things happen to me…"

"You said the doctor told you it was no big deal. You told me *she* passed herself out when she was our age. And look at her! She's a friggin' doctor!"

"I know…" Sophie was feeling wimpy. There was no way to deny it. She felt a wimpy look settle across her face, part a squirmy sort of fear, part shame at the fear, with a tinge of a plea for mercy from her merciless friend.

"Don't wimp out on me, Swankowski," Ella said sternly. "If I don't play pass-out with you, who will I play with? Come on, it's still fun, don't you think?"

Sophie recalled the dreamy visions and the sweet body-buzz. She *did* think it was fun. But passing out felt linked now with those strange feelings and visions, and that desperate need for salt. When she had fixed her bowl of cereal earlier that evening, after her mother had drifted into the living room, Sophie had swiped at the fat, round salt canister in the cupboard and plucked out the spout, sending a fall of the stuff into her Cheerios. *Weird.* But it had been delicious.

"Just one time," Ella pushed. "Once for me and once for you. Come on, why did you even want me to meet you out here, if not to play pass-out?"

"Because we're friends," Sophie said dumbly.

"Yeah, we're friends, and this is what we do when we hang out. I smoke and talk too much, you don't smoke and listen to me, and we pass each other out." Ella flicked her lighter in the dark, casting enough light for them to find a slight clearing free of dog poop or condoms or jagged smashed bottles. Smaller bits of glass sparkled in the light and reminded Sophie of the recycling shack, of Angel and the tumbler and the bright bins of glass, and she found herself actually excited to return.

"Okay," Ella said. With her knees in the dirt Ella bent her head and began her huffing and puffing. When she flung herself up Sophie tensed behind her, waiting for her body to begin its slump, to catch her and lay her gently on the ground. She did. She pushed some weeds aside so that they framed her face. Ella, she realized, was beautiful. She always had been, and Sophie had always known it, but Ella's beauty had always been neck and neck with Sophie's own. Looking down at her friend's cheeks, the relaxed pout of her mouth, the way her lashes swung up at her smooth eyelids, rapid with the movement of her dreaming, Sophie thought that Ella's beauty had pulled ahead, was in the lead, would almost certainly win.

Ella's eyes shot open, and Sophie felt like she'd been caught doing something creepy, staring at her friend while she was gone. "What?" Ella demanded.

"Nothing," Sophie said, nervously. "You were out for a while, I was just checking on you."

"How long was I out for?"

"Like, five minutes, maybe ten," Sophie lied.

Ella thought about it, then shrugged in the dirt. "I felt like I was out for five or ten hours," she said.

"What did you see?"

"Nothing. Maybe a dog. Yeah, a dog, a big sweet dog. God, I want a dog so bad," Ella mourned. "My mother is such a cat person, she'll never let me get one." Ella closed her eyes, trying to get back to the fading sensation of some soul mate dream-dog. "It felt so nice to be next to it!"

The thing about playing pass-out was it felt so nice to be next to *whatever* was in your dream. Once Sophie had gone under and had a vision of a kitchen table. She came out of it filled with a tender, almost mystical affection for the furniture. It was the weirdest thing. But Sophie could see her friend getting a little hooked on the dream dog. At least she hadn't had a vision of the beach boy, Sophie thought. *That* would for sure be unbearable.

"Go," Ella said to Sophie, arranging herself on the ground. "I got you."

Sophie resisted laughing as she began to pant and huff. Her hair did not cascade to the ground like Ella's; she felt loose strands catch and bunch around the snarls, like seaweed caught on a rock. Her heavy breaths puffed the dust of the ground back up into her face. She sat back on her heels and held her breath, gripping the edges of her throat tightly. She felt it in her face first, a hot tingle. Next in her hands, they seemed to disintegrate, atom by atom vanishing with a lovely shimmer, followed by the rest of her body, buzzing and gone. Sophie was faintly aware of Ella's hands on her, laying her down. She was in a fluid place, slow and liquid, a cave perhaps. She was underwater. Things floated around her slowly, things too dark to see, but before her eyes one simple thing glowed, a starfish trapped in a hunk of sea glass illuminating the bare chest of a wild-haired mermaid. The sea glass cast a pale blue light, giving the fish-belly-white skin of the mermaid a sickly fluoresence.

Sophie thought *her* hair had problems. The creature's inky mane hung suspended in the water around her head. Tangles unraveled into long, tough locks, only to join once more in a round weave of snarl, snarls stuck with slimy ropes of seaweed, with fragments of seashells and urchin shells and the curving, fragile bones of fish. Her endless hair floated out past her tail, which was a great and muscled thing, shining in places and dull in places, sometimes healthy and sometimes looking like a fish kept in a neglected aquarium, its body coming off itself in ghostly tendrils.

In her vision, Sophie pulled her twin jewel out from her shirt, the seashell buried in the frosted, ancient glass, and showed it to the mermaid. And the mermaid opened her mouth and spoke inside the water.

"Yah, I know," she said, sounding annoyed. Her words were heavy, each one sounded carved from rock. It was an old voice—not the shaky timbre of an elderly woman but old like bedrock, a hard voice, solid. "Why do you think I am doing here, anyway? I come for you."

The current of the waters pushed the mermaid's hair in front of her face, obscuring her. She pulled a six-pack of plastic rings from the creek bed, tore a circle free and pulled her hair through it at the top of her head, subduing a bit of the wild mane. Sophie could see more six-pack rings and other bits of garbage stuck in the mermaid's hair, trying to control it.

"You came for me?" Sophie asked. The mermaid's heavy accent, her struggle with English, made Sophie unsure she was hearing right. They spoke in the glow of their jewels, their faces lit but the water dim around them. Sophie was glad about that. She had come to understand that they were submerged in the creek, and what floated around them was the terrible flotsam and jetsam of Chelsea. She would be completely grossed out if not for the absolute wonder of a mermaid, or the bizarre ability to speak and breathe underwater. How was that possible? Sophie thought it was better not to question it. *Of course I can breathe underwater,* she thought. *That's what happens when you hang out with a mermaid.*

"You have the amulet, yes?" the mermaid gestured to the jewel. "I know you are the one. Now, put it away. Do not flaunt."

Sheepishly, Sophie dropped her amulet into her shirt, which ballooned around her in the water.

"I come all the way from Poland to be here," the mermaid said, her voice thick with her country. "I watch over my city, and now, come to get you, who watches over my river? No one. Is unprotected. Will turn into a mess, like this place. I try and try not to come. I try to get out from it. I try to come later. No, no, no, everyone say, time is now, the girl, you do what you call—pass out?"

Sophie nodded.

"Very great way to come to you, in this special place, half-real, half-dream. Is own space. Girls find it when they come into power, at certain age." The mermaid sighed with deep resignation. "So, was time to come for you. And here we are in this—what you call this? Not a river—"

"A creek," Sophie offered.

"Yes. Is terrible! So skinny, like a girl that doesn't eat. I am used to my big river, water all around me." The mermaid spread her hands grandly, to indicate space. One hand banged up against a rusted, submerged shopping cart, the other slapped against the earthen wall of the narrow channel. Sophie noticed shining rings on the creature's pale fingers, iridescent shards of seashells. "My back is very sore from having hunch to be in this small water," she continued her complaint. "And the water, so dirty! But all the waters everywhere, very, very bad. I see in my journey here. One place in the ocean is so evil, a machine pours darkness into the water, pure darkness, and if it touches you, you become the darkness, you get caught in it like this—" She caught a floating tangle of hair and thrust it at Sophie. Sophie saw a hermit crab, its tiny shell imprisoned in the snarl. "You cannot move, the darkness ensnares you, you sink down down down until you die." She shook her head. "I would think that machine is where the night comes from, except night comes from the sky and is gentle. This is something wrong."

"It's oil," Sophie offered. "There was a big spill or something." She had seen it on the news, flickering across her mother's sleeping face.

"Well, it fucking sucks. Excuse my language, but I try to speak words you know. You know 'fucking sucks,' yes?"

Sophie nodded.

"To leave my beautiful river—I keep it very nice, I promise you. I have lived there for many, many hundreds of years and the people, they are very good to me, they put my picture on the seal of the city, even. I am—what you call—a celebrity. Parents scare your children with me. They tell them, 'You throw trash in the river; Syrena will come and get you.' And I do! I come in their dreams, like I am in your dream right now." Syrena took a moment to consider herself. "I am not like the mermaids in your books and pictures, no? They are very—they are like dolls. They are pretty, but they are not real. I am real mermaid. *Rusalka*, river mermaid." She bunched her hair and twisted it in a long bundle, like a baguette, pulled it over one bare shoulder. An eel poked its confused head from the garland, and the mermaid plucked it free, sent it zooming into the dark of the creek.

"That is probably bad," she said. "Eel in your creek. Not right to have eels in this creek. But it's so filthy, he will die before doing any harm." The mermaid took a deep, sad breath, and coughed in a heavy sputter of bubbles. She pulled her hair in front of her mouth and hacked into the tangle. "This is like, humans smoke cigarettes? Being in this creek is like being in the smoke of eighty million cigarettes smoked all at once."

Sophie wrinkled her face. "That sounds horrible."

"Is fucking disgusting. That what humans say? Fucking disgusting?"

Sophie half-nodded, half-shrugged. "Certain kinds of humans," she said.

"I was told here, this creek, where I find you—Chelsea?"

Sophie nodded.

"I was instructed—much 'fucking sucks,' 'fucking disgusting.' What else? I don't know, put 'fucking' in front of much words, no? Then you understand?"

"I would understand without it," Sophie said. "It's sort of a—bad word."

"This is bad place, no?"

Sophie nodded. "I guess it is."

"I come to you to help you fix it," Syrena said heavily. She didn't seem happy about it, but she didn't seem sad either. "I have show for you. Something to feel. Will be hard. I would ask, *Are you ready?* But I don't think you are, and is time for you regardless. Everything has own time, and time much bigger than us all." The creature sighed and with her long, bony hands pushed her hair strongly from her face. The amulet lit up her sharp cheekbones; they were almost finlike, lifting from the contours of her blueish-white skin. Her clear eyes shone at Sophie and in them Sophie felt something to be trusted. But she didn't like the sound of any of this, and began to shake herself around beneath the water.

"I'm going to wake up now," she told the mermaid. "This has been cool, seeing a mermaid, but I've got to wake up before I kill my brain cells. Okay?" She tried to twist herself awake but felt the weight of the water upon her like a straight jacket, constricting her.

"Brain is fine, brain is fine," the mermaid said dismissively. "You wake up when allowed. First, you must understand. Here." The creature's hands, cupped together, opened like the shell of an oyster, revealing something small and gleaming, round and pale but not an oyster.

"What is that?" Sophie asked.

"Is salt." The mermaid smiled, a real smile now, her mouth, thin and wide, cracking into her face. The mermaid was terribly old, old as the rocks in the furrows of the deepest valley at the ocean's bottom, but in her smile she was just a girl, a girl like Sophie, or Ella. "At start of journey, this salt as big as house! I wrap in seaweed for one day. From everywhere everyone help me—my sisters help, and fish help us, and seals, you know, everyone pitch in. And together we wait for whale shark to come, and into its mouth it goes. So big! The whale shark not like, not at all. Too salty! All along it spits and spits." Syrena laughed, again becoming young, just for a flicker. "Slowly, the salt melt. From sea to sea we travel, it melts. The salt is not regular salt. This the salt that make the ocean." The mermaid's fisted hand loosened, and Sophie caught a silvery flash of the crystal in the dark.

"Two giant women, they make it far from here, at the bottom of the ocean. Women so big, if they here now, water would dribble at their feet! They are *ogress*. You know them? Big, big women! An ocean king take them many years ago, when they were just girls. King thought they were women already, they were so big, but no, they are just baby ogresses. Strong little babies! The king make them slaves, tell them to mine gold from the earth beneath the ocean. And they do for a little bit, because they were just babies and the digging was fun, but they grow older and become wise and they try to escape but they cannot. And so they begin to dredge salt instead of gold. So much salt! The ocean becomes full of it! The king cannot take it, he flee to some fresh water somewhere, he there still, what you call—refugee? In little bitty spring. And the ogresses keep bringing the salt to the ocean. They don't mind, many creatures like the salt, and so they do it and do it, even now." The mermaid smiled with the thought. "I hear story of ogresses since baby mermaid. Was something to see! Their big toe as big as your whole body. You could sleep on their toenail!" The mermaid laughed, shimmering globes of air bubbling up around her. Sophie tried to imagine a woman so big. "Ogress would let you sleep on her toe," the mermaid continued. "They—sisters—they know all about you. You famous for them like they famous for me. Say you will need their salt, they dig out big piece for you, they say will dig you more. They say you will—make them feel better."

Sophie liked the thought of being famous with friendly ogresses, but her concern was growing into a higher pitch of panic. This wasn't a normal pass-out vision. It had been too long, she was too conscious, too participatory. "I don't mean to be rude," she said to the mermaid. "But I really think I ought to stop. To wake up or whatever."

The mermaid ignored Sophie and moved closer. "We must begin," she said sternly, her joy at having met the ogresses gone, her ancient face set back to steel and determination. She brought her face to Sophie's so that her hair hung about them like a tent. Her eyes sparked brighter. It seemed that the darker the water, the more the creature's eyes glowed, like lightning bugs were trapped in her skull, illuminating the murk. Was the mermaid good or bad? Sophie felt she was both—her badness a hardness like a rock inside her, and her goodness the light in her eyes. "I will give you feeling," the mermaid spoke. "You ready to feel?"

Sophie laughed, a skittish hiccup that bubbled to the surface like a lone jellyfish. "I guess," she shrugged. The mermaid placed her forehead to Sophie's brow. How smooth it felt, like a dolphin Sophie had once touched at the aquarium. The mermaid's fingers, long and gnarled as coral branches, cupped her cheeks, slick as seal skin. Sophie felt something like love flare inside her, and wondered if that was the feeling the mermaid was giving her, this leaping feeling of love, of excitement.

"You guess," the mermaid said, hearing her thoughts.

"This is it?" Sophie asked with a smile.

"Not yet," the mermaid said, moving the glowing talisman around her neck so that it clanked gently against Sophie's. "This your feeling."

"Oh," Sophie giggled. The giggle was like a school of tiny silver fish bursting in the water around her face. "I'm starting to feel silly."

"Okay, now I give you feeling," the mermaid said. She closed her eyes like snuffing a candle, and the water grew dark around them. Her face pressed closer and the fingers on the girl's face grew tight.

"Sophia," the mermaid whispered. "I very sorry."

Chapter 9

Sophie *felt*, feelings like a black wave risen from the middle of the ocean and then crashing down on her, crushing her, pounding the air from her lungs until all that she breathed, all that filled her was an infinity of pain. Each pain as exquisite, as singular, as a snowflake, or a human being. The pain of a mother, her child torn apart before her. The pain of the torn child, helpless, conscious of their brief horror. The pain of a village in flames, as seen by the one villager who ran, who turned back to see the orange and the black gusts of smoke, to smell the terrible smell of people burning. The pain of soldiers torturing a man, their hearts a manic sickness inside them, the pain of the tortured as he tries again and again to leave his body, to die, but only remains here, in the body he once adored, now its own chamber of punishment. The pain of the old and the pain of the young, the pain of the hurt and the pain of the violent, it blew through Sophie like a rough wind through a corridor, and Sophie felt such a wind would never die, that it had blown forever and for-ever now would batter her, wearing holes in her heart for it to whistle through.

Sophie was frozen still, paralyzed. The sensation in her body, if she still had a body, was like tumbling and being stuck at once. She thought of a carnival ride that spun and spun until you stuck to the wall and the floor fell down. She was falling with the feelings, the anguish of a creature as its beloved is slain, the devastation of the pulse of love in the midst of terror and war, so that the love turned upon itself and became a misery, a pinching crab where a heart once was. A child immobilized, a child pushed into the sea, a woman screaming in a dark place, all the women screaming in all the dark places. Sophie could not bear it. She could not bear even a single strand of the pain, but how they looped and wove together, how the pain tangled with other pain into tangled snarls, tumors, pulsing and snaring yet more cords of horror. Sophie could not bear any of it, and slowly she felt herself cease to be Sophie. Sophie was easing away. There were only the feelings, thick and cold and endless and alone, bleaker than death. *Death,* flickered the last wisp of Sophie's intelli-gence, death was a pleasure, a welcome, a gateway. Death was kind, a flare in eternity. This, Sophie realized, this *was* eternity. And then there was nothing but pure and terrible sensation forever.

Feeling her lost now, the mermaid took the salt in her fingers and pressed it into the girl's slackened mouth. She pinched Sophie's lips with her twisted, elegant fingers, and on her tongue the crystal continued its slow dissolve. From a rock the size of a house to the bead the mermaid had clutched in her fist, now melting to nothing.

The ogresses had thundered across the ocean floor, to a bed of coral they'd never touched. With a twist of their wrists they'd snapped the coral from the sea like popping a top from a bottle of soda, sending a spray of tiny creatures scuttling. *A special stash*, one ogress had grunted as Syrena circled their heads in the water, pushing through their forests of hair, looping before their faces. Gorgeous as a woman carved into a marble cliff, golden eyes and the soft curve of their mouths. *Special for Sophia.* And they began to dig. To have seen the magnificent crystal, gestating so deep within the earth for so long; to watch it become small enough to slip through a crack in your fist—a pebble, a pearl, but still so powerful.

When the mermaid felt Sophie become lost, she experienced it as a flicker of peace. The pressure of hundreds upon hundreds of years— her age—lifted away in a single throb. For a pulse, she was ageless. Before her gills could complete a breath the peace was gone, and her time on this earth crashed back down upon her. Syrena was *old*. It was time to give the girl her pearl.

Chapter 10

Water tunneled backward through Sophie's nose until it ran bitter down the back of her throat. Her mouth tasted like drowning. She took a breath; there were boats where her lungs were. The mermaid was gone and everything was as ink-black as the hole bleeding oil at the bottom of the ocean. Sophie rolled onto her side. Her opening eyes cracked the darkness and brought her a vision of her best friend dumping creek water from a scummy beer bottle onto her face. She brought up her hands to block the filth of it. Sophie opened her mouth to shout, and a rogue wave of water spilled out from her lips. Her body contracted, and more water rolled out. Grimy, oily creek water. A single hardy fish surfed from Sophie's mouth and flopped onto the dirt to suffocate. Sophie lifted him by his tiny tail and flicked him back into the creek. Who knew that anything lived in that creek? Ella stood over her, clutching the old beer bottle and crying. She flung it at the ground where it did not shatter but bounced precariously close to Sophie's soggy head.

"You were out," Ella said, "for *so long*." She was not even going to try to convey the panic and grief she'd spent the last hour gripped in. The terror at Sophie being gone, the sorrow at Sophie being gone. The dread of having helped her pass out, the guilt at the sight of her, her breathing gone weird, slowed down, stop and go, had Ella helped her best friend into a coma, had she killed her, even? Would she go to jail, was she an accessory to something horrible? In her frenzied panic she'd grabbed a bottle from the weeds and plunged it into the creek, filling it with rancid water. She dumped it onto her friend's soft face, loving her, hating her, weird dopey Sophie, sweet funny Sophie, Sophie who didn't understand anything, Sophie who understood her. Again and again Ella poured the water over Sophie's face, crying, until her actions ceased to make sense. Crying, *Sophie, Sophie, Sophie,* smacking her friend, first because she'd seen it on television, a fainted woman getting smacked—that's what you were supposed to do, wasn't it?— and when Sophie refused to stir, when nothing in her face responded to the blow, Ella smacked her again, this time in anger, this time in fear, and she smacked her friend three times like that before her sense came back to her and she pulled her ringing hand away and clutched at her own face, not even caring that the muck of the creek was upon her, though later she would. She returned to the water, because she had seen this on television, too—someone throwing water in the face of a fainted woman. And the water was gentler, and didn't bring Ella face to face with the violence of her own fear. The water splashed off Sophie's face in every direction. And finally, Sophie came to, spurting an ocean of water, fish and everything, from her mouth, and Ella felt like maybe she was losing her mind. She grabbed her purse from where it lay in the weeds and pulled out her cigarettes, her wet fingers shaking like the branches of a tree in the wind of a storm.

Sophie sat up. She was soaked from the water that had poured from her mouth. Her mouth tasted terrible. Though Sophie had never smoked, she imagined it tasted like she'd thrown up cigarettes. "What happened?" she asked. Her face felt sore. She remembered the mermaid, the blue glow of her in the dark water, then a cyclone descending on her heart. Her chest ached. "Did I fall in the creek?"

"No!" Ella cried. Her talking came fast. "You passed out and then you just stayed that way, you stayed that way and your breathing got weird and I poured water on you, I smacked you, I shook you, I was yelling in your ear, I was fucking praying for you, Sophie, I was praying to god, I thought you were dead." In its heat and speed Ella's voice took on the tone and timbre of her mother's, her everyday voice suddenly enlivened with accent, a backbeat of Spanish giving her words a new pulse. Ella shook her head and wiped her face with the back of her hand, her face still wet with its own water, her nose gooey. "Not dead," she said, taking a manic drag from her cigarette. "Brain-dead. I thought you were in a coma. You were out for an *hour*. I thought that was it."

Sophie was stunned. She'd been out an *hour*? Even her dream vision didn't feel that long, maybe fifteen minutes, and dreams always felt much longer than they actually were. A normal pass-out lasted five minutes max, and most of that was just being too enamored with the tingly, relaxed sensation to break the spell by moving your body. An *hour*? She felt a chill dread play through her. Why had she let Ella talk her into playing pass-out?

"An hour," Sophie breathed.

"Why was there a fish in your mouth?" Ella demanded. "What the fuck? Am I on drugs or something? Like acid, LSD? Did someone put something in my—" Ella wracked her brain for what she had eaten that day and came up with very little. Even the pizza from the boy on the beach had gone uneaten; as cute as he was, Ella was certain his hands were dirty, and she wasn't going to put the food he'd touched in her mouth. She'd ingested hardly anything that day. She looked down at the cigarette fuming in her hand. "My cigarette!" she exclaimed. "Did someone put something in my cigarette?" She let it fall, half-smoked, from her hand and scuffed it out with her flip-flop.

Sophie sat up and considered her vision. A mermaid had come for her. Her hair was a disaster and she had a bad attitude. If not for being a mermaid, Sophie thought the creature would fit right at home in her very own family, or probably anywhere in Chelsea. She was grumpy and tired, not at all what Sophie thought a mermaid should be. Mermaids were happy, weren't they? Happy to not be human, to have fish tails, to get to swim through the ocean without a shirt on, friends with all the animals. Wasn't her father a king or something? Weren't all mermaids underwater princesses? They had great, burly dads with dripping silver moustaches and golden pitchfork-y things. When they got mad, the ocean made waves. Mermaids were supposed to spend their days idly grooming their hair with fishbone hair combs, singing sweet songs, gazing at their reflections in a polished seashell. Sophie's mermaid wasn't even pretty. She looked like she hadn't combed her hair in hundreds of years, her face was tough and sunken, maybe an edge of beauty hung there but it was the eroded beauty found of a wicked villainess, not the innocent beauty of a mermaid. Sophie's mermaid was not innocent, not sweet. Sophie remembered the curse words streaming from the curl of her lip; she swore worse than Ella, who had the vocabulary of a truck driver or sailor. Or a girl from Chelsea. Sophie's mermaid's tail was not a curling hunk of jewels but the scabby flank of a sick fish for sale in a mall pet store.

"Were you even passed out?" Ella asked, accusingly. "Did you even have a vision?"

Sophie yanked down the wet collar of her t-shirt, so Ella could see the sea glass. She was afraid to touch it. It felt different on her skin, hotter or colder, Sophie wasn't sure. Just electrified somehow, charged. Sophie was surprised to see it look so ordinary. She thought it should still be glowing, that there should be an image of the mermaid imprinted on the seashell.

"Yeah?" Ella peered at it. "What about it?" She regretted stubbing out that cigarette. She was in the grip of a nic fit. It was either smoke, or begin to obsess on the multitude of germs she'd just gotten on her body. Creek bacteria, festering diseases from that dirty bottle—there was probably dried spit on it somewhere, from whoever had drunk from it. Stuck in the weeds for so long, some animal had probably peed on it. Some animal or some boy or some man. She snatched at her purse and rifled for her pack.

"This is what Angel gave me. Remember, I told you? I had a—"

Sophie was hesitant to call it a vision, or a dream. She knew it was real. "I saw a mermaid, and she had one like it, and both of them were glowing and we were in the water. We were in the creek, right there." Sophie pointed to the water gleaming flatly beside them. It barely picked up the moonlight, so dense was it with ick. "She's some famous mermaid from Poland. She was sort of gnarly, like she wasn't beautiful, her hair was really awful, and she said she's going to help me fix Chelsea. I was talking to her underwater. We had this whole conversation. Then she did something." Sophie's lungs felt heavy with the memory. A twinge of the darkness she'd been shown shuddered through her. She coughed a tiny cough, and spat a splat of creek water. "Do you have any gum?" she asked her friend.

"A famous mermaid?" Ella tossed Sophie a pack of gum from her purse. "What's she, like, Beyoncé mermaid? Does she sing? That's a weird vision." Ella lit up and breathed deeply from her cigarette. Her words jumbled out on a wave of smoke. "Usually not so much happens."

"Usually nothing happens!" Sophie exclaimed. Usually you just had a feeling, a strange and dreamy moment, and *poof*, it was gone, and you tingled. Sophie didn't tingle. Her jaw hurt as she worked the gum around her teeth. She touched it.

"I smacked you," Ella admitted. "I'm sorry. You were out for *an hour*." She stabbed her cigarette in the dark, toward Sophie. "I didn't know what to do. I thought you were in a coma." A wave of the fear, still so close, broke over her again and tears squeezed out her eyes.

"It's okay," Sophie said. "That's what they do on TV. And salts. Smelling salt." Something tugged at Sophie at the thought of salt. She felt the sear of it on her tongue, and rubbed her tongue to the roof of her mouth, seeking the flavor of it.

"Yeah, well, I didn't have any smelling salt," Ella said. "What about the water? How was there so much water inside you? That was even scarier than your coma or whatever."

"From you pouring it on me?" Sophie suggested, even though she knew it wasn't so. She'd felt the dribble of the creek water hitting her face, a weak splash. Not the tsunami her body expelled.

Ella shook her head. "No way," she said.

"It was from talking underwater," Sophie said. "It had to be. I must not know how to do it right. I must have gotten a bunch of water in my lungs."

Ella stared at her. "You weren't *really* underwater, Sophie."

Sophie nodded. "I think I was."

"I fucking promise you," Ella said, "that you were right here. You were lying right here hardly breathing while I smacked you and threw water on you. You were not in the creek. I fucking promise you."

Sophie thought of the mermaid. "You don't have to swear so much," she told her friend. "I would still understand your point if you didn't."

"I don't fucking think you would," Ella raged. "I don't fucking think you understand right now how scary it was that you almost *died*, and then you go and puke *fish*, and now you sound crazy, like maybe you're brain damaged or something. Sophie!" Ella started to cry again.

Sophie appreciated her friend's point. Sophie totally *sounded* crazy. She supposed one of two things was happening. She was either crazy, or she wasn't. She mulled it over. Thinking that she might be crazy made her *feel* crazy, right away. If she doubted any one thing that had happened to her over the past twenty-four hours—the way she'd felt her mother's feelings, or Laurie LeClair's; the way she'd come at Angel's and found them hard, hidden, and now the mermaid and something wide and dark beyond her, something she wasn't allowing herself to remember—if she doubted any one of these things then she'd have to doubt everything, and she knew so much to be true. If she thought that maybe, just possibly, something incredible was happening, that didn't make her feel crazy at all. It made her feel upside-down and a little bit scared, but exhilarated, too. *Not* crazy.

"Ella," she addressed her friend. "I don't think I'm crazy. I think I was just hanging out underwater with this totally busted, sort of mean mermaid."

Ella stared at her friend, waiting for her to snap *psych!* or at least bust up laughing. It didn't happen. "Oh, no," wailed Ella, watching Sophie's wide-eyed, earnest face. "Great. Fucking great. You totally ruined your brain."

Chapter 11

Ella left in shambles, more disturbed for what she'd seen and couldn't understand than Sophie, who'd been its source. Sophie, who she'd left sitting on the bank of the creek, dripping and stunned, watching her walk away. Collecting herself on the walk home, Ella assembled a fake story about how *mellow* things had been at her tia's house—which tia not important, her story would be brief, vague, delivered with a shrug, the low-grade sulkiness her family had come to expect from her, dismissing it with humor as *hormones. What a relief to get some time alone!* Ella would cry, grateful and complaining at the same time. She would be a regular girl, a teenager, a fashion magazine rolled glossy in the hand. Not a girl whose best friend had almost died from a freak drowning accident while not actually *in* any water. Not a girl whose best friend had lost her mind. Ella's heart felt tight with sorrow and panic. What if what was wrong with Sophie was *contagious?* She rued their choice of the creek as their secret meeting place. Who knows what toxins had seeped into the banks, what invisible fumes had wafted up from the crumbly dirt, poisoning them? Ella's mind spun. She would go home to her computer and google remedies for toxic waste exposure, she would find the antidote and she would scrub the vapors from the inside.

. . .

AT THE CREEK, Sophie lingered. She wasn't ready to go home, to walk her changed, stranged self into her regular old house, to see everything so normal and dull when she felt extraordinary. She sat at the bank, the night around her ringing in empty silence. The echoes of her fight with her friend had faded, but Sophie felt charged from the conflict, from the mermaid. How would she be able to sleep? How would she ever be able to sleep again?

Stabbing at the ground with a dusty stick, Sophie half-wished she smoked. It gave you something to do when you weren't sure what to do next. She dropped the stick, took a snarl from the base of her skull into her hand and began to unweave it. The untangled hair frizzed in a kink, like the strands were just dying to snarl themselves together again. Sophie smoothed them with her fingers. She thought of the mermaid's hair. It would be a full-day project, untangling that mess.

Sophie heard the pigeons before she saw them, alerted by the music of their feathers. The bamboo whistles fluted gently, almost like wind in a tree. The flock of them descending before her was something.

Their dark mass not fully visible in the night, just shapes landing, the noise of their flutter, the wind of them coming to a stop in the air and settling to the ground.

Sophie faced them. *Am I crazy,* she asked herself, *or have these pigeons come to see me?* The head pigeon waddled forth from the pack, her tiny, bobbing head flicking on her neck, trying to get the best angle with which to regard Sophie. Her bamboo flute stuck stiffly behind her, like the cumbersome but dignified sword worn by a long-ago soldier. Behind her, the flock took a collective, respectful step back. *Not crazy,* Sophie decided, and pulled her sea glass from her shirt. It didn't have quite the regal affect she wanted it to have, strung as it was to a piece of grimy cord, her house key dangling beneath it. *It should be on a golden chain,* Sophie thought. *It should be hung from a rope of pearls.* Still, it caught the bit of moonlight the night sky had to offer and lit with a dull gleam, an echo of the undersea glow it had shared with the mermaid.

"Is it okay," the pigeon began, "if we talk to you? We don't want to scare you."

The pigeon's voice was beautiful. It was a soothing sound, melodious. It was a lullaby, a noise made with love to address the beloved, a coo. Sophie wondered if the bird spoke in such a way to everyone, or if she were special. Then she realized that a *pigeon* was *speaking* to her, and realized she was in fact quite special. Special, not crazy.

"You don't scare me," Sophie responded. "Are you Livia, Dr. Chen's pigeon?"

The bird ducked its head in a deliberate nod. "Dr. Chen takes care of us. We roost in the home she keeps for us on her roof. But we are all our own birds." The flock cooed in agreement.

"Sophie," Livia began. "We know so much about you. We've been waiting for you for so long; generations of pigeons speak of your coming. We can't believe we are so lucky to be here, in Chelsea, at the time of your arrival. We've been keeping your story for you, and the greater story you are to become a part of. We've taken such care to repeat the story carefully, to remember all the details and not confuse them. Your story is so old, none of us can trace its origin, it's just the story we have always been told and have grown to tell our fledglings. Back when there were carrier pigeons, the carrier pigeons told the story of you. Back before we were degraded, when we were called rock doves and lived in barns and trees and were regarded by humans the way other birds are regarded, respected, even then we told your story."

"But then there was rebellion—" another bird stepped forwarded, his waddle more pronounced. Sophie could see that one of his pink bird legs ended not in a pronged claw, but in a mottled bundle, a blob. It looked painful to walk upon, and she watched the bird shift its weight, holding the wounded foot gingerly above the ground. "When the wars with the humans began, when they started leaving us poison, poison to eat and poison to land in, just poison every-where, and that foolish rice they think we'd be dumb enough to eat, and throwing nets over our homes so that we were separated from our babies and our babies would die, and when they nailed jagged things to where we slept so that we had to roam the streets, looking for a safe place to sleep that wasn't netted or poisoned or nailed with jagged things—"

"Arthur," Livia cooed at the bird, who had gotten quite heated, his feathers trembling.

"All I mean is, throughout all of this, still we kept your story, all of us here." Arthur's wing swung out from his side and motioned to the shifting crowd behind him. "Many birds refused. They almost had me convinced, too, after my accident." Arthur shook his melted foot at Sophie. "I was so hurt and in such pain. I thought, *Why should we do anything for people, when they are trying, day and night to kill us?*"

"Arthur," Livia cooed.

"I know," he assured her. "Livia brought me to my senses. It's the darkness in the humans that makes them do such things. I tried to explain this to the rebellion, but they didn't want to hear it. They refused to keep your story, or worse, they tried to scramble it, tell a false story, and fill it with misinformation."

"Why?' Sophie asked, distraught at the thought of a flock of shit-talking pigeons out to smear her name.

"Because they hate humans," Arthur explained with a feathery shrug. "And you have been sent here to save them."

"Save *humans*?" Sophie asked. "Save them from what?"

"From themselves, dear," Livia spoke. "From the darkness inside them. You have felt it, is that correct? How old are you?"

"Thirteen," Sophie said. The birds cooed and fluttered.

"Well, thirteen, yes, surely you would have felt some of this, this human darkness? The mermaid, there in the creek. She showed it to you, is that right?" The bird spoke with a politeness that seemed to belong to another era. If she were a woman, Sophie thought, a straw hat would sit on her head, and her hands would wear white gloves. Sophie held on to this idea of Livia as the reminder of what happened in the creek began to curl the edges of her memory. If all the pain the world had ever felt, the pain of the predator and of the victim, if all that madness had been stuffed into a cave to fester and ferment for a hundred thousand years—that was the hole Sophie had been dropped into. The recollection made the hair across her body stand as if surged with electricity, and her bowels churned like she'd eaten something foul.

"Oh," said Livia, waddling toward the girl. "Oh, now, I didn't mean to—" Livia lept upon Sophie's shoulder and placed the soft tip of her wing to her clammy forehead. "Salt!" Livia barked, and a handful of

birds took the sky, scattering in different directions. Livia unfolded her wing and fanned Sophie's sweating face.

"I'm sorry," Sophie murmured. "I don't know why I feel so sick all of a sudden. If I could lie down..."

A trio of birds swept the dirt with their wings, brushing back rocks and chip bags, plastic soda cups and smashed glass. Sophie laid her head on the soft patch of dirt they'd combed for her. She could feel where her wet hair had crusted to her cheeks, stuck there with mud and creek grime. She placed her hands to her gurgling stomach. "The creek water," she said to the bird. "I was in the creek... or the water got in me, I don't know..."

"It's not that, lovey," cooed the bird, pushing cooled air through her feathers and into Sophie's face. Sophie inhaled the smell of the bird. Not the stink of a rat, though Sophie now realized she had never smelled a rat. Livia smelled like hay, Sophie imagined, something woodsy and warm. Like the pavement, yes, but like the pavement on a hot day, baked like clay, a clean-dirty smell. Livia smelled like Sophie did after a day playing in the sun. A sort of golden sweat. But she smelled like flowers, too. Like lilacs, that faint, watery fragrance. It calmed Sophie.

"You smell nice," she complimented the bird.

"Oh, why thank you," Livia cooed. "I try to take care of myself, you know."

Beside them two birds soared to the dirt, their wings high, their beaks stuffed. Quickly they spat onto the ground.

"I've got rock salt from the big pile," said the one, his words twisted with the terrible taste of the salt. Sophie had never seen a pigeon spit before, and watched with interest as the bird spat and spat again, its tough little bird-tongue sticking out from its beak.

"That's enough," Livia scolded. "Thank you very much." The bird waddled away, an agitated sound like an endless sneeze coughing from its beak. The other bird dropped its offering.

"Salt packets," it explained proudly. "From the McDonald's on the parkway." The small paper packets sat in the moonlight.

"Very good," Livia praised. "Both of you, well done." The second pigeon waddled back into the flock, indistinguishable.

"Sophie," Livia said, "you must eat the rock salt now, please. You will feel better."

"The mermaid gave me salt," Sophie said.

"Yes, that salt saved your life, dear. That is a powerful salt. But this will help."

"Help what?" Sophie said, tossing the gravelly salt into her mouth. The searing sharpness soothed her. She sucked on it like a piece of candy.

"When you experience the darkness, it takes a toll. A very real toll. On your mind and your body. The salt is purifying. It's healing. You will need to take in a lot of salt, Sophie, after what you've seen. You've seen the—the—well, I'm not sure what to call it. The darkness? The, the evil?"

"Hell?" Arthur suggested. "I mean, it sounds like hell to me."

Sophie imagined all the words and images she knew to represent that place, *hell*. What she had seen contained all the despair, all the violence and eternity of those pictures of wailing humans and creepy demons, but worse, because words and pictures weren't *feelings*. No matter how hard a writer or painter would try to make someone *feel* the pain of such a place, they could never come close. Only the mermaid could, and Sophie, and the conduit of the talisman, and the water, the charged and salty water, with all its contaminants.

"You must take lots of salt," Livia said. "To heal yourself. So that you may remember without becoming sick."

"But—*that*?" Confused, Sophie tried to make sense of too much. "I'm going to do something about *that?*"

"Oh, yes," Livia nodded, which, Sophie noticed was a different motion than her regular constant head-bobbing. It was deeper, with a stronger purpose. "You will train for it, with the mermaid and with others, but—yes, Sophie.

You are going to take that, all of that, into your body. And from your body it will be released. Here." The bird tore open the McDonald's salt packet with her beak and waggled it at the girl. Sophie took it from the bird's tiny mouth and poured it onto her tongue.

"Thank you," she said.

"Of course."

"What if I don't want to do it?" Sophie asked. It felt like worrying a cut, poking a loose tooth with her tongue. Maybe she didn't want to know the answer.

"Oh, you *will*," Livia insisted.

"But, what if I don't?"

"Impossible," chimed in Arthur.

"No, I can! Like I can just be all, *No, sorry you guys, sorry mermaid, peace out,* and take off. I can never come to this creek again. I can leave Chelsea, even. I can run away."

"No, no, you can't!" Livia's melodious voice sounded anxious. "It just never, ever would occur like that. You are the one. We've all been waiting, longer than I can understand. You will do it."

"It's a done deal, kid," Arthur seconded. "It's as if it already happened. You won't go nowhere. You're one of us."

"So," Sophie said, not exactly glumly, but with very little cheer. "I'm going to feel everyone's pain and eat a bunch of salt."

"Well, ultimately, yes." Livia nodded. "But so much is going to happen between now and then."

. . .

SOPHIE SAT WITH the birds late into the night. The flock of them clustered around her. Some hopped into her lap and cooed, not unlike purring cats. Sophie felt like a bizarre Snow White. She half expected a happy creek rat to join their gathering, or a pompous sea gull or goofy raccoon. She petted the pigeons' feathers and found they enjoyed being scratched deeply on their necks, like dogs or cats. "Ooooh, that feels good," said a bird hunkered on her thigh. All of the birds spoke in the most calming of voices, the sound of the first drift of sleep as it washes over you. Even Arthur, rankled and crotchety, had a voice that lulled, even as it shared tales of injury and battle.

"There are some you can trust and others who mean you harm," Livia said solemnly.

"Angel," Sophie said quickly. "Angel is good. She knows things. She gave me my necklace."

Livia bobbed her head affirmatively. "Yes, Angel is good. Hennie, too."

"Hennie? The old lady at the grocery store? The weird grocery store? She's—good?"

"She's on your side," Livia said. "She knows things. You can trust her."

"She looks like a witch," Sophie said uneasily.

"She is a witch," Livia confirmed.

"See?" Arthur snapped. Even his snapping was still sweet to the ear. "See what I mean about humans? *Oh, she looks like a witch.* What does that even mean? She's old? She's, what, she's a fat lady? She wears a funny hat on her head, what, she's got a big nose or something?"

"I didn't mean anything," Sophie said quickly. "Her place is just sort of creepy is all."

"Creepy," Arthur spat with a coo. "Why, it's all dusty inside? Dust is of the earth. Feathers are of the earth, your skin is of the earth. All of it will be dust." Arthur rose up on his feet, one good and one bad, and he stretched his wings grandly, beat them upon the air. "Never think you're better than any other living thing."

"Arthur," Livia chided.

"Here, here," some birds in the back cooed, clapping their wings against their bodies.

"I have kept your story," Arthur addressed Sophie. "Even when I haven't felt sure it was the right thing. The right thing for pigeons. So I am here to help you, but you are not a pigeon." Arthur stared his tiny orange eye into Sophie's large brown one. "And my trust in you is not complete."

"Okay," Sophie said.

"*Anyway*," Livia continued. "We've only been waiting hundreds of years to tell this girl these things, may I continue?"

"Continue," Arthur said, with one last, grandiose beat of his wing.

"Hennie is a witch, and she will help you always. Angel—you knew that."

"My mother?" Sophie asked.

Livia twitched. She bobbed her head at Arthur, at the others. The pigeon on Sophie's thigh looked up at her briefly, and then buried her face into her feathers.

"We are unsure," Livia said, regret in her voice like a new harmony. "This is the thread of the story that has been tampered with. Even with all our watching and observing, we have not been able to say for certain. She is either to be trusted, or she means you terrible harm." Sophie could detect sadness in the pigeon's eye.

"Okay," Sophie said. She supposed she knew that already. "My grandmother?"

"Kishka—" Livia began.

"The worst!" Arthur shouted. "The absolute worst, most wicked woman in all of humanity. Oh, the pigeons she's killed! With poisons, with her own hands! She has wiped out generations of our young! She's even used a gun! She's a cold-blooded murderer! Shooting at pigeons for fun, for a thrill! She's a psychopath," Arthur said darkly. "She's evil to people, too."

"You cannot trust her," Livia said simply.

Arthur carried on. "She treats humans like pigeons, pigeons like humans, rats like humans, pigeons like rats, humans like rats. If it's alive and it gets in her way, it's all the same. A terrible woman, a monster."

"She does not have your best interest at heart," Livia said.

"Really?" Sophie pushed skeptically at the birds. "Are you sure Kishka just isn't—I mean, I know she is very bad to pigeons, and I know she is a cranky old lady, but—what did you call her, Arthur? The worst, most terrible—"

"The absolute worst, most wicked woman in all of humanity!" Arthur proclaimed. "And no, it's not just because of all she has done to hurt pigeons—though that would be enough! But she does not stop there. She means great harm to every living thing on this earth. She is barely *of* this earth, she comes from another place, a terrible place where everything awful in the world comes from."

"But—" Sophie wanted to debate the bird. Kishka? Kishka was not a warm woman, but she was not very different than most old women in Chelsea. Old women who had had hard lives, worked tough jobs, who had immigrated, had left a whole other life behind. All the losses they'd had in this world. It's hard to be an old woman, with all the bad parts of life piling up on your old lady shoulders.

"No *buts*," Livia said sternly. Sternly, but softly. "It is important that you trust us. That you beware of her."

Sophie shifted uncomfortably. It was true she felt a little scared of her grandmother, but everyone did. That didn't make her evil. But there were *things* about Kishka, there always had been. She knew everything Kishka did—things that happened at home, at school, in her own head. Sophie had thought it was just something that grandmothers had, some special sense of their grandkids, because they were old and wise or something, but it was sort of weird. The cold feeling Sophie got when Kishka studied her like that. The way her perfume smelled, like nothing Sophie had ever smelled, lovely from a distance but close up—almost like a poison. Maybe she was just allergic?

But there were also her nightmares of Kishka, where her grandmother morphed again and again into figures and creatures, strange monsters that followed Sophie and could see her always, Sophie could never hide. Kishka was evil in these dreams, and when Sophie awoke from them her room always felt thick, like the air had become spongy, and she would pinch herself to be sure the dream was gone, because she could still feel this monster version of her grandmother there inside the room with her. Sophie shuddered.

"I don't mean to scare you," Livia said gently.

"I'm not scared, exactly," Sophie said. "I'm just—you know, this is all a little crazy. It's a *lot* crazy. I don't think *I'm* crazy, but you got to admit all this is pretty seriously crazy."

"Deciding you're not crazy," crowed Arthur, "is always a step in the right direction."

"I will consider the possibility that my grandmother is evil."

"You better consider it, kid. For all of our sake. Whatever stuff that mermaid showed you, that's your grandma."

"And what about the mermaid? She's good, right?"

"Syrena is very good." Livia nodded. "She has done you a wonderful favor, to come so far. You must take care to obey and respect her. She will teach you very much. Be kind to her. A little kindness goes far."

"And Ella? My best friend, Ella?"

Livia was thoughtful. "It's not that you can't trust Ella," she explained. "It will just take her a little while to understand."

"By a little while, she means years," Arthur butted in. "Don't sugar-coat it, Livia. The girl needs to know."

"People in their ignorance can often seem bad," said Livia. "Ella will not be of help to you for years to come."

"*Years?*" Sophie asked. "This—thing—is going to take *years*?"

Livia clucked, and the flock cooed behind her. "Oh, darling," her lovely voice soothed. "This is going to take the rest of your life."

Chapter 12

Sophie traced her steps through Chelsea, back toward home. In the dark of night Chelsea almost felt safe. It was people that made the city dangerous, and the people were mostly asleep. Sophie passed their houses, dingy colored; their concrete steps, cracked; junk in their front yard, sneakers dangling from the phone wires above. Towels and sheets hung where curtains should be. One home even had a beach towel for a front door; the nubby image of a dog on the shore hung limply from the frame in the breezeless night.

Sophie walked and the pigeons came with her. Some had flown ahead to make sure everything was quiet at home, and a couple stayed with Sophie, riding on her shoulders. The rest flew to and fro, high in the sky above her. They were too heavy to fly slow or low— "What, do you think we're hummingbirds?" Arthur asked—too short and cumbersome to waddle alongside her on the pavement. Sophie loved the movement of them high above. They swooped like bats, the

fluted ones making their eerie, beautiful sound. She also loved the weight of the birds on her shoulders, the faint *coo* of their cooing so close to her ears.

About a block from home, Arthur touched down on the pavement before her, his proud chest broad and tufted. Sophie marveled at his wing's perfect peaks, the striations of feathers—even in the dim light Sophie could see the stripes and shading. His wings were were muscular and elegant at once. Why *did* people hate pigeons, Sophie wondered? They were more attractive than seagulls, and while many found the gulls a nuisance, no one tried to kill them. They were more nuanced and interesting than crows, and their noises far less abrasive than that *caw-caw-caw*ing.

Sophie had heard just about everyone call pigeons "rats with wings." At the close of this most fantastical of nights Sophie wondered, what was so bad about rats? If a group of rats had come to her at the creek, standing upward on their hind legs to *speak* with her, a sweet, plump lady rat like Livia and a proud, showboating rat like

MERMAID IN CHELSEA CREEK

Arthur—well, if that had happened Sophie figured she'd be walking home with rats on her shoulders, and happily. People didn't *look* at the animals they claimed to hate, Sophie thought. They paid them no real attention, just agitation, and missed the ways they were as sweet as any other creature, *were* any other creature. They were dirty, and they scavenged for food, but in this way the pests—the pigeons, rats and cockroaches of Chelsea—were not so different from the people they shared the city with.

"Fast asleep," Arthur said. "That mother of yours. I recognize her. She's one of those who put dry rice out on the street 'cause they think our stomachs will explode."

"I know," Sophie said. "I told her to stop."

"Tell her when I want to eat rice, I hit the dumpsters behind Comida Criolla and get the good stuff. We don't like chomping on dry rice anymore than she does."

"Arthur," Sophie said. "I'm probably not going to tell her about you guys."

"Why?" the bird challenged. "Ashamed to be seen with a flock of pigeons?"

"Arthur," Livia stepped in. "Leave Sophia alone. She can't tell her mother about us, she'd never be believed and it would put her in danger. We don't know that her mother isn't an enemy."

"I'll say she's an enemy," Arthur grumbled. "Listen, it's not a coincidence that humans who put dry rice on their sidewalks tend to find a lot of bird doo on their cars."

"Arthur!" Livia trilled, and Sophie giggled. "You are coming very close to compromising your dignity."

"There *is* a lot of bird doo on my mom's car," Sophie said. She knew her mother deserved it for what she'd tried to do to the pigeons.

"Now you know," Arthur said with what would have been a wink, if pigeons could wink, which they can't. But he dropped the subject, because Livia had said the magic word. Dignity was deeply important to the pigeons. In a world where they were persecuted, it was important that they retain their nobility and not stoop to retaliate in a manner that only degraded them and enforced the humans' views.

On the long block of Heard Street where Sophie lived, the houses were dark as the sky. But not Sophie's. Through her window she could see the flash and glow of the television against the walls, like the Northern Lights, she thought, only not. Not like the Northern Lights at all. More like a television left on long into the night, a television playing its shapes across the face of a sleeping single mother. There was nothing natural or mystical about it.

Sophie surprised herself by kissing the face of the bird on her left shoulder before lifting her off. The bird cooed shyly, dipping her face into her feathers. "I washed my face today," she assured Sophie. "But I don't know how clean the water was. It's hard to find clean water, you know. Angel leaves us rainwater baths on the tumbler shack roof, but aside from that, it's puddles and the creek, and you know Chelsea is a very dirty city."

"Dirty cities have dirty pigeons," Arthur quipped. "The problem is systemic."

"My name is Giddy," the bashful pigeon introduced herself.

"I'm Roy," said the pigeon on Sophie's other shoulder. "Giddy's mate. Mind lifting me down? My wings will make a racket."

Sophie placed the birds side by side on the sidewalk. They yawned in unison.

"It's really past our bedtime," Giddy apologized.

"Mine, too," Sophie said, and climbed the stairs to her home.

Inside, she gently switched the television off. The sudden silence awoke her mother like a noise. "What?" she jumped from her prone position, struggling to sit up in her sleepy disorientation. Her eyes widened as she peered deeply into the room. Her curly hair rose and fell about her head like a disturbed sea. "Am I late? What time is it?"

Sophie was pulled to feel her mother's feelings right then, but she feared it would make her heart too sad. Andrea worked and worked and worked and even when she wasn't working, even when she slept, her body was a clock ticking its way to her next shift, anxiety winding the gears.

"No, Ma," Sophie said softly. "You've been sleeping with the television on and it was keeping me awake. Why don't you sleep in your bed?" She herded her mom into the bedroom as if she were a sleepy child. Andrea collapsed on the wide mattress with her shoes still on. Sophie plucked the laces from their bows and slid them to the floor. She climbed into bed with her mother. The fan from the living room spun back and forth, back and forth, filling the bedroom with moments of cool air. Sophie's clothes were gummy from the dried creek water, but she was too tired to change into something better. Plus, the briny smell meant something different now, something new. She knew she'd be grateful in the morning, when she awoke and wondered if it all had been a dream, to feel the stiff salt of the mermaid's cave on her t-shirt. She snuggled backward into her mother, who threw a sleeping arm across her shoulder. It was too hot to cuddle, but Sophie feared that forces more powerful than the humidity would soon make it difficult to seek comfort from her mom. As the sun began to rise Sophie slipped into sleep, the cooing of pigeons outside her window lulling her.

Chapter 13

"**D**o you want to come to the dump with me?" Sophie asked hopefully into the telephone.

"You definitely sustained brain damage last night if you are asking me that question," Ella said coldly. It was the sort of tease Ella could have said in a friendly way—but she didn't. Sophie's stomach swirled.

"I'm sorry about last night, Ella. I didn't mean to scare you. I know you were trying to help me—"

"Sophie, I don't know what's going on with you, but it's freaky, okay?"

"Ella, it's not that freaky, I swear," Sophie spoke quickly, stalling, lying. *It was wicked freaky.* "Listen, if you just come to the dump with me today you can meet Angel, and I think you'll understand—"

"I've got a lot of work to do at the beach today," Ella said coolly.

"Oh," Sophie was surprised. "I didn't know you were getting a job. Where are you working?"

"On my *tan*," Ella snapped. "I'm sorry you're grounded, but I can't stop my life just because you're having some weird problem. And you're right, you shouldn't pass yourself out anymore. You can't handle it."

"Ella," Sophie said. The more they fought, the more Sophie felt like a kid, just a whiny, pleading kid. The friendly part of Ella felt unreachable. "Well—okay," she said stupidly.

"Well, okay," Ella dully repeated, and hung up the phone. Lying on her bed, she pressed her hand to her churning stomach. When she got home last night, desperate for a remedy to the toxins she was certain had gotten into her, she drank half a pint of mouthwash. The liquid had seared a groove down her throat and into her guts and quickly retraced its steps, heaving out from her mouth and into the sink. Ella's stomach muscles still ached from the effort, like she'd done a million sit-ups. It ached with the heaving, with the burn of the mouthwash, and with a painful knot of emotion.

On the other end, holding the dead line in her hand, Sophie's stomach throbbed in sickening synchronicity. She and Ella had fought before, though usually her friend was eager to accept an apology. *I'm sure she'll come around*, Sophie assured herself weakly. She pushed the girl from her mind, vowing to call her again, soon. She had a whole lot of work ahead of her; moping about her room all day was not an option.

. . .

"OH, MY ACHING neck," Andrea complained, wincing, one hand kneading the soreness, the other clutching a cup of coffee. The coffee maker on the counter was full of the vile, brown liquid. Sophie didn't like the burnt stink, but her mother could not function without it. Sophie sat at the table, drowsy, her own body aching. Angel had warned her it would, that she'd been using muscles she didn't know she had, but at the time Sophie was so caught up in the work she couldn't feel it. Now she felt it, a new ache in a new place every time she moved. That plus the weird feeling in her chest, her lungs she supposed, which had been full of Chelsea creek water. Her sinuses too felt clogged. The events of the night before were clear to her, her memory of them sharp, and she had no doubt that any of it had happened, was real. What she was less clear about was what it all meant. The mermaid had danced around a certain point, as had tender Livia the pigeon. Even gruff Arthur couldn't seem to spit it out. Was Sophie meant to save humanity? She was a girl in grimy clothes, drinking orange juice from concentrate that her mom had bought five for a dollar at the supersized supermarket a town over. She hadn't had the time to make good on her promise to arrive at the dump with better grooming; indeed, she was more dusty and tangled than the day before. She swiped a ponytail holder from her mother and lassoed the mess of her hair into a dense bun on her head, checking her reflection in a tablespoon stained brown with coffee. This was humanity's savior?

"Wash your face," Andrea said, reading Sophie's mind. "I don't want to hear it from your grandmother about how I'm not taking care of you."

In the bathroom Sophie splashed cold water onto her cheeks and dried them with her mom's leftover shower towel. "Ready," she announced. Climbing into the car, she took note of the chalky white pigeon droppings splatting the roof of the car and giggled.

"You think that's funny?" Andrea asked, annoyed. "You think I have time to bring this thing to a car wash? Not to mention the money?"

Sophie felt a wave off her mother. She arranged herself, inside, to catch it. It was like a new set of arms had grown inside her, and the arms opened in a gentle curve and caught the toss of her mother's scratchy feelings. How the state of her car made her feel like a failure. It felt bad to drive around in a poop-mobile. She wanted to tell everyone who looked at her lousy little vehicle that she *knew* the droppings were there; she didn't want anyone thinking she was the kind of person who would be oblivious to such a thing. She knew about it, she didn't like it, and she didn't have the time to deal with it. Or, when a pocket of time presented itself, she did something else with it. She napped, or spaced out, or watched a television program. And later she would think, *I should have brought the car to the car wash. What was I doing, sitting reading the newspaper?* And she would not only feel like a failure, but that the fact of her failure was her very own fault.

Sophie hopped on her mom with her real arms outstretched, her psychic arms still holding the sad bundle of emotion. She hugged her mother tight. "It's not a big deal," Sophie promised. "I'll wash the car. Don't feel so bad about it. All the cars in Chelsea have bird poop on the roof."

Her daughter's tenderness was too much for her—too unexpected, too unusual, too tender. Andrea shrugged her off. "It's okay," she lied.

"I don't feel *that* bad about it." Andrea worked to harden herself to the onslaught of feelings. The problem with feelings was, first you had one, which was generally bad enough. But then you had a feeling about your feeling, and then a feelings about how you were feeling about your feeling, and then another feeling would pop up at the sight of it all, this teetering pyramid of emotion, and all of it would look wrong to Andrea, all her feelings somehow incorrect, too much or too little, too soft or too hard, and another feeling would emerge at the thought of *that*. It was endless, having feelings. And god forbid someone *noticed* you having them, as Sophie just had. Then you had feelings about *that*, about having been seen, and more feelings still about the other person's feelings. Oh, it was awful. Andrea started the car, her eyes steely on the streets ahead. If she was driving she wouldn't have to feel anything, and Sophie wouldn't expect her to, couldn't need anything from her in those moments but for her to drive the car, bring her safely to the dump. Sophie watched her mother shut down behind the wheel. The ring of her mother's sadness still bounced through her body, fainter and fainter, until it was gone.

· · ·

RONALD TRIED UNSUCCESSFULLY to escort Sophie up the hill and over to the tumbling shack. His ankles caught on the width of his pants and his feet shuffled like he was dancing. Ronald toppled. "Oh, great," Sophie said aloud. She stood over the man. The booze on his breath shot up like a geyser with each exhalation. Sophie remembered what the pigeons had said, about dignity. Of all the damage the drinking was doing to Ronald, from the swell of his liver to the blood vessels bursting on the tip of his nose, Sophie thought the corrosion of the man's dignity was perhaps the worst of all. Sophie felt a shame on his behalf as she tugged the man to his unsteady feet, a shame he didn't know to feel at all.

"Going to see your nana?" Ronald hiccupped.

"Sure," Sophie said, though she wasn't. There was no point trying to actually talk to Ronald, whose very tongue was pickled from all the liquor it had lapped.

"Your nana," he shook his head back and forth. Sophie thought he was smiling. "She is something else. Whatta lady." He tugged from the front pocket of his filthy, baggy jeans a bottle of rum. The liquid was clear as water behind the label of a pirate.

"Did she get that for you?" Sophie asked.

"She always does," Ronald nodded. "That's the deal."

. . .

THE TUMBLER WAS silent when Sophie approached the shack, but she could hear intermittent, cacophonous smashes. Angel was busting up bottles. The shack was breezeless, and Angel was sweaty. She wore pants chopped at the knee, but her feet must have been hot, stuffed inside what looked like army boots. Her goggles covered her eyes and fat earphones were clamped onto her ears to muffle the crashing of the bottles. She whipped of her protective gear when she saw Sophie enter, her stance suddenly eager and nervous, excited.

"Hey there," she said casually, but Sophie thought, *She knows everything.*

"I saw the mermaid," Sophie said immediately. She'd been planning to wait, sniff things out, but Angel pretending everything was normal made her start blurting. "And the pigeons came to me, too."

Angel smacked her forehead. "Crap!" she said. "The pigeons! It hasn't been raining and I forgot to fill their baths on the roof."

"Well, you better," Sophie said. "They're getting grimy, and Giddy feels bad about it."

Angel tossed the goggles and headphones at Sophie, followed with a toss of gloves that smacked her in the belly and fell to the ground. "Finish this bunch of bottles," she instructed. "I'll be right back. Then we'll talk."

Angel grabbed the nozzle of a long green hose and tugged it outside. In between deafening smashes, Sophie could hear the spray of water into the glass bowls on the roof. She busted up the bottles with ease; it felt so great to make them smash into pieces, the crunch and spray of the pulverized bottles. It felt fun and destructive, like something she shouldn't be allowed to do, but it was her job. She laughed out loud, crushing the bunch in no time. Sophie pulled off the gear and surveyed her glittering creation, the wider work room strewn with shards and sparkle. In the corner of the shack one of the junkyard cats lay lazy in the heat. It was a big orange and white cat with unusually long legs, a boxy face and ears chewed from fighting. Angel called it Creamsicle. Sophie sidled up to it.

"Hey," she said. The cat blinked at her, then dozed its eyes. Sophie tugged her sea glass from under her shirt. It was cool and heavy in her palm. She shook the cat awake. "Hey," she said. She showed the cat her necklace. "It's okay. I know everything. You can speak to me." The cat blinked, yawned and slid its pointy chin onto its long legs. It purred a light purr. Sophie shook it again with her hand, eliciting an annoyed mew. "Tell me what you know," she ordered the cat. "It's okay. I'm not going to freak out, okay? Just say something." She brought the sea glass closer to the cat, who sniffed it, gave it a lick, and pulled its head away.

"Sophie," Angel was behind her. "What are you doing to Creamsicle?"

Sophie jumped, tucking her talisman quickly beneath her shirt. "I just, I was just letting it know that it could—talk to me," she said. It sounded dumb, but then, a flock of pigeons had escorted her home last night. She couldn't be blamed for not understanding the rules of this magic new reality. She tucked the sea glass back under her shirt.

"Creamsicle doesn't speak to people." Angel smiled.

"So, the cats don't know anything? Only the pigeons know things?" Sophie felt annoyed. "Or do, like, rats know things? Can I expect dogs to start talking to me, or bees or raccoons? Can I expect to start reading a seagull's mind anytime soon? Will I be getting a visit from, like a UFO full of space aliens?"

"Creamsicle probably knows everything," Angel said. "But he's not talking." She walked over and dumped a bucket of glass shards into the tumbler. "Hold on," she said. She dumped a bag of grit into the machine and switched it on. The noise was a lion's roar and they were inside the beast's mouth. The ground beneath them was alive with the tumbler's power. Angel came close to Sophie. "We can talk about it here," she said, "But only when the tumbler's on, okay? It scrambles your grandmother's powers or something; she can't hear when it's going. Not just ear-hearing, but her other hearing. She can hear your feelings, your thoughts. And you don't need to be right in front of her for her to do it."

Sophie was alarmed at this. "She can read my feelings?"

"Yep," Angel nodded. "Where do you think you got it from?"

"You know I do it? Do you know everything? Will you explain it all to me?"

"I don't know everything," Angel said sadly. "I only know my piece. I know that Kishka can spy on your insides."

Sophie ran through a catalog of feelings as if through a violated diary, trying to gauge what her grandmother might know. "I have... bad feelings about my grandmother," Sophie confessed. "Like, I've always been scared of her. Or, kind of repulsed by her."

"She knows." Angel nodded.

Sophie felt terrible. "Should I apologize?" She tried to conjure sweet feelings for her grandmother, but found it impossible.

"No, no," Angel waved her hand. "It's all as it should be, you can't help it. Even if you didn't know your grandmother is bad, you'd at least know she's sort of crazy. Don't worry about your feelings. You can't ever change them, anyway. You can't control them. That's a good first thing to understand—you can't control how you feel. It's pure honesty, feelings. But you can block them. That's what I can teach you."

Sophie remembered her attempt to peek into Angel's emotions, how it felt like diving into an empty swimming pool. "You've blocked yours, right?"

"I couldn't be here otherwise," Angel said. "You felt it, right? You ran into it yesterday. You were snooping."

Sophie felt ashamed but Angel didn't seem to mind. "I was glad you did that, actually," she said. "I wasn't sure how far along you were in your powers, or in your understanding of them. I was glad to feel you playing around with it."

"What *is* it?" Sophie asked. "At first I thought there was something wrong with me. I do this—thing, with my friend."

"The pass-out game." Angel nodded. "Don't, anymore. The mermaid will find you without that."

"Did it hurt me?" Sophie asked. "Last night I was out for so long..." She thought of Ella and her heart hurt.

Angel pulled a knit cap from the back of her pants and pulled it over her head of sweaty tangles. "There is so much for you to know," Angel said. "Have the pigeons bring you to me tonight. It's not safe here." Angel brought the tumbler to rest with a switch, and the echo of it rung in Sophie's ears for the rest of the afternoon.

. . .

THE DAY WENT quickly, Sophie and Angel smashing glass silently, side by side, the sounds muffled from their foamy headphones. Sometimes Sophie would try to look into Angel, slowly, carefully, sneaking up on that hard, protective wall as if it were a living thing she could outsmart. Her sly pace prevented her from smashing against it, but Angel was impenetrable. And Angel could feel Sophie, too—every time the girl tried to pry inside, Angel would lift her head and look out from goggles, shaking her head with a smirk. "Nice try," she mouthed above the smashing.

"I'm sorry!" Sophie hollered, though she wasn't. She felt something, a breeze inside her.

"No you're not!" Angel yelled, shattering an empty jug of wine.

"Was that just you?" Sophie exclaimed. She dropped her shovel, her hands crossing her body as if she could somehow hide her insides. "Did you just peek at me?"

"Yes," Angel said. "That's what it feels like."

"Don't do it again!" Sophie ordered. It felt like her brain had been cracked open, pools of thought and opinion, fantasy and memory exposed to the elements. Like she'd been singing in the shower and someone had turned the water off and pulled open the curtain.

"I won't," Angel promised. "Not without telling you first. But, keep trying to peek at me. It's okay."

And so Sophie did, becoming familiar with the perimeters of

Angel's wall. In her mind it was a steely dark gray, tall and sleek, impossible to climb, impossible to penetrate. Sophie didn't know the wall was made from it, but she imagined it was iron. She leaned in to smell its slight metallic smell. Angel laughed.

"Okay, Sherlock," she said. "Give it a rest for a while."

. . .

SOPHIE SPENT THE entire day at the dump without running into her grandmother. It felt strange, especially with all she'd learned. She wanted to have a normal interaction with the woman, to see if she *could* act normal, what with all she knew and didn't know.

"Don't worry," Angel said. "You'll have plenty of time to see your grandmother."

"Is she really bad?" Sophie asked.

"Um, yeah," Angel said with a little laugh. "I mean, *she* doesn't think so. It's like she's just a businesswoman or something. She's just looking out for number one. But, trust me. As far as the rest of the world is concerned, she's really bad. Especially for your work in the world."

My work in this world, Sophie thought. *I've got work in this world. Work to do. Work that is all mine.* She felt excited and anxious, filled with a pride of purpose quickly deflated by the understanding that she didn't know quite what that purpose was. Or if she'd even want it.

Passing by the Airstream, Sophie thought, *There is the lair of my wicked grandmother.* Wicked people lived in lairs, didn't they? Could an Airstream trailer be a lair? If her grandmother was so bad, wouldn't she have a castle? A dungeon, a cave? Sophie sidled up to the trailer. She placed her hand on it, and the hot metal seared her palm. The Airstream looked like a bullet or a spaceship, and Sophie had always liked it. They were meant to be hitched to cars and dragged around the country. This one was beached, beached in a garbage dump in Chelsea. Sophie imagined it would have preferred a different life, one spent winding down roads blasted into the sides of mountains, rust-colored canyons rising and falling as far as the eye could see.

Sophie knocked on the door. "Nana!" she yelled. Angel had turned off the tumbler, she realized. The dump rang with quiet, and Sophie felt vulnerable, like a rabbit caught in the sight of a hawk. "Nana?" There was nothing. She nudged open the door. The place was hot. The air conditioner was off, the lights were off, the interior held a swampy humidity and a wonderful smell—like bubble gum, but sweeter and fainter. It took Sophie's eyes a moment to adjust. "Nana?" she said, softer. The pile of sheets and pillows on the couch was only that, sheets and pillows, not the slumbering body of her grandmother. At the kitchen table covered with papers, no grandmother. The door to the narrow bathroom was open, no grandmother in there, either. Sophie walked deeper into the trailer. There wasn't much space; the place was small but so stuffed with junk it seemed bigger for the mysteries it stored. There was a crate of antique bottles, words bulging from the glass. Another crate held glass balls, some of them caught in stiff, ropy nets. There were dishes of rusty object—nails, locks, skeleton keys. On a countertop beside a pan of old buttons sat a hot pink stargazer lily, the source of the trailer's wonderful smell. The flowers splayed open like starfish, their petals stained rosy as tongues. Their pollen-crusted stamens dangled. The back of the trailer was so stuffed with pots bearing trees and climbing plants, succulents and ferns, it appeared to be a jungle. Sophie couldn't spot where the trailer ended for the lush wall of foliage. How could someone so bad take care of such beautiful, natural things?

She stepped gingerly toward the greenery, dodging the chipped teacups and torn scarves littering the scratched floor. The Airstream was small but it felt so large inside, it seemed to stretch before Sophie as she moved through it, a sensation that left her a bit dizzy. She realized she hadn't eaten enough today, or drunk enough water, and it was so hot and the work she'd done was tough. The shady coolness of Kishka's trailer should have been a relief, but as Sophie moved toward the plants her breathing became difficult. She reached out and brushed a vine with her fingertips, peering into the plants. Something caught on the back of her throat and she choked. She needed water. She thought briefly of the sink behind her, right behind her in the trailer, but now it seemed sort of far away. This wall of plants, shimmering, creating their own environment, their own mixture of smells, was way more interesting than a *glass of water*. *Phew*. Sophie took a deep breath, and moved closer.

Were there more plants behind those plants? And more behind them? Sophie felt disoriented. Was there a mirrored back wall, presenting an infinite illusion? Sophie reached her hand to touch it, but her hand kept going. Through more
plants and more plants and

more. She made her breaths shallow, just little breaths, like teeny sips of air. Didn't plants and trees help make *more* air? Wasn't that what was so great about them? If Sophie looked close she could almost *see* the leaves making the air in front of her, the thinnest fog drifting out from the green. But was that air? Sophie tried for a regular breath and choked. She poked a bit deeper into the forest, a claustrophobic panic rising within her. *Where was the wall?*

As far back as she could see, Sophie caught a rustle in the leaves. A tremble, a rough shaking, a creature scampering.

"Hello?" A tiny voice quavered, and Sophie jumped, then screamed. She watched the leaves in the distance quiver as the creature dashed away, deeper into the grove, deeper and deeper, the trees trembling and twigs crackling in the quiet, deeper and deeper the thing scurried until it was gone. Somehow.

Sophie's last breath felt like someone had taken a can of hair spray and blasted it down her throat. She pushed herself back out from the plants, shocked to see how deep she had crept into them. Pushing through rows of vines, their leaves prehistorically large, slapping her in the face, blocking her view, she ran. Her Vans slid on the undergrowth, tripped on low vines. She wanted to scream but could not take a breath to. Was the forest growing before her? *Not a forest!* She yelled at herself inside her freaking-out mind. *No forest inside a little trailer!* Finally, Sophie could spy her grandmother's disheveled couch. With a cry she hurled herself out from the plants and onto a pile of sheets, gasping and wheezing at the cool, clean air around her. Sophie was surprised to taste the drip of salt that hit her lips, and lapped at it hungrily. She hadn't even known she was crying.

As she caught her breath Sophie felt a tickle on the inside, someone peeking in on her. Was Angel checking in or was it something else, maybe even the plants themselves, conscious and prying? Sophie tried to make herself iron on the inside, lead, metal, wood, anything, but she could feel the tickle worming its way into her, deeper and deeper, the feeling spreading. From her seat on the sofa it just looked like a wall of plants, but the harder she looked she could see them shimmer. Sophie hopped to her feet and ran for the door, stumbling on a pile of old magazines, the pages curling in the damp heat, curling like the leaves. Outside the trailer, Sophie ate at the humid air, oblivious to the junkyard stench. She lapped at it like a great bowl of water. Ronald watched her leap down the wooden stairs, her legs as wobbly as his.

"She's not there," he told her. "She's at a meeting. With the city people. She's at the City Hall."

"Great, thanks," Sophie stammered. She propped herself against a tree, the rough bark somehow soothing. Her breathing became even.

"I'm not allowed in there," Ronald said. "You allowed? She let you in there?"

"Ahhh..." Sophie shifted guiltily against the tree. "I don't know. I was just looking for her, that's all."

"I can tell her you stopped by."

Sophie wondered if Ronald had drunk slightly less today. His stance was pretty steady even without the stool, his speech slurred but quicker. Sophie was surprised to think that Ronald might actually remember to mention this visit to Kishka.

"I wish you wouldn't," Sophie said. "I wish you wouldn't tell her I stopped by, okay? It was a mistake."

Ronald nodded, no longer looking at Sophie but at the Airstream. The shine of the sky against it was such a violent flash it was like staring straight into the sun, but Ronald didn't blink

"Fine," he slurred, shrugging. "I won't tell her. But you can't surprise Kishka. She always figures it out."

Chapter 14

Sophie waited for her mother to fall asleep in front of the television before she snuck from her house to meet Angel. The smarmy host of a nighttime talk show took the stage in his suit and tie, and Sophie stepped quietly through the flat, opening the front door with the teeniest click, flinching as she shut it with another tiny sound. None of it was as loud as the laugh track the TV barfed out, but Sophie was nervous. She didn't really sneak out of the house, ever, and now it was two nights in a row she was acting like a juvenile delinquent.

Livia stayed behind, huddled in the shadows outside the open living room window, her orange eye on Andrea. If Sophie's mother woke up, Livia would speed to the girl. The alibi was, Sophie was too hot to sleep in the sweltering house and was just standing out front, or taking a walk around the block. The poison ivy she'd gotten on her hands and wrists was keeping her awake and miserable, the calamine cooling it for a precious millisecond before the unbearable itch flared once more. Andrea had clucked and hissed at the sight of the angry rash, pissed at Sophie for being so foolish, playing around in the trees when she should have been working. This is what Sophie had told her, accepting her scolding with sheepish regret. But in her chest her heart pounded fearfully. It *wasn't* poison ivy. It was her grandmother's trailer greenhouse, and she had no idea why the plants had burned her skin so bad. She was anxious to get to Angel. Angel knew so much. Angel would have all the answers.

Angel lived with her mother on the second floor of a three-story house on Spencer Avenue. Sophie walked there quickly, cutting through parking lots, Giddy and Roy on her shoulders, Arthur leading the rest of the flock high above her head. She swung her arms as she walked, appreciating the coolness on her hands.

"Turn here," Giddy said in her baby voice. "Turn here. Stop. This is the place."

A glow on the second floor seemed like candles to Sophie, sort of orange, the way the flame flickered the light. *Like breath,* Sophie thought. Angel was waiting on the porch. She bounded down the stairs to receive Sophie and the birds. "Hello," she said, moving in to give Sophie a hug, then thinking better of it with the pigeons balanced on her shoulders.

"Hello," said Giddy, and Roy gave a coo.

"Is that where you live?" Sophie asked, nodding at the flickering window above.

"Yes," said Angel. "My mother, she's a *curandera*. A witch, basically. She's been lighting candles for you, and for the pigeons, too."

"Oh!" Giddy exclaimed. "Please thank her for us." Humans offered few kindnesses to the pigeons.

"Wow," Sophie marveled, thinking *it must be so cool to have a witch for a mom.* "Does she know everything?"

"Yeah, she's known of your coming. Plus, she can read emotions, like we can. She's a snoopy mother, you know, and I live with her. She could tell something was up. I had to tell her."

"But your shield is so strong!" Sophie was shocked. "Your mother is so powerful, she can get through it?"

"Awww, she's my moms," Angel said, shy. "I don't keep that wall up with her. It would be too exhausting. The thing about the wall—" Angel's view swept up and down the street. "Come on, let's go in the shed if we're going to talk about this."

The shed was a regular wooden storage shed built under the back stairs in Angel's yard. The yard itself was spacious, ringed with slender juniper trees. Wrapped around the shed were lush viny shrubs, shrubs tipped with white blossoms and crimson berries. She thought of Kishka's garden and blew on her fingers. The pigeons pushed off her shoulders with a kick of their strong legs. *Chicken legs*, Sophie thought affectionately, watching them tuck their spindly orange limbs into their bodies as their wings pulled them to the top of the shed. *No, pigeon legs.*

The inside of Angel's shed was shelved with glass candles, which Angel lit with a long kitchen lighter. There were jars of herbs marked with pieces of masking tape, Spanish words labeling the contents. Sophie's hands and wrists throbbed. She looked at them in the bobbing glow of a candle. The skin was laced with painful welts. "Angel," Sophie started, suddenly overwhelmed by all she had to say and learn. "Uh, my grandmother has all these plants in her trailer, and I think I'm allergic or something." She held out her arms.

"What?" Angel shook her head like she was clearing water from her ears. She wasn't wearing her hat, Sophie realized. That's why Angel looked different. Her hair was pulled into a messy ponytail at the back of her skull, and her choppy bangs were flung around her face. She didn't wear heavy boots, just some sort of plasticky sandals. She seemed relaxed, Sophie realized. She started to peek into her, was shocked to find not the leaden wall but a certain space, maybe a feeling of alarm—yes, it was alarm, the sense of alarm you have when you recognize that something has spiraled beyond your control.

With a thud the iron wall came down, giving Sophie the sensation of having been shoved. "Don't do that." Angel shook her head. "Not now. I'll let you later. What are you talking about? You went into Kishka's trailer?"

Sophie shrugged a sheepish, guilty shrug. "I just wanted to see her. After everything, you know? I know she's bad, but she's my grandmother. I just wanted to see if she looked different to me now. If I could see the badness."

"You can't," Angel said sternly. "You can't see badness. She just looks like any old batty lady in Chelsea who needs to quit smoking. You went into her *house*? Sophie, you can't—when you're in someone's house, snooping like that, they can feel it. If they're a witch or whatever."

"Is Nana a witch?"

"I don't know what you want to call it. She's got mad powers. My mother has powers too, but they're simple, good powers, that's what a *curandera* is. She knows things and can heal people with herbs and her prayers. I have it, too; that's why I'm meant to help you. We have it in my family, the powers. Look."

Angel lifted a picture from where it leaned against a candle.

"This is my great-great-grandmother, Teresita Urrea. She had the powers, big time. She was very righteous; she helped the indigenous people in Mexico."

"What's *indigenous*?"

"The people who were there first. Like, the Native Mexicans. They were there, and then Spanish people came from Spain and messed it all up, and all the Native people, like, Indians, they were enslaved by the government. The government was so bad."

"Like..."—Sophie searched her mind for historic examples of bad governments—"Nazis in Germany?"

"Yeah, totally." Angel nodded. "Or, you know, America with Native Americans. The Mexican president wanted to kill all the Indians, or use them as slaves, yeah. And Teresita really felt them. She would use her healing powers to help them, she did everything for free because she'd seen God and God had told her not to like, charge for her services. So she was this amazing curandera, and she inspired the

Indians to revolt, to riot, right? And there were all these battles, and they did it in Teresita's name. She inspired them, and empowered them with her powers. She was like Joan of Arc. You know her? They teach you about her in Catholic school?"

"A little," Sophie said. She knew Joan of Arc was French, she heard voices, she got a bunch of people to go to war and then got burned at the stake.

"Teresita's like the Mexican Joan of Arc. She got thrown out of the country and came to America and kept healing people. She opened a clinic for poor people. Her magic was so strong it gets passed down person to person, but it gets weaker, too. My mother's magic is weaker than her mother's, and I am not as powerful as my mother."

Angel looked at Sophie, nodding her head. "You are like Teresita, and like Joan of Arc, and all those girls, you know, there are so many stories. Girls who knew things and had powers and a certain destiny." Angel smiled. "It is very, very exciting to get to know and help you, Sophie."

Sophie felt sick from the intensity of Angel's admiration. She didn't really deserve it. She didn't know anything, actually; the pigeons knew more than she did. Sophie knew nothing, was waiting for everyone to tell her everything. As for her powers, they seemed not very special in the light of birds who could speak human English and the simple existence of mermaids.

"Are you going to teach me how to read minds better?" Sophie asked.

"It's not reading minds." Angel laughed. "It's reading hearts. You want to read a mind, turn on the television. That's what the mind is—chatter, thinking. Loopy, repetitive thinking. It's like being in a birdcage with a bunch of angry parakeets. What we're doing is reading hearts. Most people do it a little bit every day. You know how you can feel when someone is upset, or really sad, or if someone is happy it can make you feel happy, too?"

"Yeah, totally."

"It's really not that magical. We can all just feel each other. It's how people fall in love, or have friends. It's why I can't block myself when I'm home with my mother. I *want* her to feel me a little." Angel grabbed her ponytail and tugged it tighter to her scalp. "But most people can't get inside like we can. It's tricky business. My mother taught me respect and caution with it. It's like reading someone's diary, but worse. It invades people's privacy. But it is important. Very powerful healers can peek into a heart and take out what sickens it. I think that is what you're meant to do, Sophie."

Angel turned to the shelves of jars behind her. Sophie watched as she took a dark powder from one, dried green leaves from another, and another. With her own spit she made a paste, and she motioned for Sophie to giver her her hands. Angel spread the paste across Sophie's fingers and wrists, massaged it into her palms. Sophie smelled familiar smells—coffee, and pizza, smells she could eat. "Try not to move your hands," Angel instructed.

"They feel like they're in casts," Sophie said. "Or, like, papier-mâché or something."

"Is it helping?"

Sophie was thoughtful. "More than the calamine lotion," she said, nodding. "Yeah, I think so."

Angel's face had a rueful look. "This is very bad news," she said. "This garden. I guess it is good that we know there is something strange in her trailer—but it is so bad of you to have gone there, Sophie! Your grandmother must have felt you in her home. I'm sure she knows you were snooping. Who knows what else she knows? You don't know how to protect yourself." Angel sighed, grabbed an indigo mussel shell from the shelf and dunked it into a dense, gritty jar of salt and honey. She smeared it over Sophie's hands. The sting of it felt good, and the smell made Sophie's belly rumble. She realized she hadn't eaten dinner—she had been so anxious for her mother to fall asleep that she hadn't joined her in a bowl of dinnertime Cheerios. She brought her mouth down to the medicine and slurped some off her skin. The taste of salt, her favorite.

"Here," Angel said, handing her the jar and the seashell. Sophie scooped the paste out and fed it to herself, rolling her eyes in pleasure at the sweet, salty goo.

"You are very strange," Angel observed.

"I didn't eat dinner," Sophie explained. She wondered about what she'd heard in the trailer, a voice, if she should tell Angel. The voice and the way she couldn't breathe. Maybe she had imagined it? She felt too sheepish to confess more to her mentor. She figured if Angel really needed to know she could barge into her brain and find out.

"You've got to take care of yourself," Angel instructed. "You're going to need your health and your strength."

"My nana read my heart when I was in her trailer," Sophie admitted, knowing the truth of the tickle she'd felt. "I could feel it."

"That's good," Angel said. "It's good that you know when it's happening. That's the first step to being able to protect yourself. Most people can't feel anything. They are so up in their minds"—Angel tapped her temple—"they can't feel what is happening to their hearts."

Sophie ran her finger around the edges of the now-empty jar, sucking the last of the paste. She regarded the coat on her arm hungrily.

"Leave it," Angel ordered. "Who knows what poisons you got? The salt will draw the posion out and the honey will keep the wound clean so it won't be infected. And the other paste is coffee and basil and marjoram. It should heal you. Now, we have to get started."

"What are you going to teach me?" Sophie asked. She arranged herself so that her posture reflected that of an eager, obedient student.

"First, protection. You need to learn to hide your heart. Then you'll need to gain control of your power, so you don't accidentally go invading someone's heart and feeling all their feelings when you don't want to. And you need to get stronger. If you're as big of a deal as you're supposed to be, you should be able to break through my wall. Let's go."

. . .

IN THE DARK shed that felt like a magical clubhouse—that *was*, Sophie realized, a sort of magic clubhouse—Sophie and Angel worked into the night, the candles burning low, sometimes sputtering out and filling the small room with waxy smoke. With Angel's smooth voice to guide her Sophie went deep into herself and found her own bedrock, as if she were a planet with a molten, iron core. Sophie never knew she possessed such hardness.

At first it was a sort of lava rock, rough and curling, dotted with holes. "Too porous," Angel said, her own eyes closed. "I can get right through. Plus, it's like, absorbent or something. Here, feel this." Angel thought of her mother, the curandera, and a liquid, warm affection surged through her body and leached into Sophie.

"Oh!" Sophie said. "You love your mother so much!" *That's what it feels like*, Sophie thought. *To have a mother you just wholly and simply love.* Sophie felt a sad, flat envy. Angel felt it, too.

"Okay, okay," she said. She lifted a bundle of dry, greenish sticks and twigs and dipped them into a candle, igniting it. She blew out the flames until a fragrant smoke fogged the little shed. "Let's start over. You're looking for hard stuff," Angel repeated. "The hardest you can find. Mine is iron. Use that as a guide."

Inside herself, Sophie went down, down, past the porous lava rock that seemed to smash like china as she tunneled through. She went deeper. She felt the iron, and recognized its lightly textured surface from her contact with Angel. But Sophie knew she could go even deeper. She seemed to be entering a place that had never seen light, a place perhaps older than light. There was something there to grab, though it didn't feel like a *thing* as much as a place. She tried it anyway. She pulled it up and around her insides like a cloak. It was impossibly heavy, but Sophie could move it. She was scared as she felt it stretch across her feelings. Was she going to obliterate herself? The sensation of it, the incredible weight, felt like it could block herself off from her very own self, if such a thing was possible. Was it? Sophie was trembling, half from the effort of lifting the material, half from fear. What was this stuff? What if it cut her off from other people? What if it cut her off from the world?

"Yes!" Angel said, excited. "Yes, that, that whatever it is! What is it? Where did you get it?"

"I don't know," Sophie said. She was completely covered by the shield now. And she felt herself without change, her feelings still there, all of them, her fear and excitement, her affection for Angel, the dull thump of envy for her mother-love an echo in her heart. Sophie observed the symphony of her emotions. "Can you read me?" she asked. "Anything? I'm having so many feelings!"

Sophie could feel a sort of numb pressure, Angel peeking in on her. Sophie didn't even try to repel her; her shield, brought up from some other place, made it simply impossible for Angel to get in.

"Nothing, I can't get any read off you at all. That thing, your material—" Angel marveled at it, touching its edges with her heart and mind. "It's like from outer space or something. Mine is just earth minerals, I think. This is, like—I feel like if I touch it too much it's going to suck me into it, make me a part of your wall." Angel pulled back with a shiver. "It's scary. Good job. Not only can I not read you, I don't want to."

Angel had Sophie cast the wall away and bring it back again and again, until Sophie wanted to pull out her hair with boredom. She wanted some talking animals or a fabulous creature, a myth or story or a piece of magic sea glass. Her wall came down and Angel read her discontent without even trying.

"Get over it," she said. "This is work. You're going to, like, save the world or something."

"From what?" Sophie demanded. "What am I even going to do with all this crap?"

"I'm not sure," Angel said. "I don't have that part of the story. I'm just here to help you with this."

Next, Angel helped Sophie master control of the impulse to eavesdrop on someone's emotions. "You don't want to keep getting sucked into everyone's feelings," Angel told her. "There are a lot of people who feel really, really bad."

Sophie remembered what it felt like to be Laurie LeClair, a dense, rotting misery. Or to feel her mother's feelings toward her, so sad and angry and afraid. She wished she never felt that. "Okay, show me how to do it."

Sophie became very still, noting the cues of her body, making time feel slow so she could sense how it felt right before she got tugged into the whirlpool of another person. She noticed there was a tremor, the air taking the hint of a liquid shiver, as if all its water was gathering in a thin fog. She felt a part of herself open toward Angel, and could feel Angel opening in response. Normally all of this happened at a level that neither Sophie nor the object of her attentions could feel. She stepped a little closer, beginning to feel Angel.

"Whoa," she said.

"You got it?" Angel asked.

"Yeah, it's like first the air, right, and then this feeling." She put her hands on her heart.

"Yeah, like magnets, I always think."

"Like warm, slow magnets," Sophie agreed. It felt sort of nice at the start, but once you got inside the feelings it often wasn't nice at all.

"Just cut it right when you feel that. Pull yourself back in."

Sophie knew to do it. It happened in a snap, like elastic. She boomeranged back into herself, landing with a giggle. It all felt like some strange internal gymnastics, bouncing and flipping.

"Now for the hard part." Angel smiled, pushing her bangs behind her ears. "Crack my shield."

This took Sophie hours. They took many breaks, first so she could eat from a bowl of beans simmered with fat chipotle peppers. She wolfed it down without chewing, an animal. When she was sated Angel handed her a giant glass mug, water with bits of dried-up twigs floating inside it. "To keep you awake and focused."

Later they took breaks so that Sophie could catch her breath and steady herself, for it felt like walking up to a mountain and trying to push through it with your hands. Her body shook with the effort, her face red as if she had been running. Eventually, they stopped so that Sophie could cry, with frustration and exhaustion and an angry sort of boredom. She *hated* this. Maybe it wasn't worth it to be so special and see talking birds and mermaids if you then had to do *this*, whatever *this* was, a sort of psychic pummeling, like trying to lift the earth itself onto your back. It felt impossible, and Sophie spun out in a tantrum, kicking and smacking the smooth, iron wall of Angel's heart.

"Hey, hey!" Angel could feel the blind, emotional slaps upon her surface. "Let's take a break." And Sophie burst into tears,

"I'm terrible at this!" she cried. "I can't do it! No one could do it!"

"You're not terrible at it," Angel said. "I'm just awesome at staying protected. It's very hard to break in. It's not going to be easy."

Sophie leaned against the rough wood wall of the shed with a sigh. She missed Ella, missed being a goon, just laughing, passing out, wasting time. What would she say if she spoke to her friend again? *You know, I've just been chilling with a bunch of talking pigeons, hanging out in a shed with that chick Angel learning how to read her mind and shit. How's the beach?*

Sophie took a glug of the herbal water and focused on focusing. *I don't want to let Angel down,* she thought. *Or the pigeons, or the mermaid.* A terrible thought shook fresh tears from her eyes—what if they were all mistaken, and she wasn't the girl they thought she was? Somewhere else in Chelsea the true girl slept, ignored by talking pigeons and Polish mermaids, and so humanity would never be saved, or whatever. *Help me help me help me,* Sophie repeated inside her head, though she didn't know who she was talking to.

Help her help her help her, Angel prayed in her mind to her great-great grandmother Teresita. *I think she is like you,* Angel spoke inside her heart. She thought of the woman who had helped free so many people from their enslavement, using her magic and her heart, her magic heart. *I think Sophie has a magic heart, full of the good magic, the helping magic. Help her grow strong and sure inside it.*

The two looked at one another, Sophie wiping the tears from face, gathering herself and smearing herbs and salt on her cheek. "One more time?" Angel suggested. It turned into two more times, then twenty, then fifty. On the seventy-eighth try, Sophie walked through the thick, iron wall and into Angel's heart. She could feel Angel rooting for her there, how anxious she was for the girl to succeed, how much she believed in her. How good was Angel's heart, pulsing a giant *Hooray!* in Sophie's direction. Angel's smile was so big it could crack her face in two. "You did it! You did it!" Sophie luxuriated in the excellent sensation of being Angel Barrera, until a wave of motion struck her and she was back on the other side of the dark stone wall. "Now, get out!" They fell into a fit of exhausted, laughter that, once started, they had a terrible time stopping.

"We're done for now, but not forever," Angel said, after they'd collected themselves. "You need to learn to stay there, even when someone is trying to kick you out."

"That doesn't seem right," Sophie said, not liking the thought of hanging out where she wasn't wanted.

"It's what you're meant to learn," Angel said. "It's what you already know. You just need to get really, really good at it." She took a clean rag damped with something that smelled like the earth, and wiped Sophie's hands. Her skin was cool and pale, the angry welts gone.

"You did it!" Sophie cried with joy. Angel smirked and shrugged her shoulders, full of fake modesty.

"Of course I did."

. . .

ANGEL REFUSED TO send Sophie home with only a flock of pigeons as her protectors. "No offense," she said to the flutter of them rising and falling around her head. Arthur swam a crazy backstroke in the air before them, looking Angel right in the eye.

"Should trouble go down," the bird began, "I am certain that the total of us, dive-bombing some chump's head, is going to be a lot more effective than you trying to talk yourself out of a fight."

"Death from above!" another pigeon shouted, spinning toward the ground, then arcing up sharply, tumbling in a loop-de-loop.

"Wow." Sophie was impressed.

"Well, if, um, trouble goes down I will be your man on the ground," Angel offered. "Safety in numbers."

"Totally," Giddy cooed, nestling into Angel's shoulder. Roy settled onto Sophie's, and they headed toward the square, turning down Heard Street, just short of the city's center and all its late-night activity. Anyone out at this hour was up to no good, and anyone up to no good would head to Bellingham Square to find it. It did the trick of keeping the rest of town relatively safe and quiet until the sun came up, releasing hoodlum boys and girls into the streets.

They walked down Heard Street, passing the house with the glut of lawn ornaments spilling across the lawn, then the vacant lot with overgrown weeds springing from the busted concrete, finally stopping at Sophie's house, the dark green house with mismatched, chipped lion statues resting on either side of the stairs. It faced the dark rails of train tracks a block away.

"This is where you live." Angel looked around. She noticed the tracks. "Wrong side of the tracks," she teased.

"There isn't any right side of the tracks in Chelsea," Sophie teased back, but serious questions nagged her. "Angel, how did you know that I was coming?"

"My mother told me," she said. "She'd thought maybe you would come in her generation, and she prepared, and when you didn't she taught me everything she could. I got hired at the dump as soon as I got old enough, and I've been waiting there for you."

"For how long? How did you know I would come there?"

"I've been working for your grandmother for five years, since I was fifteen." Angel shook her head. "And I'm not crazy. That's how I know I got strong magic."

"But how did you know I would come?"

"We knew you were Kishka's granddaughter."

"How, how did you know that?"

"Awww, Sophie." Angel shifted uncomfortably. "I told you, I don't know everything, I just know my part."

Sophie rushed at Angel and got in before she knew it, before she could yank her iron wall up around her. It felt so different inside Angel than it had earlier; Sophie marveled at how quickly a person's feelings could change. The love was still there, Sophie knew it was true, and that Angel had goodness in her heart, but now there was fear and discomfort, a claustrophobic feeling inside her, like the walls of her own self were closing in on her. It was an icky feeling, and Sophie could feel that Angel didn't like it, either. It was the feeling of a lie.

"Stop it!" Angel yelled. Sophie could feel her pushing her out, the dense vibrations of the wall coming, but Sophie stayed. She went deeper. *That's how you stay,* she thought. *When they try to push you out, you go deeper.* Sophie burrowed into Angel like a tick. "Ugh!" Angel twisted like there was an insect crawling up her back, just beyond her reach. It was true that many normal people had their psyches invaded all the time and didn't even know it. But Angel was sensitive, attuned. Her walls were the strongest. She had never felt someone break inside and stay there. Her mother was probably powerful enough to do it, but she was too respectful. It felt terrible, like an ant had crawled into your brain, to feel this small, invading motion in your most tender parts. "Please!" she begged Sophie.

Sophie had been on the edge of learning something more about the lie Angel had told her. There were waves of information, shimmers, she only had to catch them, braid them together into the truth.

There was *mother*, her mother, and *salt*. A baby. A terrible sadness, a sacrifice. She pushed for more, but Angel's anguish at Sophie's invasion grew, until all Sophie felt was her feeling of violation, her despair at not being stronger, able to protect herself. Angel had never felt so unprotected. It was a frightening feeling. Though she'd known that Sophie possessed incredible magic, it was hard to match that knowledge with the easily frustrated, sometimes bratty girl she'd been tutoring. Sophie's strength, her fierce perseverance, stunned her.

When the understanding that she was hurting Angel became more painful than the feeling of being lied to, Sophie leapt back into herself, feeling the iron wall spring up behind her as she left. *She was trying to pull her wall up that whole time,* Sophie realized. *She couldn't do it. I'm stronger than her wall.* And Sophie knew she had learned her final lesson, how to stay where she wasn't wanted. That she had in fact known how all along, and even without Angel she would have figured it out, the way she had understood to pull back from Ronald and not enter his boozy, decrepit interior. The way she'd known she could send herself into Angel that day she first saw her at the dump. Was that yesterday? That was only yesterday.

Angel sat on Sophie's front steps. She looked broken from the experience, her head hung, her bangs clumped to the sides of her face—wet, Sophie noted. Angel was crying.

"I'm sorry," Sophie rushed to say. Whatever had happened, whatever lie Angel had told, there certainly was a reason for it. Angel was good, had been only good to her, and Sophie had hurt her. "I'm so, so sorry Angel. I didn't—" Sophie started to say she hadn't meant to do it, but she had. And maybe she hadn't meant to hurt Angel, but once she did, she'd stuck around a while. Why? Because she could. Because she was pissed at Angel's lie and wanted to know the secret of it.

"I don't," Sophie corrected herself. "I don't like what happened. That I did that." *Don't cry don't cry don't cry.* There was something gross, Sophie thought, about crying while offering an apology. The tears gathered at the corners of Sophie's eyes and dried there. Angel rubbed her wrist across her face and looked up at her student.

"I can't be mad at you," Angel said. "You are more powerful than me. I've known that all along, it was just really intense to feel it." She stood up. "I guess our work is done," she said. "That was my last lesson for you, but you know it. How to stay when someone is trying to make you leave. You just go deeper. There is no end to how deep you can go. You can go so deep in a person, even a person fighting you, that they stop feeling you're there, they think you're gone." Angel shook her head, still stunned from Sophie's invasion. "I knew you were the one and everything, but damn," she said. "You just kicked my ass. You're really, really powerful Sophie. I thought it would take a lot longer to teach you what I know but, you got it. That's it."

"Our work can't be done!" Sophie cried. "I—I—there's a lot I don't understand, Angel. What if I go too deep and I can't get out? Can I get trapped in a person?"

Angel shook her head. "No. They might begin to feel you again when you come out, there could be a struggle, but you can hold your own in a struggle. Jeez." Angel tried to smile, to lighten the moment, but truthfully she didn't feel light. She felt battered and exhausted, and sad. She had been training for this moment her whole life; she didn't expect it to be over so soon. The girl knew everything she could teach her.

"Well, what about Teresita?" Sophie said, desperate. "You barely told me anything about her, she seems really important."

"She is important." Angel nodded. "Honestly, Sophie, I have thought that you might be her. You might be her, and Joan of Arc, and all those saints, those girls who had crazy magic and didn't know what they were doing, who didn't have helpers like you have, and the people of their time just punished them for it. I've even thought you could be, like, the big revolutionary heroes who spoke about love, you know? Like Jesus Christ or Gandhi. Maybe it's the same spirit coming back again and again to try to help. Maybe this lifetime, it's you."

Sophie thought of the images she'd seen of the men Angel talked about. Fragile-looking Gandhi, too skinny, but he seemed cheerful, a happy man in his little glasses. Jesus Christ on the cross. She'd looked at him every day for eight long years of Catholic school. And Angel was suggesting she *was* him. *In your face, Sister Margaret,* she thought with a spiteful pride. Angel caught it.

"I shouldn't be saying any of this to you," Angel said. "This is not the story. This is not the prophecy, not at all. These are just my thoughts. Maybe it only means that you are part of a powerful lineage, Sophie. It is good for me to remember. Because when I see you,

I see a young girl with snarls in her hair, and I need to remember your lineage."

"What's *lineage*?"

"Like ancestors. But, it's like you're part of a bigger family than the one you have here on earth. Anyway, it's good for me to think like this."

"I'm sorry I didn't get out of you when you wanted me to," Sophie said.

"It's okay. Please don't do it again. I hope to never give you a reason to."

"But Angel—" Sophie started, stopped. "Why did you lie? What won't you tell me?"

"Someone else should tell you these things. It is not my work to explain everything to you."

"Hennie," piped Livia, who, like all the pigeons, had been watching them quietly. "Hennie will tell you more; go to her when you can."

"Okay," Sophie said. She wanted to look at Angel but felt she might cry. "We'll still hang out at the dump, right? Smashing glass and stuff?"

"Sophie," Angel was shaking her head. She busied herself pulling her hair from its ponytail, then roping it back into a ponytail. She fussed with her bangs. "Sophie, I have been waiting to quit the dump for years. I was only there to wait for you. I can't keep working with your grandmother, in that smell, watching how she treats Ronald— she's killing him, giving him all that alcohol, she might as well give him rat poison. Having to keep my wall up all day in case she comes snooping, having her think I'm a guy all the time—I can't do it. It's really stressful."

"Well, what will you do?" Sophie cried. She couldn't picture Angel anywhere but the dump, smashing old jars in her goggles, harvesting gleaming beads of perfect glass from the tumbler.

"I want to help kids," she said. "I want to be a juvenile drug counselor. It bums me out, seeing so many kids in Chelsea messed up like that. There's a program at that college that just opened a campus right here in town, in the old post office. I bet I could get financial aid, I think I could do it."

Sophie thought about Angel counseling drug addict kids, her ability to go inside them, her ability to keep them outside of her. It seemed perfect. "You're a really good teacher," Sophie said shyly. "It would be kind of like teaching, wouldn't it be?"

"Maybe." Angel nodded. "So... I won't be at the dump tomorrow. I'm sorry to leave you there. The pigeons will be with you, but you have to steer clear of your grandmother as much as possible. Okay?"

"Okay." Sophie hurled herself impulsively at Angel, gripping her in a clutching hug. "Can I please come visit you sometimes? What if I need you?"

"Yeah, yeah," Angel said. "Of course, if you ever need me, come find me. You know where I live. My mother will always be home, she would always be happy to see you, okay?"

"Can I just come and, like, hang out sometimes?"

Angel laughed. "Yeah, sure. In all your free time. When you're not, like, saving the world, come by and I'll tell you the whole story of Teresita."

"Okay, great," Sophie felt relieved. Angel handed her a paper bag she'd brought along.

"One white candle, dressed by my mother. Light it and pray to Teresita. Make an altar. It will help you stay focused and strong, and it will call help to you." Angel kissed Sophie on her forehead. "I will be praying for you all the time, always know that Sophie."

Sophie clutched the paper bag to her chest and watched Angel walk away. A sweet fragrance, like lilacs and peonies, floated up fro the sack. One of the pigeons, a bird named Bix, settled onto her shoulder and lifted his feather to soak up her tears. " 'Parting is all we know of heaven,' " he intoned, " 'And all we need to know of hell.' That's Emily Dickinson. She was a poet, perhaps you've heard of her?"

"Don't start with the poetry crap," Arthur bellowed. "She's having a moment, let her have her moment."

"I find that poetry aids the having of such moments, greatly," Bix sniffed.

"Thank you, Bix," Sophie said. Together with the pigeons she watched Angel move up Heard Street, unti she was around the corner and gone.

"Who will put out water for us to bathe in?" Giddy asked sadly.

"I will," Sophie promised. "*If* you guys promise to stop taking dumps on my mom's car."

"You drive a hard bargain, lady," Arthur said. "But you got us over a barrel. We need a bath. It's a deal."

"I would offer to clean it for you," Bix offered generously. "But we do not possess the appendages for such a task."

The pigeons took off into the sky, the tail-whistles of Livia and the others like audible streamers in the night. Sophie waited at her door until she could no longer hear them, then pulled her house key from her shirt and let herself in.

Chapter 15

Sophie was too exhausted to wake her mother from the couch and coax her into bed. She felt a pang, thinking about her mom waking up in her work clothes, her body crumpled and sore, but she felt a flare of annoyance, too: *Why keep falling asleep on the couch, then?* But Sophie knew she should be grateful for her mother's narcolepsy. Without it she would not have been able to sneak away these past nights, out of her house and into her destiny.

Sophie walked through her mother's empty room and into her own cramped space, her twin mattress on its twin frame facing a stout wooden dresser, old looking. It had been Andrea's when she was a child, something Sophie hadn't learned until after she'd found how easy it was to carve onto the surface with her house key, and spent an hour on the phone with Ella idly carving spirals, stars, and hearts into the dresser. Andrea had been so upset she simply stared at the furniture, her tongue working to conjure the proper words from deep in her throat. "That was mine," she said simply. "When I was your age. That was an antique." She rubbed her fingers over the vandalism. Sophie felt defensive. She hated getting in trouble for things she hadn't known she wasn't supposed to do.

"I thought it was mine," she said. "I thought I could do what I wanted to it."

"Just because something is yours doesn't give you the right to ruin it. It doesn't mean you get to treat it disrespectfully." Andrea ran her fingers in the deep, rough grooves of a heart her daughter had bore onto the surface. "Or, I guess it does. Do what you want. Draw all over the walls, why don't you? It's 'your' room."

But Sophie would never do such a thing; she knew it wasn't her room at all, but the landlord's room. She'd thought the dresser was hers. She didn't know why she'd carved on it, it didn't look good, she'd simply wanted to do it at the time and so she'd done it. She felt embarrassed, and hated how beaten down her mother was being about it. She preferred Andrea angry to this limp and hopeless version. "I'm sorry," she offered, wondering what other things she thought were her own were in fact not. Her mother had left the bedroom, and the defacement was never spoken of again.

Lying in her bed, with the candle in its paper bag stashed beneath it, Sophie watched as the slowly rising sun lit her room, illuminating the carvings on her dresser. She was perhaps more tired than she had ever been. She wondered if she had to pull up her shield right then, if she could even do it. She'd surely collapse. She lay flat on her back because she liked to feel the weight of the sea glass on her sternum, cool and flat and precious. At least that was hers, she was certain. She pulled her sheet over her head to shield her eyes from the coming day, and tried to get some sleep before heading back to the dump.

. . .

IT SEEMED LIKE Sophie had just shut her eyes, and her mother was calling her. But it wasn't her crisp, drill-sergeant mother, it was some croaking, weakened, frog version of her mother.

"Sophie," her voice was raspy. "I'm sick." Andrea was seated on the edge of her bed, in a room adjacent to Sophie's own. Sophie pulled herself up with effort; her eyes did not want to be open.

"What's wrong?"

Andrea felt around her throat. "My lymph nodes are swollen," she said. "And my throat is sore. I think I have a fever. Will you feel my forehead?"

Sophie climbed out of bed and brought the cool inside of her wrist up to her mother's forehead, feeling the throbbing heat of the skin there. The air around her shimmered, and a part of herself magnetized toward her mother. She reined herself in. "You have a fever."

"That goddamn old man sneezed on me," Andrea grumbled. "I washed my face and Purelled and everything but it's no use. I work in a germ factory. They should give us all extra sick days." Andrea took off her work pants and slid into bed in her t-shirt and underwear, bringing the sheet over her body limply. Her head sunk into a pillow. "Ooooh," she groaned, a mixture of relief and pain. "I forgot what it's like to lie down in a *bed*. It's so *nice*."

"What about me, Ma?" Sophie asked. "How will I get to the dump?" She held her breath hopefully, keeping a cheerful, earnest look on her face. Even though her mother couldn't read her, she brought her wall up anyway, just for practice. She felt snug and safe inside it, like a tree house had sprung up beneath her, and from its heights she spied everything but no one spied her.

"No dump," Andrea said. "You'll stay here. I'll need you to stick around and go to the store for me later. Call your grandmother and tell her you're not coming. And call the clinic, would you? Tell them I'm not feeling good. Ugh." Andrea kicked off the sheet and spread her limbs across the bed as far as she could, feeling for a spot that felt cool. "Nothing is worse than being sick in the heat," she said. "I feel like a dog, a sick dog."

Sophie walked over and kissed the burning top of Andrea's brow. Her hairline was damp, the hair sticky with sweat. She petted her mother's head, pushing the full roundness of her hair back onto the pillow. Bobby pins jabbed her hand; Sophie removed them so they wouldn't poke her mother in the skull, laid them on her bedside table. "Okay, Ma," she said. Then Sophie walked solemnly into the kitchen and, once out of Andrea's view, did a happy dance. She wiggled her hips and punched her fists in front of her, kicking her legs. Her mother falling ill was the best thing that could have happened.

She called the clinic first. Who was her mother's boss? She wasn't sure, actually. There was a long list of people at the clinic her mother complained about on the regular, and Sophie wasn't sure who was who. She let the voice mail take her through the workforce. None of the names were familiar. *Betsy Chen,* the robotic voice intoned. Sophie hit pound, and the phone began to ring in Dr. Chen's office.

"Hello," the doctor answered.

"Hi, Dr. Chen?"

"Yeeees." Something about the way the doctor spoke made Sophie feel like she was half-singing her words. It was similar to the pigeons, she realized. How they spoke in such soothing, cooing melodies. Dr. Chen's voice was not so different.

"Hi, it's Sophie Swankowski. I'm calling about my mother. She woke up really sick and she's not going to be able to come in today."

"Oh, no!" Dr. Chen exclaimed. "Well, I'm so sorry. What is wrong with her?"

"Um, her lymph nodes are swollen and her throat is sore and she's got a fever."

"Uh-huh." Sophie imagined the doctor's face nodding, her smooth bob swaying above her shoulders. "That's what's going around. She'll probably need some antibiotics. Perhaps I can stop by later and look in on her."

"Sure," Sophie said, suddenly alarmed at the thought of Dr. Chen inside her dumpy house. Dr. Chen was a *doctor*. The perfect, sharp cut of her hair suggested a person with money to blow on a fancy salon, someplace in Boston, Sophie bet. Though she knew the doctor grew up in Chelsea, lived here still, Sophie couldn't imagine why. Dr. Chen was too *good* for Chelsea. The thought sat uncomfortably inside her. Sophie didn't like thinking anyone was too good or not good enough for anything, ever.

On the line, the doctor could sense Sophie's reluctance. "Well, you let me know, okay? I'm only thinking about your mom. I'll let reception know. Please tell her I hope she feels better. *And*," she finished, "Livia says hello."

Sophie felt a burst of excitement at the dove's name. "Is Livia your favorite?" she asked the doctor, knowing immediately it was a sort of lousy question.

"They are all my favorites, but Livia is so special, isn't she?"

"She never gets ruffled," Sophie said. "She's very capable. Very sensible."

"It's true. But there are good things about Arthur's temperament, too. Arthur gets very ruffled, but he's passionate, and passion can accomplish quite a lot. What about Giddy?"

"Giddy is so sweet!" Sophie gushed. "She makes me want to take care of her."

"Well, she's still young. But yes, she's very purehearted, very sincere. Roy, too. They're good mates for each other. Roy is very loyal. But then, all the pigeons are. Loyalty is a pigeon trait. They mate for life, you know. How about Bix, have you met him?"

"Yes!" It felt good to talk about the pigeons with someone else who knew them, who knew them so well.

"Bix is a poet," Dr. Chen said. "He is very learned. He's yet to find a mate; I think his standards are too high." Sophie caught her breath as she realized the conversation they were having. A casual conversation about pigeons being capable, or passionate, or learned poets. "You've caught some of Bix's quotations, no?"

"I have," Sophie said. She felt like she was admitting to, or confirming, much, much more.

"Well, if you would ever like to see their dovecote you're welcome to visit. Let them know, they'll bring you over. I'd be happy to see you, Sophie."

"Okay," Sophie said.

"You're doing okay with everything?"

"With everything?" Sophie couldn't be sure what the doctor was asking, and even more, she could not be certain she was doing okay. "Yeah," she lied.

"No more passing out?"

"Once more," she said. "I did it once more."

"What happened?"

"I saw the mermaid. I was out for an hour and woke up with water in my lungs and a fish in my mouth and now my best friend is mad at me."

She heard the doctor take a deep breath on the other end. "Oh, Sophie," she said. "You really must stop. *The mermaid will find you,* please stop doing that. To be out for an hour—you could have put yourself in a coma. It's quite serious."

"Okay," she said, feeling small.

"When do you start high school? A couple months?"

High school? The thought was ridiculous. All this insanity—talking pigeons, Polish mermaids, mind reading or heart reading or whatever that craziness was, and she was supposed to go to *high school*? Chelsea High at that, to get shoved in the halls by kids tougher than her, to suffer through the dull classes by day, and what? Save humanity by night? The effects of two nights without sleep were working to derange Sophie a bit. Her emotions felt right at the surface, tears felt close. "I guess," she said. "I guess I'm supposed to go to *high school*."

"Well, you'll need another physical," Dr. Chen said in a clipped, business-y voice, still musical, though, still a voice with a flute tied to its tail, whistling pleasantly as it spoke. "I'll make you an appointment. A follow-up for that last one, just to make sure you're okay. I'll schedule it for when your mother is working, just you and me. And no more passing out."

"Okay," Sophie felt grateful to the doctor. With so many strange characters watching out for her, it felt good to have a *doctor* on her team. Even if it was a rather strange doctor.

"And maybe I'll see you later," she said. "Goodbye."

. . .

BEFORE SOPHIE DIALED up the junkyard she pulled her shield up high over her emotional body. She made sure it went above her head, imagined it closing over her skull, sealing her inside an impenetrable bubble. Kishka picked up on the first ring.

"Sophia," she said before Sophie said a word. "You're late."

Her grandmother was being aggressively psychic. The boldness of it threw Sophie off balance, but her shield stayed strong around her.

"H-Hi, Nana," she said, composing herself.

"Let me guess," Kishka began. "Your poor, overworked mother is sick, and there is no one to take you to the dump today."

Sophie's body rang with alarm. How did Kishka know all this? She remembered Ronald's dull pronouncement: *She knows everything.* She imagined her grandmother hovering over a crystal ball, like in *The Wizard of Oz*, Sophie trapped in the orb like Dorothy.

"Anyone could have guessed such a thing," said Kishka, annoyed with Sophie's breathless silence. "*All* that woman does is work and work and work, with a bunch of slobs who don't know how to take care of themselves. It's a wonder she doesn't get sick all the time." Kishka exhaled heavily on the other line. Sophie imagined a burst of smoke leaving her mouth, like steam from a train. "I could come get you," Kishka suggested, freezing Sophie's heart. "But I'm sure you want to stay at home and help your mother like a good daughter. I bet you have *lots and lots* of little things to busy yourself with."

Sophie could feel a patter upon her shield, like raindrops on a windowpane. The patter grew harder, rain becoming hail. The insistent shower of it stung, but Sophie felt snug inside her shield. A new fear bloomed inside her, though—that her grandmother would know that

Sophie could hide her emotions. That in itself was confirmation of so many things. Satisfied, Kishka pulled away from her granddaughter. The hailstorm ceased. Sophie breathed a sigh of relief, but kept her shield strong. Her grandmother could not get in, at least not this time. She thought of her mom lying sick in bed. Kishka must have read her when they didn't show up at the dump on time. Sophie realized that she would have to keep her shield up more often, possibly all the time. The thought made her worried. Didn't Angel say that it was *good* for humans to pick up each other's emotions? Sophie didn't want to be cut off from the world. The thought made her lonely, and her feelings rose wildly inside their container. *A can of feelings,* Sophie thought.

"I do want to take care of my mother," Sophie said. "She needs me to run errands for her, and just hang around. The house is dirty. Dr. Chen might come by."

"Dr. Chen?" Sophie felt another rain of Kishka's attentions upon her. "That loon who keeps the pigeons? I'm about to have the city do something about her. Those goddamn winged rats are all over my dump. I've got enough problems with the seagulls and the actual rats."

"I'll mention it to her," Sophie said, alarmed. "I'm sure you don't have to talk to the city. Dr. Chen is really nice; she wouldn't want to be a problem to anyone."

"What do you care?" Kishka snapped, then softened. "Oh, my poor granddaughter," she cooed, sounding almost like an actual, loving grandmother. "Look what it's done to you. Being a latchkey kid, an only child, no father, your mother barely looking after you. You've grown up too fast," Kishka said. "You're a little adult, trying to take care of every-thing. The responsibility you must feel! But you're just a little girl. You don't have to take care of it all. Who is taking care of you, Sophie?"

The truth in Kishka's observations made Sophie's eyes sting, and she wrapped the shield around her like a blanket. Sophie knew who was taking care of her. She brought them up in her mind: the pigeons, Angel, even Angel's mother had fixed her a candle and cooked her those beans, would cook her more food if she was hungry, Sophie knew it. Was the mermaid taking care of her? The mermaid caused her to nearly drown, Sophie thought, but she knew the creature would be there for her in her strange, cranky way. Dr. Chen would take care of her, of this Sophie was certain. She felt a tingle in her heart, a loneliness growing. These were her people, weren't they? Her strange crew. Would they be enough to make up for no father, and an overworked, neglectful mother?

"It's probably enough to make you feel a little cuckoo," Kishka continued in her falsely soothing voice. "Neglected children often make up imaginary friends to make themselves feel better. You're not doing that, are you, Sophie? Hmmmm, but maybe that's the wrong question. Because you would *think* the friends were real..."

Sophie had to get off the phone with her grandmother. The woman was trying to crack her shield, make her question her sanity.

"Sophie!" she heard her mother croak from the bedroom. "Would you bring me some water?"

"I have to go," she said to her grandmother. "Ma has a sore throat and she's asking for water."

"Well, maybe I'll stop by," Kishka sighed. "I should check on my girls. You are still my girl, aren't you, Sophie? You would never betray your own grandmother, would you?

"N-No, Nana!" Kishka rattled inside Sophie's shield. "Of course not."

"You do know it's always worse to lie than to tell the truth, don't you? Because when you lie—well, that makes *two* infractions. Double the trouble. You don't want to trouble your grandmother, do you? Your flesh and blood?"

"No, Nana, of course not!" Sophie tried playing it cool. "I don't know what you're talking about."

"Yes, you do," Kishka said coldly. "You know exactly what I am talking about, Sophia. And you can bury yourself in that rock of yours, but you cannot hide from me. And your friends, all your little friends, they are all even weaker." Kishka exhaled, and Sophie could almost smell the cigarette smoke through the telephone. "You will not win a fight with me, dear. Whatever lies these people might be filling you with. You are just a girl, a simple, common girl. You are not special. And you will lose every battle you try, so if I were you I would call pest control and tell them you are having some problems with the pigeons in your neighborhood. And stay away from the creek."

Her grandmother hung up the phone, leaving a crackle in her ear, the sense that even though the connection had been cut, the conversation continued.

. . .

SOPHIE BROUGHT HER mother a glass of water clacking with ice cubes. She shook a bottle of aspirin. "I brought you this," she said. "But I think you should take *this*." She waved another bottle at her, nighttime cold medicine. "It'll knock you out, so you can sleep off your cold. You really need to sleep, Ma."

Sophie's guilt was bunched up inside her shield, known only to her. To her mother she sounded like a concerned and thoughtful daughter, and she was—Sophie did want her mom to be well, to sleep a deep and healing sleep. But Sophie also wanted her mother *out*. Knocked out. Sophie had a lot to do, and she could do it best, and safest, with her mother zonked out on cold medicine. *Am I trying to drug my own mother?* Sophie worried. She kept the medicines held out to her mom. "Your choice," she chirped. Andrea selected the cold medicine, and Sophie felt a rush of relief and excitement.

"Did you make those calls?" Andrea asked. Her hair was triple bedheaded, first from the couch, then from her restless slumber, and then from the sweat of her fever dampening the tangles. Her face was flushed and her eyes looked dull. Sophie kissed her warm cheek.

"Dr. Chen might come by, to see if you need antibiotics," she said, and Andrea rolled her eyes.

"Right. Get me better quick so I can go right back to work," she said cynically. It occurred to Sophie that maybe her mother *wanted* to be sick. Maybe this was the only break Andrea could manage to take.

"No, she's just concerned for you, Ma. She wants you to feel better. Nana might stop by, too."

"Gosh, I'm so popular," she quipped. "I'd better put some pants on. Will you bring me some shorts from my dresser?"

Sophie rifled through her mother's drawers, a sweet lemony smell filling her nose. Her mother kept little bundles of herbs stashed among her clothes, the perfume of it rose into the air. Sophie found a pair of pajama shorts patterned with ducks and brought them to her mother.

"Go to the store and get orange juice, and those instant soup packets. And some honey and lemon."

"Right now?" Sophie asked.

"Whenever," Andrea said. "Go later. Take my purse with you. Just let me sleep. But remember, you're still punished. No running off with Ella or passing yourself out or anything. I'll know if you do," Andrea threatened, full of maternal bravado. Sophie knew she could do all that and more and her mother would never be the wiser. It gave Sophie a sad feeling, that her mother should be so easy to trick.

"Okay, Mom," she said. "I'll be right here."

. . .

THE FIRST THING Sophie did was take plastic bowls from under the sink and fill them with tap water. She carried the sloshing containers out into her yard and lined them up against the back fence. Livia swooped down from a telephone line with a whistle.

"How lovely of you," she thanked Sophie, and entered the bowl with a splash. Sophie cupped some water into her palms and poured a stream over the pigeon's grimy head. Livia shut her eyes as Sophie massaged the dirt from her wet feathers. "Oh, my," she cooed. "That feels wonderful." Soon the yard around her was fluttering with pigeons wanting a hand washing.

"Me next, me next," Arthur insisted.

"Would you do that to me, Sophie?" Giddy asked in her tender voice. Beside her, Roy bobbed his neck from side to side.

"I think I really threw something out doing loop-de-loops," he complained. "Would you mind giving it a rub?"

"And me," Bix inserted. "If you would."

And so Sophie spent the next hour of her morning bathing each pigeon, one by one. She stole from her bathroom her mother's shampoo, which smelled like bright fruit, and she lathered their feathers into a froth. "Ooooh," they cooed uniformly. "Aaaah."

They emerged from their baths with their feathers wetted to their wings, looking ugly and drowned. Sophie was certain the birds had never been so clean. They rose to the telephone wires to dry in the sun, growing fluffy, sticking their beaks into their bodies to huff their candy-sweet stink, becoming pretty and noble once again.

"I smell so good I want to take a bite outta myself," Arthur said happily.

Sophie refreshed the water and left it out for them, then got to work washing the birdshit from her mother's car roof. The pigeons sat shamefaced above her, watching.

" 'I watch, and long have watched, with calm regret,' " spoke Bix. "William Wordsworth. Poet Laureate of Great Britain, 1843 to 1850. I am so, so sorry that any of my kind has shat upon your carriage."

"It's fine," Sophie said. The sponge removed the crust of excrement fairly easily. She scrambled up and over the roof of the car. "I just want to finish this now, in case my grandmother comes."

"Wordsworth had a dreadful grandmother too," Bix said. "She nearly drove him to suicide. But the romantics, they were very weak, and dramatic. You are something different, dear Sophie."

Sophie cast half an eye at the bird, and kept scrubbing.

" 'Queen of my tub, I merrily sing, while the white foam raises high,' " Bix carried on. "Louisa May Alcott. Best known for *Little Women*, but she was a poet as well, you know."

"Bix, you are becoming annoying," Livia said.

"Oh, dear." The bird shuffled his feathers nervously. "I'm very sorry."

. . .

WITH THE BIRDS and the car clean and shining, Sophie returned to the house to check on her mother. The cold medicine held her in its druggy grip; Andrea breathed deeply, her sleep solid. Sophie found her purse in the living room, on the edge of the couch. It was a roomy bag, fake leather slowly peeling where the strap wore against Andrea's shoulder. Sophie fetched the paper bag from beneath her bed and stuffed the candle into it. "Mom?" she spoke softly into the bedroom. Andrea answered with a snore. "I'll be back in a little while."

Sophie left the house, the birds following above, flying ahead and roosting on wires as Sophie made her way down Heard Street, mercifully ignored by a pack of boys clustered on a porch, their dirt bikes in a tumble upon the sidewalk, further still, past the rows of neglected houses. *Neglected.* Sophie mused upon the word. Neglected like her. What Kishka said had truth in it: Sophie was a neglected kid, she knew she was. Her mother didn't mean it; Andrea just worked so much— she was consumed with their tiny family's survival. Consumed, too, with her resentment of it; how unfair it was, how she wished it wasn't so. In the swirl of Andrea's mind Sophie got lost, bobbing into view only when she misbehaved. Sophie felt a sort of respect for Kishka. Her grandmother was not a fool. She knew Sophie's weak spots, so Sophie had better know them, too.

Chapter 16

Hennie's store was on the last populated block of Heard
Street. Beyond it there was just a single house, dark
green and crumbly, pointed and strange. Strange to be a house
in a congested city and have no neighbors. On either side, straw-
colored weeds sprang, and across the street ran a long, abandoned
warehouse, its small, tough windows cracked and shattered, graffiti
looping across its corrugated walls. The pavement here gave way to
packed dirt, and dust hung in the humid air. The city never repaired
the street since the block's sole resident never complained. The few
times Sophie had walked that block, to dodge a gang of boys or take
a quicker route to the park, she felt creeped out and confused. How
could this be the very same street she lived on? It seemed like she'd
crossed over into another region entirely, perhaps another era. She
saw a snake slithering on the edge of the weeds, and a big German
Shepherd on the porch of that one weird house, a big pink tongue

hanging sideways from his mouth. Sophie didn't like such big, not-cute dogs. She liked dogs that were tiny and funny looking, or else she liked larger dogs that were mellow and friendly and brought you things. She did not like big dogs that stared and panted, or drooled. She had wondered, seeing the Shepherd, what would happen if the dog attacked her. Weren't they attack dogs, terrible police dogs? She supposed she'd simply be mauled, as there was absolutely nobody to help her on this strange strip of Heard Street, nobody but whoever lived in the crumpled, green house and they clearly did not like people enough to care if one was getting eaten by their dog in the street.

That day Sophie didn't continue on to that abandoned block. She stopped at the corner, noting the way the dust yellowed the air down the way, like looking at a sepia picture from another time. The place that marked the crossroads was Hennie's Grocery. She turned and entered the store. It took a moment for her eyes to adjust to the darkness. The bright sun outside struggled to cut through the layer of grime on the grocery store's windows. Sophie thought that probably some people didn't shop at Hennie's because they thought the place was closed. As for the rest, they just thought it was nasty. Sophie's eyes came to rest on the glass countertop. Arranged on its center, a carton of orange juice, a box of instant soup, a lemon, and a jar of amber honey. Behind it all, Hennie, her thin scarf containing her hair, her eyes lit like a magic piece of sea glass.

"Hello, Sophia," she greeted the girl. "At last, my niece."

. . .

HENNIE SWUNG A bolt of rusty metal, locking the door of her shop. "Not that anyone comes." She winked at Sophie. "Right?"

"I have always wondered how you stay in business," Sophie admitted.

"I stay in business for you," the old woman said. "I know when you come. I peek at your mother, I read what she wants, I make it be here for you."

Sophie thought about the loaves of bread she'd brought back, eaten as baloney and cheese sandwiches at school. The ground beef her mother fried up with Hamburger Helper. The gallons of milk and fizzy liters of soda. All magical, conjured by Hennie. A glance around the shop and Sophie could see there was no deli case, no fridge stocked with colorful cans of soda. Even the glass candy jars she'd seen when she first entered had asserted their rightful existence as great glass orbs of dried herbs and flowers. Hennie eased up on her illusion, and the grocery store relaxed into the witch's workshop it really was.

"But the food," Sophie insisted. "The food was real."

"Magic is real," Hennie said. "Illusions are, in their way, completely real."

"Was it bad for me to eat it?" Sophie dug. "What *was* it?"

"I care very much about your growing bones," Hennie said. "I make sure it have all the nutrition. Charmed food maybe the very best food." She winked.

"Did it make me even more magical?" Sophie said hopefully.

"You don't need Hamburger Helper to make you more magic." She chuckled. "Now, Sophie—where do I even begin with you?"

. . .

THEY BEGAN WITH an altar. It was a relief for Sophie to lay her mother's heavy purse onto the counter next to the magical groceries. She unloaded the heavy white candle Angel's mother had dressed for her. A sweet smell filled the dusty room, a smell of flowers. The inside of the glass was dusted with what looked like glitter and pencil shavings, and Sophie thought she could see the letters of her name dug into the soft wax.

"Angel—you know Angel?" Hennie nodded. "Her mother made these for me. She's a curandera." She tried to say it like Angel had said it, with a roll to the *r*, and felt embarrassed, like she was trying to sound like someone she wasn't. But she didn't want to disrespect the pretty word by butchering it with her rough Chelsea voice. "Are you a curandera?"

Hennie nodded, smelling the candles. "Yes, but we call it different. I am *znakharka*. That is how we say *curandera*. Here, you say *witch*. Is all the same." She brought the candles to a low shelf already holding bundles of herbs, some rocks and feathers, what looked like a piece of an animal pelt, a chunk of fur. "Znakharka," Hennie spoke the word like taking a chomp out of it. It sounded like a powerful word. In general, Sophie liked words that began with *z*, because they were unusual. "You are znakharka," she told Sophie, taking the candle from her and bringing it beneath her nose for a sniff. Sophie pulled a strand of hair into her mouth and began biting the split ends. Her hair tasted salty, and she realized that though she had bathed an entire flock of city pigeons, she had not taken a bath since puking creek water all over herself. *Gross*, she thought, and spit out her hair. She hadn't chewed her hair since she was a kid, anyway. But something about the way Hennie watched her made her feel like a child.

"You light this candle. You pray for clarity and protection." Hennie gave Sophie a box of wooden matches. Of course Hennie wouldn't have a damp pack of paper matches, or a plastic Bic like the ones Kishka lit her cigarettes from. Her matches were hardy little torches from another place and time. Sophie pulled the tip down the rough wooden wall, and the tang of sulfur filled the shop. She lit the candle, wondering who she was praying to. She recalled what Angel had said about *lineage*. Teresita, Gandhi, Jesus. Was it blasphemous to pray to Teresita *and* Jesus at the same time? She knew the nuns at school would think so. But the nuns would have a lot to say about Sophie hanging out with Hennie, an actual znakharka. Sophie hadn't ever paid much mind to the nuns and wasn't about to begin now. *Hi, lineage*, she thought inside her head. *Please look out for me, okay? Please help me pay attention and not space out.* She thought for a moment. *Is that it? I don't know. Thanks.* She opened her eyes. Hennie, who'd been clutching at her own hands, reached out and clasped Sophie's.

"Sophie," she said. Sophie flinched, but did not pull away her hands. It startled her to be touched by the woman. She realized she was still a little bit scared of her. Even though everyone had said she was good—and she *was* good, Sophie could feel it—she looked so much like a witch from a fairy tale, it was hard for Sophie not to think about Hennie pushing her into an oven when she wasn't looking. Her nose even had a mole on it, for god's sake. A mole sprouting a hair. If you did an internet search for *witch*, Hennie's picture would pop up.

"Sophie, when I say you are my niece, I mean, you are my niece. You are my blood. I wait to meet you a very long time."

"But—but I've come in here before!" Sophie exclaimed. "I bought hamburger meat and soda and butter. You *have* met me before. You could have—you could have met me then."

"It was not time," Hennie said, simply. "Now is time you know all. There is much to know, I tell you everything. Much is bad. There are many bad things to know, I am sorry to tell you. But maybe good, too." She tightened her grip on Sophie's hand, giving it a squeeze. Hennie's hands were cool and plump, like a mound of dough being chilled for cookies. Sophie squeezed back.

"I am your aunt," she said. She tugged a copper-colored necklace out from her blouse, a strand of thin links. For a moment Sophie anticipated sea glass, but it was an oval-shaped locket on the end of the chain. A disk of porcelain painted with faded roses was affixed to the metal. Hennie pulled it over her head, taking care not to knock off her head scarf. "Oh, my babushka," she laughed. Hennie had a big laugh when she laughed, a big smile when she smiled. Sophie could see a missing tooth at the edge of the woman's mouth. She held the locket in the palm of her hand and flicked it open to two tiny pictures of two tiny babies, one on each side, mirror images.

"That's me?" Sophie asked. She recognized the photo, her mother had copies of it stuffed into the plasticky photo albums. The joke was that Sophie, whose unruly head of hair taunted Andrea with its wildness, had been born bald as a marble. The nurses had to stick a pink bow on her head with a piece of Scotch tape. *I don't see what the big deal was anyway, who cares if I'm a boy or a girl, I was a baby!* Sophie would grumble, slightly humiliated by having a bow taped to her head. In the photo on the other side of the locket, Sophie wore no such demeaning bow. In fact, she had hair on her head, a dark little cap. Sophie blinked and peered closer. The picture was small. The face was hers, but like she was wearing a wig, a baby toupee.

"What's this?" Sophie asked. She tapped the photo with a grubby fingernail. "How'd I get so hairy? That's me, right?" She laughed a stilted laugh, like she was foolish. Her head was buzzing with questions. *One thing at a time,* she thought, trying to calm herself. She cleared her mind. The heat of the burning wax intensified the scent of the oil the curandera had dressed the candles with, and the smell of warm, white flowers was thick inside the room. She stared at Hennie. She still couldn't trust this woman, but she trusted the pigeons and she trusted Angel. "Will you explain to me how you are my aunt? Why you have these pictures of me in a locket?"

Hennie grabbed a couple of lumpy mugs that looked to be made from the mud of the earth. She filled them with a steaming beverage that *tasted* like the mud of the earth. Sophie made a *blech* face, sticking out her tongue, sputtering. "This tastes like dirt."

"Come, sit with me," Hennie said. She was reclining on the floor, on a pillow stuffed with straw. Beside her was a fireplace, alive with a glowing orange fire. Sophie knew there hadn't been a fireplace when she'd arrived at Hennie's. She was also fairly certain that outside of the shop Chelsea was in the throes of an insufferable heat wave. To drink a hot drink before a roaring fire was insane, but Hennie's shop felt cozy. "I make like winter in here, sometime," the woman explained. "I miss my old land. I am winter witch. I feel most powerful when there is snow, and cold." She regarded her niece as she settled down into a puffy hay pillow, folding her legs beneath her. "You, I think, are summer witch. You are most powerful now. Kishka too, is summer witch. When she was a girl like you, maybe little older, in Poland, she run around with *Poludnica*. Nasty girls. Very beautiful, like Kishka. Poludnica wear pretty dresses and walk around fields where farmers work, make them sick with heat and sun, make them crazy even, sometimes."

"Were they were, like, a gang?" Sophie asked. "A Polish girl gang?" The thought sounded sort of cool.

"No, no girl gang, not real girls. Poludnica are, how to explain—ghosts? Not real. Magical girls. Their magic bad, like Kishka."

"Is Kishka a znakharka?"

"Yes, dearie. Bad znakharka."

"Did she learn magic from the... Poludnica?" The heavy Polish words felt cumbersome in Sophie's mouth.

"No," Hennie laughed. "Poludnica probably learn from your grandmother. She is much more powerful. She was, how you say, *slumming*, running around with the Poludnica. She being rebellious. They are small magic, but mean magic. But, Kishka is summer znakharka, big magic. As are you."

Sophie listened to Hennie talk about Kishka as a young girl, in Poland. Hadn't Kishka come over as a baby? Who was Kishka's mother? Why didn't Sophie know *anything* about her family? In Hennie's eyes she saw a shard of Kishka's blue; in the hair beneath her babushka, a streak of Kishka's yellow. "Are you my grandmother's sister?" she asked, and Hennie nodded.

"Yes, we are sisters, and enemies. We hold opposite magic. We do not speak."

"Does my mother know? That you are her aunt?"

"Yes, Andrea knows me. I loved Andrea very much. A little baby, I watch over her. I babysit when Kishka and Carl go dancing." Hennie sighed. "Those were nice time. Kishka very beautiful, more so than the Poludnica. With red lipstick, and she make her eyebrows like so," Hennie moved her finger in an arc above her eye. "She wear such good dresses. But still, she have her powers always, she run with the bad ghosts, she become *mora* very young, she leave her body and fly around. That's *mora*, ones that fly. She do it without out the flying herbs, without *zagavory*."

"I don't know what you're taking about." Sophie was overwhelmed.

"*Zagavory* is magic spells. But Kishka need nothing to fly. We were children, she just leave body, she fly around, she come to America, she come back to Poland. Whatever she like. In the morning, she tell me wild story, and I believe."

"Who is older, you or Kishka?"

"We are same," Hennie said. Sophie was shocked.

"I know, you shocked," Hennie said. Sophie quickly drew up her shield around her emotions. "No, no, I do not read you, dumpling. I know you shocked because every person shocked. Also, your mouth hung very open. Kishka look very younger than me, no?"

It was true that Hennie looked like a very old woman, her face folded with wrinkles, while Kishka, though old, had a spry youthfulness about her. Her skin was tighter, it caught light and hurled it back at you—a miracle really, considering how much the old woman smoked.

"One of her powers," Hennie said, with a tone of acceptance. "She has the glamours, I do not. But still, I look good when you think. How old am I to you?"

Sophie hated these questions. There would be an insult buried in whatever answer she gave.

"No, for true, please tell me. I throw away my vanity long time ago." Hennie smiled, and the dark space where a tooth once was seemed to wink from the cave of her mouth.

"I don't know, my grandmother is, what, fifty? So you must be, too? But I guess I would think seventy."

"You are very good," Hennie smiled, nodding. "You could feel a seven. I think I am seven hundred years old."

"Okay." Sophie sat, thinking about seven hundred. It was too large for her to grasp. She imagined seven hundred dollars—too much money, couldn't grasp it. Seven hundred people. What was that, everyone in Chelsea? Seven hundred years. Sophie was thirteen. Seven hundred years was outer space, it was science fiction.

"I am, how you say, blowing your mind? Yes. Sophie. We are not regular people, Kishka and I. We are *Odmieńce*. Magic creatures. First creatures on whole planet. Before humans, Odmieńce."

"So, you're not human," Sophie said flatly. She didn't know why this was harder to swallow than grumpy mermaids or pigeons who spoke, but it was. Maybe because of what it implied.

"No, not human, Sophie."

"Am I... I'm human, right?" Sophie wracked her brain for proof that she was human. She breathed air. But she breathed water too, didn't she, that night? But that was a dream, a vision! But who brings back a lungful of water from a dream? She slept and ate, she cried tears, she got her period, and she was a human, a thirteen-year-old human girl. Who could read minds and talk to pigeons and stuff.

"You are part human," Hennie said. "And you are part Odmieńce. Kishka is all Odmieńce, your grandfather all human. Andrea half Odmieńce, half human. Your father, human. You, some and some. A little less every time."

"Wait!" Sophie felt insulted. "My mother is less human than me? Does she have power, too?"

"It skip generation," Hennie explained. "Sometimes it does, sometimes it does not. Kishka very angry. Wanted Andrea to have much power, Andrea have none. Kishka very cruel to your mother. Your mother, she run away. She come back with baby in her belly. That is you. She come back with a man, too. Your father."

"You knew my father?" Sophie felt awkward. She had come to rest in a certain feeling, the feeling of not having a father. It was hard to miss something she had never had, so she had decided it was no big whoop. Fathers were something that other people had. She had Andrea. She'd had Kishka. Now, she had Hennie. Hennie, and an entire mythology. She felt scared at the thought of having a father. It made her feel vulnerable, and embarrassed. Would she meet him? Would she be expected to cry, to have feelings? Would it be a sentimental reunion, like a cheesy television movie? Sophie loathed situations where she was expected to have a feeling. She feared she would have the wrong one, or have none at all, and then what?

"I know your father," Hennie said. Sophie noted the present tense. "But we talk of that later. So much to tell, Sophie. Are you okay?"

Sophie nodded. The mug in her hand had gone cool. "Your drink," Hennie said, "is whatever you like. What you like it to be?"

Sophie looked down at the cup, confused. The liquid was dark in the dark earth color of its vessel. *Watermelon juice?* she thought, remembering the heat outside. But she realized it was a hot chocolate, hot chocolate with a twig of cinnamon *and* a striped peppermint stick inside it. Teeny puffs of marshmallow bobbed on top. It was the perfect winter drink. She took a chocolatey gulp. "Wow."

"Is nice to have fun with the magic, too," Hennie said, nodding. "Can't always be, *Read minds, remove zagavory, cast zagavory, become mora, yadda yadda yadda.*"

Sophie closed her eyes and thought, *Watermelon juice.* She could smell the fresh, summery smell of the melon before her eyes were opened.

"Sophie, your grandmother very bad." Hennie's eyes were intense, the play gone from them as quickly as it had come.

"I know." Sophie nodded. "Everyone has told me. The pigeons, Angel, they all think she's the worst person in the whole world."

Hennie nodded. "She pretty bad. Always drawn to the bad magic, ever since tiny baby so long ago. Spending so long in the bad magic, it takes hold of you. Soon, no way to come back. Darkness claim you."

"What about you?"

"I pure good." Hennie smiled, and the *pure good* was in the smile, and it made Sophie smile, too. "Always good girl. Drive Kishka crazy. But good take hold too, good can claim you. Kishka and me, we sisters, but not sisters. Is different from human way. All Odmieńce related, descended from the first creatures, all Odmieńce are sister and brother. Because Kishka most bad and I most good, we were placed with humans together, side by side. The *Boginki* bring us.

Boginki, how you say..." Hennie thought about it. "Fairies, maybe? Water fairies, from rivers? They steal human babies, they replace with Odmieńce. Me and Kishka, we placed with family in village outside Warsaw, so many years ago."

"What happened," asked Sophie, "to the stolen babies?"

Hennie looked sad. "The Boginki, they love human babies. They bring them into the river."

"Into the river?"

"They drown them." The story had been in Hennie for hundreds and hundreds of years but still, the thought of the human babies dying in the water, their fat and tiny fists flailing, their futile struggle, it brought her to tears. Hennie cried. She cried like the Boginki had cried so long ago in Poland, underneath the river, shaking the tiny babies, floating them in their hands, pulling their lifeless eyelids open, howling thunderous howls that pushed through the water like currents. "They do not know," Hennie tried to explain. "Each time they believe the baby will live, be their little human friends. They are like children, the Boginki. They do things again and again and every time it is the same bad way. They are a little mad, from so long of this. A little crazy. But without the Boginki there would be no Odmieńce among the people. It is like strange system. We need Boginki."

"Do they still exist?" Sophie asked, scared.

"Oh, yes. You meet Syrena, the mermaid?"

"Yes." Sophie nodded.

"She have terrible Boginki problem in her river, she tell you. She is very concerned to return to Poland and have Boginki everywhere, and crying mothers on the riverbanks, police officers—this is her fear. Because now, less and less Odmieńce babies. Boginki just take the babies, no replacement babies. They are so bad." Hennie shook her head, a sadness still on her face. "But so sweet, the Boginki. They only want love, the special kind of love you have with baby. Anyway." Hennie pulled a fistful of straw from her pillow and tossed it into the dwindling fire. "I can make fire with mind," she said. "I can make anything with mind, but then is like—what point is life? You do everything with mind all the time, is like having no life. Who cares? I get very, how you call it, depressed. So now, I do things. I put the straw in the fire, like a human would do. Then you feel straw, you hear crackle, smell good straw smell. It is nice, to work with the world in such a way. I want tea, I take the herbs, I measure them, I watch the water become hot on the fire, I smell the tea opening its smells. You know? Otherwise, I go, *Tea!* and I say my *zawolanie*, and poof, tea! But when life is too simple it feels wrong. Like talking. I can make you hear my English perfect. It would be a zagavory, a spell. Or, another zagavory—I just make you hear in mind what I think to you. I do this many years, hundreds, hundreds of years, never bothering to learn any language. Is why my English so bad. I not try. Now, I try. I save zagavory for emergency. Or for fun, like drink." She gestured toward Sophie's magical mug. "You want cookie?"

Before Hennie could answer, a pile of cookies appeared on a hammered metal tray beside her. They smelled amazing. She touched one; it was warm from an oven, the chips gooey in the dough.

"They are perfect chocolate chip cookies," Hennie said.

"Yes," Sophie agreed, eating them. It made sense that Hennie, made of goodness, would bake a cookie that tasted like pure love. Sophie could feel that all her fear of the woman was gone. "Hennie, are you sure *you're* not my grandmother?" she asked hopefully. "If I'm good and you're good, how can Kishka be my grandmother? Did the Boginki mix me up maybe?"

"Child, you might as well be my granddaughter. You might as well be my daughter, you are so close to my heart." Hennie's eyes looked like cookies in her face, warm and full of tenderness. "But is not how goes. Kishka have Andrea, Andrea have you. You part human, you raised with human love. You have many influences upon your heart. Kishka Odmieńce, she is only what she is meant to be, she is badness. It is how it is." She looked hard at her niece. "All human, like you, have choices. Many choices. You could be bad, too, Sophia. But it is not your destiny, I think. Not what you wish for."

"No!" Sophie exclaimed, horrified at the thought that she could have a bit of Kishka's badness waiting inside her, like a cell that could grow into a tumor. "I don't want to be bad!"

"Well, most humans don't. But then—" She shrugged. "So many sadnesses pile up. Partly this is the curse. You will undo much such badness. And yes, you do have bigger ability for bad inside you, as

Odmieńce." Hennie smiled. "But you have bigger ability for good, also. Tremendously bigger. Human would say—*supernatural*. But that is only because human does not understand nature."

Hennie clapped her big, soft hands together. "I apologize. No time to—what say, philosophize? So much to tell, and you must go, you must. I can play with time, slow down some, but too much and Kishka will notice, it will draw her too us. I will hurry, now. I apologize for that, for all you must hear so quickly. To hear so quickly and then poof, I will push you out my door, I apologize for this. What else you like, what sweets?"

Sophie was going to say *banana cream pie* when the perfect banana cream pie appeared aside the cookies.

"I am like Boginki!" Hennie laughed. "I wait so long to spoil you, my niece, now I stuff you with magic pastry!"

"It's okay," Sophie said. "I didn't eat breakfast."

Hennie wrinkled her face at that, and then blinked at the cookies. "Very nutritious, now," she said. "Eat all you want."

· · ·

"FIRST OF ALL," Hennie said, "your grandfather not dead. Kishka turn grandfather to dog. She say he killed in dump, by hoodlums. He never die. Kishka turn him to dog, he live with me, in my house, down the street."

Sophie's mouth hung open. She tightened her grip on her magical cocoa, because this was the sort of moment people let glasses slip from their hands in movies. Sci-fi movies. Fantasy movies. Of course that house, that spooky, solitary witch's house, was Hennie's. And she had seen the dog, the German Shepherd on the porch, looking up and down the abandoned block, its tongue dangling from its mouth in the dust. That dog was her *grandfather*? "No," she said.

"Yes."

"No!"

"Yes, Sophie. Carl is dog. Is terrible magic. He not know he is Carl anymore, he think he is only dog. He behave like dog, he is dog." Hennie heaved a big sigh and shook her head. "Kishka let him be picked up by, what you call—pound? They have him in cage, would adopt maybe, maybe he become police dog, maybe put to sleep, no one know. I adopt him." Hennie sighed. "I more cat woman. Not much like dog. But what to do? Let Carl become drug dog in Chelsea? Too bad for such a man. He would not want."

"What about your magic?" Sophie asked. She felt a desperate anxiety rise at the simple *notion* that a person can get cursed into a dog. "Can't you free him? Can't you do anything?"

"No," Hennie said, simply. "Is brilliant zagavory. She use terrible magics, things I cannot touch. Some things, you cannot touch and remain good. Kishka, she touch anything she want. She use all kind of bad magic to make Carl dog."

Sophie took stock of what she had learned thus far: she was only part human, another part was—what was the word—Odmieńce. Hennie the creepy old witch lady was her aunt. Her grandfather was Hennie's dog. What were the Polish words Hennie was flinging around, a jumbled rubble of language, all these *z*s? "What are the words?" Sophie asked. "All the Polish words?" Words were practical, unemotional, simple. She could carry a word like a piece of sea glass on her chest, solid and helpful.

"Yes, new words for you. *Znakharka*. That is witch. You are znakharka."

"Znakharka."

"*Zagavory*. That is spell. Magic spell."

"Got it."

"*Zawolanie*. That is like, special noise only for you. A magical noise, you make it, is yours. You sound your zawolanie when you make your zagavory, and it will be full of your power. Is like you call out to all the universe and all who know you hear, and answer."

"Can't you just say, like, *magic noise* and *magic spell*?" Sophie asked. "Do you have to use those big Polish words?"

Hennie looked hurt. "Suit self." She shrugged. "Noble, ancient Polish words. Your tradition. You lose words, you lose power, lose magic. I work," she said, "to speak in your language. You come for magic, you speak in mine. In my language that is also yours. Even if you don't feel it."

Sophie felt embarrassed. "Okay," she said. "Will you teach me my—"

"Zawolanie?" she asked. "No. I teach you nothing. You know everything. My work is to tell you the stories of who you are."

"Thank you, Hennie." Sophie began to rise. "I guess, do I call you *Auntie* Hennie?"

Hennie smiled, but did not look happy. "Sit back," she said. "We are not done. I will slow time, Kishka be damned. You do not yet know your story."

. . .

THERE WAS A special hush in Hennie's shop. It felt a bit like being passed out—things felt enchanted, a sort of slow tingle, like she was on the inside of a slow globe, an aquarium, a crystal ball. The very air around her seemed warped. Hennie had taken great handfuls of salt and tossed them into the room's four corners, speaking in Polish. She'd taken a stick with a beautiful rock tied to its tip, long and sharp like a dagger, she'd cut a wide circle in the air with it, still murmuring in her native tongue. Then she spoke her zawolanie. It was a surprise to hear such a beautiful call come out of the old woman. Everything about her felt gruff and rough to Sophie, her heavy voice with its chunky English, the warts, the babushka pushing her gray hair flat, her wide face, the bulk of her. But Hennie's zawolanie was a chime. It enchanted Sophie and it enchanted time itself. The hush that followed was like a first snowfall, untouched and glistening. She thought about how Hennie was a winter witch.

"You did it," Sophie said, half-expecting to be able to see the steam of her breath in the air before her face.

"You feel it?"

"Yes," she breathed. "And your zawolanie is so beautiful."

"The zawolanie," Hennie said, "is *you*, only a sound. It is the sound of your essence. It is like the key of your magic, unlocking everything."

"How do I get mine?" Sophie asked.

"You go to the mall," Hennie said. "Is zawolanie store. Come in many colors, you buy one you like." It took Sophie a minute to realize her aunt was making a joke.

"Hennie," she said, "You can't. You can't make jokes. Because you could be like, oh, a talking pigeon will tell you, or a mermaid will bring you one, ha ha ha, and, I'm, like, scrambling over here, because a couple days ago there were no mermaids or talking pigeons, so for all I know some gremlins opened a store in the mall that *looks* like a computer store but, whoa, it's a magical zawolanie store! *Come on in, we'll customize you the best zawolanie ever, give you a great deal!*" Sophie could feel a certain hysteria rising behind her own joke, the pull of tears straining in her face. Hennie could feel it, too.

"Is true," Hennie agreed. "Too much weird stuff to make joke. Your zawolanie is inside you. When you make zagavory, you will feel your zawolanie come."

"Okay. How do I make zagavory?"

"It depend what you want. Many zagavory. You want to be invisible, you want to make person do what you want, you want to make someone love you. Some of these bad magic. Very tricky. Must be clear in heart."

"Is it bad magic to make someone love you?" she asked.

"Mostly yes. Unless big reason to have the person love, bigger than you just wanting love. Understand?"

"No. So, if I just have a crush on someone I can't make them love me back?"

"No, no. The *Dola* come for you, they very angry. *Dola* like—police. But they police of destiny. You make a person go against their destiny, Dola very upset. They haunt you. And you go against your own destiny, Dola haunt you also."

"How do I know if I'm going against my destiny?"

"You just know," Hennie insisted. "You feel."

"But, like, if I go against my destiny, isn't it my destiny to go against my destiny?" Sophie's head was spinning. It looked like Hennie's was, too. She put her palm to her broad forehead.

"Child," she said, "You are speaking like Boginki, like crazy this and that. You have destiny, I have destiny, even little Boginki have destiny. You go against your destiny, Dola come, they bother you forever. So, know your own self and do what you know you must do, and stop no one from doing what they must do, understand?"

"Yes," Sophie said, even though she didn't, exactly. "What do they look like, the Dola?"

"They look like a bad feeling," Hennie said. "Hope you never see. Now, more, fast. I don't like keeping time for long. It makes humans weary. They feel thick in their head from it. Now—here." Hennie handed Sophie a pouch on a string. It had a cool design on it.

"What is it?"

"Is your magic pouch."

"Is there a Polish *z*-word for it?" Sophie asked.

"Just say magic pouch." Hennie was getting tired. It took a lot of magic will to stop time. "Inside, for you, much salt, good stone, good herbs. Pigeon bones."

"Ew, why pigeon bones?"

"Pigeon your animal. Everyone have animal, you are pigeon."

"Wait—are you talking about power animals?" Sophie knew about power animals, everyone did. Ella liked to say she was a parrot, or a dolphin. Sophie thought she might be a cat, she liked cats a lot. She hadn't even considered a person's power animal could be a pigeon. She realized she hadn't been thinking of pigeons as either powerful, or animals. They were pests. Sophie felt sad, thought of her friends on the wire outside Hennie's shop, waiting for her. She wondered if they could feel the stopped time. If she left Hennie's house, what would the world look like?

"Okay, pigeons are my power animal."

"Good animal to have. They fly. Their bones are light, hollow, so they can lift themselves. You are light boned, you can move fast when you must. Pigeon have special magic, no one know they are magic, no one ever think such beast have magic. You are like that, too."

"I am?"

"Yah. You dirty, snarly-haired girl, full of magic." Hennie laughed. "You wise like pigeons, stick with people, and help people like the pigeons. You have noble history, like pigeon. They are really rock doves, quite lovely, and you are really Odmieńce. Half Odmieńce. Brings me to next, final story, quite bad—"

"Wait, what do I do with this?" Sophie shook her magic pouch, hearing things rattling softly inside the cloth.

"Just keep it. Wear it, put it in purse."

"I don't have a purse, that's my mom's."

"You teenage girl, should have purse and brush hair, yah?"

"I guess."

"Is your life, what do I know?" Hennie shrugged. "Anyway, just keep on you." Hennie paused. "Really, think about a purse. You will be accumulating much magical object."

"But what does it do?" Sophie asked.

"You want to make zagavory, everything you need in pouch. Is perfect zagavory kit! I make myself. Very thorough." Hennie looked proud. "You need more, you come here. Or, you think of it, say your zawolanie, poof, you will have. But, come see me, please. I like you very much."

"Oh, Hennie." Sophie was not accustomed to feeling this affection from an older person, a relation. Family. She was embarrassed at how badly she wanted it. She pushed herself into her aunt, hugging her tight. Her wide, soft body smelled like cookies and tea and herbs and flowers.

"Wait, Sophie," she said. "I have more bad to tell. Your father. Your father is man you know. Name is Ronald. You have met him, yah?"

Sophie shook her head. *Ronald.* Pathetic Ronald, drooling, drunk Ronald, gross filthy stinking Ronald was her *father?* She wasn't ready for this information. Unlike the wild revelations of talking pigeons of creek-dwelling mermaids, there was no magic in it—just sadness and disgust. She suddenly felt overwhelmed and pulled away. "Hennie, I heard enough. I have to go; I've been here too long."

"Time is stopped," Hennie said.

"I just can't hear anymore. I can't take it!" She could hear her voice, too loud in the cozy room.

"You must, Sophie. You have to know everything. And there is more—"

"No!" Sophie dashed to the counter, where her mother's purse sat. She stuffed her magic pouch inside it, and then the orange juice, the soup box, the lemon and the honey.

"Sophie, you keep Syrena waiting. The mermaid. She waits for you, but you must know everything before you go with her—"

"*Go* with her? I'm not going anywhere with her! I'm thirteen years old, I live here, in Chelsea!"

"You are Odmieńce."

"That means nothing to me." Sophie had hit overload, and Hennie had *more?* Sophie had a witch for a grandmother, a dog for a grandfather, a drunk for a dad. What more could there be? "I gotta go," Sophie said. "I'll come back some other time and you can tell me everything."

"Sophie, there is an order. It is time. You must stay." Hennie's open palm held something grainy, heavy. She flung it into the fire, and again Sophie heard the gorgeous call of Hennie's zawolanie. It almost made her stay. The sound of it fluted through her, calming her. Why was she in such a hurry? Time was stopped. She looked at

Hennie, sweet Hennie, her stricken face. She only wanted to show Sophie who she was.

"Argh!" Sophie hollered, her voice echoing off the wood and stone of the small shop. Hennie had charmed her! She could feel the zagavory stunning her mind, enacting its will upon her, making Sophie doubt herself. She *should* stay—no, she was being enchanted—*no, she should* stay, it wasn't *a bad* enchantment—that's not the point!—Sophie's will flailed inside her. She didn't *want* to stay! How *dare* Hennie! "How dare you!" she thundered at the old woman. And Sophie felt something rising inside her like a thing alive. It was *her,* had always been within her, and it flexed itself suddenly, like a muscle that ran the length of her body. From the soles of her feet to the top of her head, Sophie tingled and burned as the sound surged upward, escaping her mouth in a noise so pure, so sharp and fierce it exploded the glass in Hennie's shop, filling the room with liquids and herbs. The glass of candles shattered, releasing blobs of molten wax. And Hennie. Poor Hennie, her hands plastered to her ears to keep the sound out, Hennie was hit by a wave of sound dense as brick, flung backward onto a shelf of books. All of them—znakharka, paper, wood—tumbled together to the floor. Hennie's eyes remained closed. Sophie looked with horror at all she had done, all she had not intended to do. With her mother's purse on her shoulder, she tore out of Hennie's Grocery.

Chapter 17

Sophie slammed out of the grocery store, Chelsea's humidity hitting her like a wall of water. She stood on the dusty corner, the crossroads. If she kept walking forward down Heard Street she would arrive at her house, where her mother slept, where Dr. Chen and her grandmother were possibly headed. Behind her, the homes and pavement fell away and there was dust, abandoned buildings, her grandfather in the form of a German Shepherd. The cross street was Maple. What if Sophie just took off? If she walked Maple in one direction it would take her beneath the looming green overpass that delivered cars to Boston. She would hit train tracks, vacant lots, an abandoned playground. She would come upon the shopping mall, almost all the stores inside closed, the ones still open strange boutiques, dollar stores selling shelves of toxic toilet cleaners next to rows of ceramic swans. Sophie was never allowed to go down Maple, because dead women had been found there. On the tracks, under the overpass, in a dumpster behind an industrial building. Sophie grew up hearing stories of the dead women; in her mind, they were solid landmarks, as present as the Tobin bridge, and as normal—surely most cities had bridges and playgrounds, shopping malls and dead women. Standing in front of Hennie's, the air eerily still, she realized that it maybe wasn't so. Maybe having so many dead women was particular to Chelsea.

In the other direction Maple was lined with the same shabby houses common to Chelsea. In the summertime they didn't look too bad; most all of them had wide, leafy trees in their yards, or outside on the sidewalk, the muscled roots busting up the pavement. But if you looked beyond the canopy of green you would see how worn the homes were, the siding cracked, the stairs a hazard. Graffiti sprayed over doors and windows. Overgrown front lawns hid treasures of garbage. In the winter, with everything green receded and dead, the depressing face of Chelsea was undeniable. Maybe that was why Sophie liked summer best. That and no school, no mean nuns, no wearing the same ugly jumper every day, jumpers that began to smell a little by Wednesday, that absolutely held an odor by Friday, that hopefully would get washed over the weekend. At least that part of her life was over, Sophie realized. No more Catholic school. Hello, Chelsea High. The thought made her laugh out loud, breaking the strange quiet. She was supposed to go to *high school* after this?

The pigeons were stirring above her. Sophie realized they weren't frozen by the stoppage of time; they were, like Sophie, somehow immune to it. There had to be another reason for their stillness. Could Sophie read a pigeon? She scanned them, huddled in a line on the wire, the way birds gather before a storm. Which pigeon would have the least disturbing interior? She selected Livia, and pushed her way inside the bird.

What it felt like to be so small! That struck Sophie first. She realized she perceived her own emotions as running the length of her body, and to feel such a fullness of feelings compacted inside the tiny body of a bird was new. Like a tightly wrapped bouquet as opposed to a sprawling garden of flowers. And Livia's feelings were sweet, it was sweet to be Livia, her heart was so pure, so oriented toward rightness that she could relax and follow it, and she did, and there was little conflict inside her bird heart. There were many pulses of love, and Sophie could feel how the bird loved the sky, how she loved Arthur, delighted in his cranky rants, found them noble and adorable at once. Sophie felt a pulse of love for the wind, which Livia interacted with as a living thing with a will of its own, one that Livia had learned to understand and love. And there, a pulse of love for Sophie. Sophie felt joy at this, and shame. She didn't know that she deserved it. Swarming the love was a sadness, a worry, a concern. A disappointment? Sophie didn't want to feel *that*. She couldn't feel sweet, pure-hearted Livia's disappointment in her. She pulled herself out of the pigeon.

"I didn't mean it!" she shouted up at the birds on their wire, and they shuffled and cooed, spoke in bird language, like they weren't magical at all, or like Sophie was no longer special enough to hear their crystalline voices.

"Don't talk about me in your bird languages when I'm standing right here!" Sophie hollered. "It's rude! I can tell you're talking about me!" She zoomed deeper into Livia and felt the bird's concern rise above her disappointment. "If you're so worried about me don't talk about me behind my back when I'm right in front of you!" Sophie was crying now. She didn't like the birds' silence, she didn't like the world when time was stopped. It felt wrong, the air heavy and still, nothing moving. Walking felt like pushing through soup. When would Hennie put everything back to normal?

"I don't want to know who my father is!" Sophie screamed at the flock. "I like not having a father; it's too weird to have one all of a sudden! I don't want to know anything else about my family!"

Sophie remembered the secret she felt bobbing inside Angel, something about Andrea, her mother. She thought about the twin baby pictures in Hennie's copper locket. Maybe for a moment she'd wanted to know more, but Sophie had changed her mind. She wanted Andrea to remain Andrea—cranky, overworked. As Andrea had tended to ignore her daughter, so had Sophie learned to tune out her mom. She didn't want to tune in now, with so much sad, spooky information spinning around her. "I don't want to know *everything*, okay?" she shouted. A dog howled at the sound of her voice, another animal able to move in the time-stop. Her grandfather.

Giddy lifted herself from the wire and flew down to Sophie's hot shoulder. She fluttered and cooed, still smelling sweet from her bath.

"If I had a mouth I would give you a kiss," she said. She brushed Sophie's face with her wing. "Maybe you should apologize to Hennie."

"I've been here forever. I have to go home."

"Time's stopped," Arthur butted in. "No one's even conscious right now but us and Hennie. And Kishka." He shuddered, his feathers puffed up as if a wind had hit them.

"And my grandfather, the German Shepherd," Sophie said. "I'm going home." She turned on her heel and headed down Heard Street.

She passed the gang of boys who commonly terrorized her, frozen on a front porch. Their bicycles were heaped on the sidewalk, and it occurred to Sophie that she could just take one. It occurred to her that she could go right up to the biggest one, the bullyingest one, and give him a smack, a punch, a kick. He stood with one hand low on his hip, the other gesturing outward; he had been in the midst of a story when the zagavory hit. If she knocked him over would he retain his pose, like a department store mannequin?

Sophie walked up onto the porch. She slid between the boys—one half-bent in laughter, one leaning back against the wall, scratchy with peeling paint. Another had a cigarette stuck in the *v* of his fingers, burned down to the filter, a long ash arcing precariously. Sophie bumped his arm, shocked at the feel of his skin. The ash crumbled.

"What are you doing, Sophie?" Livia said. The bird sounded scared. "Leave the people alone."

But it was mesmerizing to be here, in a lion's den of sorts, and to be unafraid, safe for the moment, so close to the boys who bothered her.

Not that Sophie could be sure that *these* were the boys who hounded her, trailed her on their bicycles, hollered names at her, suggested they would like to grab her and bring her to the train tracks, if only she wasn't so *ugly*, such a *dog*, and how they barked as they menaced her, howling and bow-wowing, ruff-ruffing. Sophie kept her head down and so never really saw the boys as anything more than a pack, a cloud, a blur of striped athletic shirts, the silver spinning of bicycle wheels. This largest boy might *not* be the bully. Sophie tried to get a read on him, pushing into his space, but it was like static on a television set, no picture, no nothing. She placed her hand flat on the muscle of his arm. It was warm the way living people are warm. She brushed his hair out of his eyes. His hair was damp with humidity and sweat.

"Sophie," Livia continued nervously. "Hennie could break the spell any minute. Then you're here with all these boys, with a bunch of pigeons. Sophie, it would be terrible. Please, let's go."

Sophie imagined what would happen if the boys all came to with her standing there, twirling their hair. Partly it was hilarious, but also, horrifying. She stomped off the porch, extra hard, wondering if the stomp of her feet would jar them like sleeping people but of course it didn't. "This is totally weird," Sophie breathed. Her crying had stopped, her sadness distracted by the strange world she suddenly occupied.

254

. . .

THE STOPPING OF time didn't really make Sophie's house feel very different. Andrea slept in her darkened room, the shade drawn against the heat of the day, making the place a cave. Sophie thought she should get her mother more water, in case the time-stop stopped and she awoke extra thirsty in her fever. She moved toward her mother's night table, reaching for the empty glass. Andrea started, rolling over in her bed, cracking her puffy eyes in alarm. Sophie screamed.

"What? What?" Andrea scrambled up in her bed, kicking sweaty sheets down her legs. "Oh my god, what? What are you doing? Why are you screaming?"

Sophie felt a bit of her mind flex, and the water glass was in her hand, broken. A crack had loosened a shard, and the shard lay in Sophie's palm.

"The—the glass broke," she said quickly, flooded with gratitude for her instinctive magic. Hennie was right, she could just *do* it. Sophie knew there was simple magic— mind tricks—and bigger magic that required stuff from her magic pouch and the howl of her zawolanie. How would she know the difference? She just would. It was part of her overall *knowing*.

"Oh my god, you scared me," Andrea said. "Are you okay? Is there glass on the floor? Did you go to Goldstein's?"

Sophie nodded, patting her purse.

"I have everything, juice, soup, all of it. The glass—it's—I'm fine, it's okay." Why was Andrea awake? Because she was Kishka's daughter. Because she was Sophie's mother. Because somewhere inside her lay a dormant gene for magic, and it made her immune to the stoppage of time.

"Bring me some water," Andrea said. "And throw that glass away. And make yourself some soup or something. I'm not going to be able to cook for you tonight." Andrea collapsed back onto her pillows before Sophie could say something smart about tonight being just like any other night. Why did she have to be so mean to her mom? Was it a piece of Kishka's cruel magic inside her? She bent low and gave her mom a kiss on her sweaty forehead. Andrea batted her away.

"Are you crazy?" she asked groggily. "Do you want to get yourself sick?"

. . .

WITH HER MOM conked out on cold medicine, Sophie rummaged half-heartedly through the fridge. There wasn't much to eat, but she wasn't really hungry. She was distracted, bunched up inside. What was she supposed to do now? Where were the pigeons? Sophie moved to the kitchen window and spotted them huddling and cooing by their bowls of water. And what else she saw sent goosebumps rising up her arms like a mountain range: Laurie LeClair, standing in her back-yard. Like a skull-faced ghost with her pale skin, black-rimmed eyes, and flat white hair. She looked into the window, staring into Sophie's face with her blank and hollow gaze. "Laurie?" Sophie stuttered.

"What?" Andrea mumbled from her bedroom.

"Nothing, Ma!" Sophie yelled back, not taking her eyes off Laurie's, empty and haunted at once. She wore black jeans, tight on her skinny legs, and black sneakers, and a black t-shirt reveal-ing long white arms spotted with bruises. Her child was with her, a toddler with amber curls, in wrinkly shorts and a t-shirt. One hand clutched Laurie's, the other held a plastic shovel. When Laurie let go and moved toward Sophie the child's hand stayed raised, her fin-gers curled in an empty grip. The child had been stunned by the time-stop, but not Laurie. Laurie glanced at the baby, made sure she was stable, and walked stiffly across the yard. The pigeons parted to accommodate her, and Sophie ran from her kitchen, dashing out the back door to intercept her.

"Laurie, Laurie, Laurie," Sophie gasped, putting her arms in front of her, touching the girl's shoulders. "How are you awake? Time is stopped. Are you magic, too?"

Sophie stared deep into Laurie's dead eyes. The only magic she could possibly have was the unnatural reanimation of a zombie. Sophie glanced over at the child, posed like a doll at the back of the yard. She looked like one of the lawn ornaments cluttering the yard of the woman up the street. She should be holding a lantern, not a toy shovel, or wearing a pointed red hat like a gnome.

Laurie's chapped mouth cracked open to speak. When Laurie spoke Sophie didn't only *hear* the words, she felt them, and the feeling was bad. "I am the Dola," Laurie spoke. There *was* a life in her eyes, a strange flicker. "I am not Laurie right now."

Sophie wished the thing would never talk again. Every word seared into her, leaving in its wake a regret that seeped into her bones. *Oh no,* Sophie thought, and the phrase began a loop she was powerless to stop. *Oh no, oh no, oh no, oh no.*

"Come here, let's talk back here." Sophie pulled Laurie back to the rear of the yard, where the pigeons had assembled themselves around the baby. "Will you guys make some noise?" she requested, and a choir of cooing started up. "Thank you." Sophie looked at the little girl, her steady breathing, her rigid pose. The sun blasted down on her. "She's going to get a sunburn," Sophie said, worried.

"You can move her," said the Dola.

Sophie lifted the girl under his arms. She was light and smelled like a baby, sort of sour. She was grimy, her hair full of dust, her clothing limp from being worn and re-worn. It was strange, placing her down in the shade like a statue. She wobbled, but stayed upright. "How old is she?" Sophie asked.

The Dola considered, reaching backward into Laurie's consciousness. "Almost two." Sophie nodded. She leaned her back against the chainlink fence, which sagged gently like a hammock beneath her weight. The Dola stood stiff before her, watching her with Laurie's face.

"Why are you Laurie LeClair?" Sophie asked.

"She was easy to get into," the Dola said. "She takes drugs, it makes it very simple to slip in. She doesn't really know herself, so she doesn't know if an entity takes over. She just thinks it's the drugs."

This made Sophie feel bad, and it wasn't just the Dola's voice spurring doom and gloom inside her body. The Dola was a creep. "That seems... unethical," Sophie said in a smart voice.

"There is no such thing as ethics," the Dola said. "There is only destiny, and much of it is bad. Nonetheless, it is such, it is destiny. It is the rule, and it must be obeyed." The Dola turned her face to the sun. "The destiny of every person is inside me," she said, her scary eyes closed. "I feel it. When it goes off track I feel that, too. You have gone off track."

"I have?" Sophie didn't want to talk about herself, she was fully sick of thinking about herself. She would rather engage the Dola in existential debates that made her feel smart. "Isn't it my destiny then, to get off track with my destiny?"

The Dola opened her eyes and rolled them. "Yes. It is your destiny to have done this. And it is my destiny to come here and bring you back to your destiny."

"You want me to go back to Hennie's, don't you?" Sophie sulked, fighting back a rain of tears. Every time the Dola spoke it was an injury upon her heart. The muscle grew heavier with every word, a solid rock in her chest.

"Yes." The Dola nodded Laurie LeClair's head. "You were meant to learn more from that woman. You need to go back to her."

"Is she ever going to put time back on?" Sophie whined. "Is she waiting for me to come back or something?"

The Dola shrugged. "I don't know, time doesn't have a destiny. It's time. I know nothing about it."

"And if I don't go back to Hennie's what happens? You keep hanging around?"

The Dola nodded. "Yes. I will be around you always."

"That's going to be really weird," Sophie pouted. "It's going to be really weird to have Laurie LeClair just hanging around all the time. Especially when the time spell is broken and that baby starts crying." They both turned back to look at the frozen child. A fly had landed on her cheek. Were flies magic? How come they got to buzz around? "Livia, will you make sure bugs aren't crawling on that baby?"

"Oh, of course." Livia set about to brushing the baby off with her feathers, cooing all the while.

"If you're just hanging around like Laurie LeClair," Sophie continued, "being creepy, people are going to call the cops or something. Or someone who knows Laurie will take her to the hospital. Then what are you gonna do?"

"Then I jump into another's body," the Dola said, simply.

"Really."

"Oh, yes. It can go on for all eternity. If I am forced to leave Laurie, I am thinking I will occupy your mother."

"No!" Sophie cried.

"Yes. She is very weakened; she would be easy to slip into."

"You are really evil," Sophie spat. "I don't know how you can live with yourself."

"It helps that there is no such thing as evil," the Dola said. "If I believed in it, I would probably have a hard time."

"I thought there was evil," Sophie said. "I thought my grand-mother was evil."

"The concept of evil serves its purpose for humans," the Dola granted. "But where I exist, there is no such thing. There is only destiny."

"Well, I wish you would go back there," Sophie grumbled.

"If you return to your destiny, I will," the Dola said. "I would love a day off. I was haunting Laurie in the form of her drug dealer earlier this week. She was going to let that child die, and that is not their destiny. After she'd salted her, she was meant to bring her to the hos-pital, and instead she did her drugs and fell into a stupor. I was very concerned she wouldn't respond to my haunting, and that the child would die."

"And then what?" Sophie asked. "You'd haunt her forever?"

"No, the child would," the Dola explained. "She would become a *Naw*, a spirit cast out of their bodies against their destiny. It would have been tragic for everyone. Naws are eternally unhappy, and Laurie would have been driven mad. So, good work last week. Now this week, I have you."

Inside her home, Sophie checked in on her sleeping mom. Andrea snored a light snore, undisturbed by the drama in the backyard.

Satisfied, Sophie made a cup of instant soup and sat at her kitchen table eating it, having a staring contest with the Dola out the window. As the sun slid across the sky, Sophie periodically returned to the yard to move the little girl into a shady place. "This is crazy," Sophie said.

"Yes," the Dola agreed.

Sophie went back into her house and grabbed her magic pouch from her mother's purse and returned to the yard. The Dola watched her, solemnly. Occasionally the being said, "You should return to Hennie," and the words ran down Sophie's spine, pure guilt. She ignored it.

Sophie stuffed her hand into the pouch. How was she supposed to know what grainy grain or sharp rock or smooth rock or sandy sand or pigeon bone was the magic ingredient she needed? She let her hand hang open inside the bag, and felt it pulled toward something. The grainy bits. She harvested them from the bag, felt the pile of it cool and heavy in her hand. Did she need fire? Hennie had used fire. Andrea didn't smoke, there were never any matches around. Supposedly Sophie was able to just make things with her mind; surely fire, so elemental, would be simple. And it was. A tuft of flames ignited on a patch of dirt in her backyard. Sophie quickly yanked a few dry sprouts of weeds that hung too close. She took a breath. The pigeons stirred.

If Sophie was as powerful as everyone was acting, she should be able to do—or undo—any zagavory Hennie could do. She found the piece of herself that was her zawolanie and flexed it, let the perfect sound fly from her lips. She hurled the grainy grains into the fire, extinguishing it. A glass bowl holding water for the pigeons cracked, wetting the dirt. Sophie heard the snap of her mother's water glass breaking on her nightstand inside the house. Laurie LeClair's baby burst into tears, flapping its arms against itself like a grounded bird. The pigeon's coos became alarmed as they dodged blind baby-stomps. She screamed and howled, waving her plastic shovel. The Dola turned to her with an annoyed sigh.

"Sophie!" Sophie could hear her mother shouting for her inside the house. The crazy racket, the strange electrical surge of time reactivated, had awoken her. The baby continued to cry. The Dola stared at it blankly.

"It's a baby," Sophie snapped at her. "Just be sweet to it. Do Dolas have, like, no maternal instinct?"

"No, we don't," the Dola said. "I actually don't even know what you mean by *maternal instinct*. That's a human thing. I'm more of a concept." She walked to the baby and petted its head awkwardly. The child looked up at her mother and, not finding her, screamed louder.

"Sophie!" Andrea's head poked out the kitchen window, then was gone. Soon she was on the back porch, her puffy, sickly eyes widening at what she saw. Andrea's head teetered back and forth between her daughter and Laurie LeClair, with an occasional dip to take in Laurie LeClair's screaming baby. The pigeons, Sophie noted, had flown away. Time was running smoothly. Her zagavory had worked. She'd kept control of her zawolanie, and it had done less damage. Sophie would have liked to bask in this victory, but the ruckus in her backyard prevented it.

"I'm sorry—Laurie? Laurie LeClair?"

The Dola looked at Andrea blankly.

"Can't you just play along?" Sophie hissed. "Act normal?"

"I don't care about the consequences you will face in your life as a result of not following your destiny," the Dola said. "As far as I'm concerned, the more problems for you, the better." The Dola fixed its steely, empty stare on Andrea, who shuddered.

"Sophie, what is going on? What is she doing here?"

"Uh, I was out in the yard, and she passed by and we just started talking," Sophie said dumbly. She could see her mother deciding whether to believe her. "I'm so *bored* with being grounded!" She affected a whine. "I just wanted someone to hang out with!"

"Really?" Andrea raised an eyebrow. "Laurie LeClair?" The baby continued to howl. Laurie stood motionless beside it, unaffected. "What are you on?" Andrea demanded of the girl. "Huh? What's wrong with your baby? Will you—do something, will you hold it or something? Sophie, really, what is going on!"

"I don't know!" Sophie sulked. The only strategy she could muster was embodying a bratty teenaged girl, which she supposed she was. "We were hanging out and she got weird!"

"Well, she's on drugs," Andrea informed her daughter. It was extra easy to talk about Laurie like she wasn't there, because she wasn't. But when Andrea told the girl to take her baby and leave, the Dola responded.

"No," she said.

"No?" Andrea repeated, shocked.

"No. I'm not leaving your yard."

"You'll do what I say or else I'll call the police. And Child Services. I think I'll be calling them, regardless."

The Dola shrugged. "I don't care," it said. "Do what you want."

"Sophie!" Andrea turned her agitation toward what she could control, her daughter. "Make her leave!"

"Sophie can't make me do anything," the Dola said in its simple, honest voice. There was a bit of weariness to it. Sophie had to strain to hear what the Dola sounded like beneath the waves of dread and regret the voice provoked. The Dola didn't sound sad exactly, just resigned. It must be wearisome to walk around all your life telling people simple truths they didn't want to hear.

"I'm calling the police." Andrea turned and stormed back into the house.

"If I am taken away, I'll jump into her." The Dola nodded at the back door. There was no threat in its voice, just the calm reportage of facts.

"Really?" Sophie asked. "So we'll be having this conversation, this same one, but you'll be in my house with me, you'll be my mother."

"That's right."

Not only was that horrible for all the obvious reasons, but the thought of seeing her mother all zombified, blank and flat, her self gone away, replaced with the monotonous Dola, gave Sophie terrible shivers.

"Oh, god, okay!" Sophie spat. "Ugh! I really hate you."

The Dola shrugged. "People tell me that all the time, but I don't know what it feels like." Beside it, Laurie LeClair's baby howled and screamed, whacking itself in the head with its shovel.

Inside the house, Andrea waited for the staticky telephone to connect her with the police department. With all the windows opened to the summer day, Laurie LeClair remained in full view. "Hello?" Andrea spoke into the phone.

Please, please, please, please, Sophie chanted in her mind. Her hand stuffed in her pouch, her fist wrapped around a cool, jagged hunk of crystal. She willed the phone to die, pushing her energy into the piece of black plastic. It exploded in Andrea's hand.

"Shit!" Sophie jumped.

Andrea turned to her, staring at her empty palm where the phone once was. The thing lay in shards around her bare feet, the edges of the shards melted. "Why are you swearing!" Andrea scolded her daughter. "I don't understand what is happening. Sophie, is something happening?" Andrea sounded desperate, and scared. She touched her head. "I think I may still have my fever..."

"Ma, the heat wave is causing all these blackouts and stuff," Sophie lied. "We're not really supposed to be using electricity if we can help it." She wrapped her hand around Andrea's arm and made to guide her mother back toward the bedroom.

"Uh, uh, uh." Andrea shook her head. "I'm not going anywhere until that druggie is out of the yard." They both turned to look at Laurie LeClair, motionless as a sundial, aimed at them. Andrea shuddered. "Do you see?" she hissed at Sophie. "Do you see what drugs will do to you?" It was truer than Andrea even knew. If it wasn't for drugs Laurie wouldn't have brought the Dola. Sophie imagined one of those antidrug commercials she'd seen on television—Laurie LeClair, all zombied out, possessed by a conceptual being. *This is your brain on drugs, inhabited by a Dola.*

"Ma, please let me handle it," Sophie said softly. She knew tone would be everything right now. Energy was contagious. If Sophie was all ruffled, Andrea would continue to be, and it would turn into a fight between them. The vibe was volatile, charged with the eyes of the Dola upon them. Sophie rounded her voice with compassion, and weighted it with maturity. "Let me walk her to her home, okay? Please don't call the cops."

"Well, I can't now," Andrea spat, kicking at a piece of phone with her foot, a battery melted to a chunk of plastic, bright, thin wires wrapped around it. "I can't believe we need a new phone. Sophie, you are not going to that girl's house!" Andrea's hands clutched at her hair, close to the scalp, a habit of hers when she was overwhelmed. Sophie could detect a low, painful sound. It made the house feel tragic around them. She looked out the window and saw the Dola's mouth moving, very slight, very quiet, almost soundless. The baby smacked her hands to her ears and wailed. Andrea pressed her thumb to the place between her eyes. "Oh, my *head*," she moaned. "And that *baby*. It's so *wrong*. The cops would actually get her help, Sophie. That baby shouldn't be with a mother like that, she's already tried to kill it,

I don't understand how she's even on the streets."

Sophie stuck her hand in her pouch, watching her mother watching Laurie LeClair, shaking her head, her lower lip bunched in her teeth. She slid her hand into her magic bag. The finest stuff, like a powder. Sophie knew what she needed, like the elements were bits of her own self. She pulled a pinch into her palm, and removed her hand. She pulled her zawolanie up inside her, but calmer, smaller. She didn't need the full strength of it, she was understanding. Sometimes a whisper would do the trick. Or a sneeze. She fake-sneezed her zawolanie into the palm of her hand, surprising Andrea with the sound. Andrea looked up and got a palmful of magic dust sneezed into her face. Sophie's mother's eyes grew heavy, she strained to keep them open, and as she tumbled to the floor Sophie saw them cross, rolling in her head like marbles.

Chapter 18

"**S**he wouldn't have let me go," Sophie explained to the Dola defensively. "She would have called the cops on you, you would have been hauled away, then you would have jumped in her and I don't think I could have handled that, the way you make the people's eyes dead, has anyone ever told you about that?"

"How the eyes look? Yes." The Dola nodded. "It bothers people."

"You really make people look dead. It's creepy."

"Well, it is best to be scared. You are more likely to change your ways."

The pair walked down Heard Street, the baby in Sophie's arms. Babies were heavier than you thought they were going to be. This one had exhausted herself crying and now was in a numbed state, drooling onto Sophie's t-shirt, occasionally grabbing a snarl in her fist and refusing to let go. Babies were also stronger than you thought they were going to be. "What's this thing's name again?" Sophie asked shifting the child's weight around in her arms.

"Alize," the Dola said.

"Right." Sophie began to explain the controversy of this to the Dola, then decided it would be too exhausting. The being didn't grasp *evil*, or *maternal instinct*. She probably wouldn't get why naming your kid after a cheap wine cooler was tacky.

They approached the house where the boys gathered, their bikes still sprawled across the sidewalk. The scrawl of their voices on the air was tangible as they talked boisterously over each other. Cigarette smoke clouded lazily from the porch. The sound of them all shutting up in unison to watch the girls pass was even worse. Sophie's face turned sunburned at the feel of their quiet eyes upon them.

"Hey, Laurie!" one yelled. The big one leaned over the edge of the porch and made a hand motion around his mouth while his tongue bulged his cheek grotesquely.

"What is that?" the Dola asked.

"It's like—ugh. He wants Laurie to do something to his penis. With her mouth."

"Laurie, Laurie!" another boy yelled, the one whose cigarette had been burned down to the quick. "Cute baby! You want another one?" He locked eyes with Sophie. "You want one, too?" He smiled and rocked his hips at her, while the boys behind him cracked up. One began to bark.

"Is it my destiny," Sophie whispered, "to kill any of them? Or to turn them into frogs?" It thrilled Sophie to know that she could actually *do* this. She ached to do it right then, could feel her *zawolanie* inside her, a snake ready to strike. But the Dola was shaking her head.

"Not now," she said simply. "And, not all of them."

"That is good enough," Sophie said. "That is actually better than I thought." She glared fearlessly at the big one, the one whose bangs she'd touched. "I hope it's that one," she said to the Dola.

"What'd you say, bitch?" he hollered, stretching his arms wide so that his pecs strained against his shiny sports shirt.

Sophie bared her teeth and hissed like a cat. The baby burst into fresh tears.

"You are moving away from your destiny," the Dola said.

"Fucking *freak!*" the boy yelled. "Did you see that? Did you see that shit?" He was smacking his friends in the arm. But he looked spooked. Sophie was happy to note it.

"I thought I was already off-destiny," she said to the Dola. "How can I be moving away from my destiny if I'm already outside it?"

"There are layers and levels." The Dola shrugged. "It was your destiny to move away from your destiny, but you're breaking further away if you continue to engage with the boys."

"I don't know." Sophie was skeptical. "This destiny stuff sounds like a bunch of crap, frankly."

"It is advanced," the Dola said. "Most humans can't understand."

"I'm only part human," Sophie said proudly. "I'm also part Odmieńce. Do you know what that is?"

"Of course. They are the first beings. But, before there was Odmieńce, there was destiny."

"Great, you win."

"I do," the Dola agreed.

.   .   .

OUTSIDE HENNIE'S GROCERY store, the wind felt strange, both still and charged. Sophie paused at the door, gazing down Maple, to the overpass. Haunted, she realized in a rush, the place was haunted by the women who died there. If Sophie tried to, she could almost see them, wispy things that fluttered like tattered curtains under the bridge, sitting on dumpster lids, kicking around the train tracks. She blinked her eyes, but it was another sort of eye inside her that could see them. "Are there ghosts there?" Sophie asked the Dola. "Women?"

The Dola nodded. "They are the Naw I was telling you about. Try not to see them," she advised. "Once you do, you see them everywhere. This world is crawling with Naw."

"It hadn't been their destiny to die?" Sophie asked. "If there are that many people going against destiny, maybe this whole destiny thing isn't real."

"It was their destiny." The Dola nodded. "Naw are also people who died tragically. Most tragic deaths are destined. But they still become Naw." She put her hands on Sophie and turned her away from that sad end of Maple Street. She looked down the other end, ramshackle homes housing people who struggled with their lives. Behind her, Heard Street and the obstacle course of asshole boys Sophie would need to dodge to get home. Then there was the dead-ended dirt road off Heard Street. The heat made the air shimmer, as if passing through it would lead you to another world. It always felt like time was stopped at Hennie's corner, Sophie realized. She pushed open the wooden door, and the bell hanging from a piece of yarn jingled their arrival.

"Alleluia!" Hennie's exclamation was joyful at the sight of Sophie, but her face quickly drooped in confusion at the sight of the baby in her arms. It deepened into a frown as she watched Laurie LeClair shuffle in stiffly behind her. Hennie nodded, her eyes wide. "Okay, okay," she said. "I understand. The destiny of going against destiny very intense." She smacked her hand to her forehead. "Oh, my. So much to do! Come in, everyone, please." A wide table of treats appeared before them, and Hennie clapped her hands happily. "Please." She motioned to Laurie. "You too little."

"Hennie, it's the Dola," Sophie explained.

"So! Dolas don't eat cake?"

"No, we don't," the Dola said flatly. "But thank you."

"That girl you are inside needs food," Hennie said scoldingly. "And this baby, oh, this baby!" Her tone devolved into the mushy voice everyone used to talk to babies. She reached her arms out and Sophie gratefully passed the baby over. The baby liked Hennie, giggling right away, pushing her face flat into the cotton of the woman's dress as if looking at her was too much, and then lifting her face to behold her again, bursting into baby cackles. "You play hide and seek with me?" Hennie cooed. She lifted a bottle from the table and placed it in

Alize's hands. She sucked on it greedily. "So sweet, this," Hennie said proudly, "But much nutrition! My own zagavory recipe."

Hennie's shop showed no sign of the disaster Sophie's zawolanie had caused. Sophie noted the perfect glass jars, the white candle undisturbed on its shelf. The floor was clean of shards or muck or water or debris.

"I clean like that." Hennie snapped her fingers and shrugged. "Sometime is better not to do things long, human way. Sometime magic really is best." She gave Sophie a soft smile, and Sophie knew she'd been forgiven.

"I'm so sorry, Hennie," Sophie said. "You were so nice to me. I don't know why I freaked out—"

"Is much." Hennie nodded with understanding. "Is very much, all of it. You are permitted freaking out. But only so many."

"It's true," the Dola chimed in. "By your destiny, you are allowed a certain number of brief but intense mental breakdowns, but then you are destined to be over it. So don't get too indulgent."

"Thank you," Sophie said, touched. The Dola was tight with her information. It struck Sophie as an act of generosity for her to share a bit.

"I put a spell on my mother," Sophie confessed. "I used the powder in my pouch." She hit the pouch where it swung around her waist, tied to a belt loop by its long strap.

"That is good powder." Hennie nodded. "I mill myself."

"What will happen to her? I don't really know what I did. It was all happening at once—time, and the baby, and the Dola, and my mother was seeing everything, and the Dola was going to jump into her if she called the cops so I made the phone explode—"

"You see what happen when you go against destiny," Hennie said. "Pandemonium."

"I know." In the safe quiet of Hennie's shop, Sophie began to cry.

"Is okay, is okay," Hennie assured her.

"Is this one of my mental breakdowns?" Sophie asked the Dola.

"No." The Dola shook Laurie's head. "I think you're just crying."

"What did you want for happen to your mother? When you do zagavory?"

"That she fall asleep," Sophie said. "I just wanted her to go to sleep so I could come here, and do this, this destiny thing or whatever."

"Is fine," Hennie said, nodding. "Sleeping spell very simple. You go home, you sprinkle more powder, you wake her up. No big whoop. Now, you," she addressed the Dola. "What do we do with you?"

"It's up to you." The Dola shrugged. "You're back on track as far as I can tell, so I'm done. I've got a romance to haunt; someone is supposed to break someone's heart but they feel so bad about it, they're not doing it."

"God!" Sophie blanched. "You're going to go *make* someone break someone's heart? Dola, your work is really awful."

"It's what I do." The Dola sighed. "A lot of great things happen because of broken hearts. It puts a lot of things into motion on this planet. Sometimes I think heartbreak is the dominant active energy.

People start things they wouldn't have started, they go places they wouldn't have gone, they meet people they wouldn't have met. It's actually one of my happier tasks."

"When you go," Hennie asked, "this girl, she be here?"

"I can walk her home, if you like," the Dola offered. "And vacate her there."

"And this baby?"

"She'd come too."

Hennie shook head. "This girl, she sick, yes?"

"She's a drug addict."

"I think you bring her here to me, this destiny, yes?"

The Dola shrugged. "Everything is destiny," she said.

"Argh!" Sophie cried. "You are driving me crazy! If everything is destiny then I can't go *off* my destiny so why did you come to bug me?"

"It was your destiny," the Dola said.

"No quibble over destiny," Hennie said gently.

"I don't expect you to understand," the Dola said, and to Hennie, "You want me to wait until you're done and then vacate and leave the girl here?"

"Yes, please," Hennie said. "Can I get you anything, is there anything you would like to have? Do you eat?"

The Dola looked wistful. "Not food. I'll be home soon enough. I'd like to just rest if that's okay."

A straw-stuffed mattress appeared, fragrant as a clean barn on a spring day in another country in another time. The Dola collapsed on it with a grateful moan. The baby in Hennie's arms was drifting to sleep as well. Hennie placed her on the bed beside her mother. "When I wake up," the Dola said drowsily, "I'll be gone. It'll be Laurie." The being squinted at Sophie. "It was a pleasure working with you."

"Dolas feel pleasure?" Sophie asked.

"Not really," the Dola said. "But isn't that what people say to each other?"

"They're supposed to mean it," Sophie said, annoyed. "Goodbye, Dola."

"We'll see each other again." The Dola said it as if to comfort Sophie, as if Sophie would miss the being. And Sophie realized that, strangely, she sort of would.

"No doubt," Sophie replied, and the Dola closed its eyes, curving into a spoon around the sleeping baby.

"First, a toast." Hennie held in her hand a great goblet sloshing with a deep, blue liquid. Sophie found one in her own hand as well. The liquid smelled like five hundred different smells, like the freshest burst of pure salt in your face while stand-ing on the ocean shore; it smelled like a fat lilac blossom, the blossom a mosaic of tinier blossoms, its smell that faint, pastel smell that made her throat clutch. It smelled like a baby that had just been cleaned, been bathed and shampooed and laid down to sleep, the smell of the baby coming through the top of its head, through the warm hair fuzzing there, the liquid smelled like that. It smelled electric like pavement before a rain, and lush and round like a field of mown grass being heated in the sun. It smelled, thought Sophie, like the sun itself, a bright burst, and it smelled like the moon, cool and lingering, like a rich woman's shoulders, and it smelled earthy in pockets, like the dirt that built the earth, like the heart of a cave. It tasted fruity and blue, like Caribbean waters, a smell that lapped at her, made her mouth water. Sophie wouldn't have imagined that so many of these smells would strike her as good smells, or that together they would smell so magnificent, or that she would ever want to *drink* such a smell, but she did. She clinked her goblet with her aunt and let the potion wash through her mouth. "Wow," she said.

"I bottled this in 1628." Hennie smiled. "It's been getting better and better all these years. I knew the perfect occasion would come to pop it open." She took a gulp and closed her eyes in reverence to the taste. "Congratulations, Sophie. You broke the time zagavory. You have done other zagavorys as well, small ones?"

Sophie nodded. "I made fire, I made some glass break, I made my telephone explode, I made my mother pass out." Sophie felt a swell of shame at the litany. None of it sounded very nice.

"All you do, you must do," Hennie said, noting the droop of her niece's shoulders. "And you do well, and you learn to do better. All is good. Cheers." She hefted her goblet and they clinked and drank again. "Now." She placed her glass on the tabletop, beside heaps of grapes and split-open figs, rounds of cheese, peaches and nectarines with their chunky pits exposed, dishes of fragrant olives, oily bowls brimming with garlic. And the bread, so soft and warm it seemed living. Sophie tore the end from a baguette and a delicious steam wafted across her face. She thought of butter and butter was upon it, melting dreamily.

"Thank you," Sophie said. "For all of this."

"You deserve all, and more," Hennie said. "You deserve magnificent send-off."

The soft bread felt suddenly hard as it passed through Sophie's throat, she looked at Hennie, alarm bursting like fireworks across her face. She swallowed hard, so as not to choke. Hennie's hand shot up, palm out, universal for *stop*.

"You not talk this time. You listen. Drink, eat, listen." Hennie snapped her fingers, and a shuffling of feet filled the room. Or paws. A German Shepherd came out from behind a tall shelf of dimly lit jars. Its eyes were bright and darting, alert to command, ready to obey. Its tongue lolled out the side of its mouth. It seemed both keenly intelligent and wholly dumb. Hennie patted its head, then looped her arm around its neck and gave it a squeeze. "This is Carl."

"My grandfather," Sophie said.

Hennie looked at Sophie critically. "Not sure to let you speak at all. Never know what you say, or do."

"I'll be good," Sophie promised, though she didn't even know what that meant. Not when she'd just sneezed a spell onto her own mother and left her conked out on the kitchen floor.

"You must. Otherwise, I put quiet zagavory on you," Hennie threatened. She looked at Sophie, and looked away. They both knew that Sophie would be able to break out of whatever spell Hennie cast upon her. "Call your grandfather," the woman said.

"Papa?" Sophie called uncertainly. "Carl?"

"Dog name is Carl," Hennie said simply. "Dog respond to Carl."

"Carl!" Sophie called brightly, trying to insert some cheer into the moment. She clapped her hands together briskly. "C'mere, Carl! C'mere!"

The dog's tail wagged, responding to the excitement in Sophie's voice. He loped around the table and came to her, panting. His big damp nose sniffed at her, and she petted the wiry fur of his head awkwardly. The animal quickly grew bored and edged over to the table, dragging a round of cheese to the floor with its teeth. He ate the cheese in large, wet-sounding chomps.

Sophie drained her goblet, and it was instantly refilled, this time with a stronger essence of seaborne, salty breeze.

"You like more ocean?" Hennie asked, and Sophie nodded. "I thought so. Never too late to play with ingredient. Me, I like the lilac best." She took a sip, and sighed. "Sophie. Your story. You are ready?"

"Yes." The Dola twitched in her sleep. *What*, thought Sophie, *does a Dola dream of?*

"Your mother, Kishka think she will be you."

"What do you mean?"

"When your mother baby, Kishka think she is girl with power. Most magic girl. She almost kill your mother, with salt."

"That myth, that thing!" Sophie cried, excited to have a piece of the puzzle.

"Yes," Hennie said. "It is real, and it is tragic. Real that a girl will become powerful girl, and she will crave salt, and salt will make her strong, never hurt her, even as baby. Real, true myth. But, tragic, so many people want baby to be theirs." She sipped her lilac potion. "Especially in this place, Chelsea. And more places like it, where people poor, confused, not knowing how to make better. They think, *Oh, my baby magic, will save me,* and they hurt, even kill baby."

Sophie pointed to Alize, asleep with her fingers in her mouth. "That happened to her," Sophie whispered. "She did that. Laurie, not the Dola."

Hennie nodded. "Very sad, very scary. Happen to your own mother. After that, Kishka not love her." She paused. "Maybe Kishka never love her. Maybe Kishka not able to love."

It made Sophie feel terrible to imagine her mother, a girl, unloved. "Did Kishka love her at least a little?" she asked desperately. "Did she at least pretend to?"

Hennie sighed. "Kishka very cruel. She do zagavory on Andrea just to scare her, make her see things, send her nightmares. She call the Poludnica, make her faint in the summer always. She invite Naw to stay in Andrea's room. If she could put Boginki in bathtub, she would. Very terrible." Hennie petted Carl, sitting beside her, posture still and classic as a statue.

"Andrea grows up, is bad girl. Always in trouble. With the cigarettes, with the alcohol. She run away with boy she love, he like the alcohol, too. Ronald. Is your father."

"Ronald." Sophie turned her mind back to the information. "Ronald who works at the dump?" The man was a clown, a sad clown. "The drunk?"

"Yes, Sophie." Hennie nodded. "Ronald your father. Andrea quite young, too young, she become pregnant. Is very scared. Was very drunk when she allow herself to become pregnant, not thinking well. But, it happen."

Sophie tried to remember what she knew of Ronald. His face, dark from the sun. His eyes half-closed always. She wasn't even sure how tall he was, as he was always stopped with liquor. He was an empty man. He was no one's anything.

"They talk of marrying, yah," Hennie continued. "Kishka say no way never. She lay energy onto Andrea—all her rebellion gone. She sink zagavory on Andrea, kill a bit of spirit. Numb it. You go to dentist? You know they numb you with the needle?"

Sophie nodded.

"Kishka do like that to your mother's spirit. To her heart. She not have the joy to fight anymore—to fight for love, for herself. For Ronald." Hennie's face turned tender. "For you. "

For a moment Sophie felt like Hennie could see all her secret loneliness, and the sensation of being known so deeply was too much. She stuck her head quickly into her goblet and felt the spray of the sea against her face.

"Is there a zagavory on Ronald?" Sophie asked into her mug. The man was clearly under a terrible spell.

"No." Hennie shook her head sadly. "Ronald just alcoholic. Ronald very sad. Kishka keep Andrea away from him, but she keep Ronald close, to watch him. Give him job, pay him good for teenage boy." Hennie laughed a mean laugh. "She pay him same now, grown man. He don't care. She buy him alcohol all the time."

It made Sophie want to cry. She thought of her mother, so cold to Ronald, indifferent. "And the zagavory on my mother, it makes her not care about Ronald?"

"Yes, Sophie. Like I said, part of your mother's heart is gone."

"Forever?" Sophie cried. "Can't I remove the spell?"

Hennie shook her head. "Some spell, the longer they happen, the more damage. For Andrea to be under spell so long, it not reversible. It hurt her spirit permanent."

Sophie thought about her mother—overwhelmed and overworked, neglectful. *Not there*, Sophie realized. Some crucial part of her mother had never been there. She felt a flare of rage at the injustice. "What about you?" Sophie demanded. "With all your good magic, what good is your good magic if you can't undo a spell like that! Why didn't you help her?"

"Oh, I did," Hennie said wearily. "I did what I could. I think I ease it, some. For you and for your mother. Could be worse, my belief. But, yes. Still bad." There were tears sparkling in the corner of Hennie's eyes. They stayed there, shining like diamonds, while Sophie's liquefied and slid down her face. "Once Kishka know your mother having baby, she make her power very strong. She know magic skip generation. She want magic baby for herself."

"She knew I would be magic?" Sophie nervously chugged her oceany drink, then watched the elixir rise back to the top of her glass. *You can't nervously eat magic food,* Sophie thought. *It just keeps replenishing itself.* She put her goblet down and fiddled with a snarl instead.

"Well, love. Yah, Kishka know you come now. But there surprise for Kishka, for everyone. You not alone, love. You have sister. Twin sister. You come together. You come, and only one is magic baby."

Sophie reached for her goblet with a compulsive hand, and buried her nose in the cup of it so she would not have to face Hennie. A *sister.* Her heart was racing. A *twin?* Twins were magic. Even regular, non-Odmieńce humans thought there was something uncanny about twins, something extraordinary. Sophie thought of television shows she'd watched, where one twin would sense another twin's feelings. The thought both charmed and scared Sophie. Had she been feeling her twin's feelings and thinking them her own? How could she be so connected to another and not know it? Was there a hole inside her where her twin had been pulled away? Sophie often felt lonely, but it seemed to her, living in Chelsea, that most everyone did.

"What, what is her name?" Sophie brought her face out of the goblet. "My sister." *I have a sister.*

Hennie shook her head. "She have no name."

"Everyone has a name."

"She have no name."

"Is she dead?" Sophie was suddenly struck by a million possibilities. Where was she? Why was she taken? Was she drowned in the creek by Polish Boginki?

"She alive." Hennie nodded. "When you babies first born, Kishka enraged! She think she know everything, she so mad to not know something like two baby instead of one. Something simple, many witch could see. Kishka not thinking, though. Now, both you baby, which is magic baby? Huh? How does Kishka know?"

"Couldn't we both be magic?" Sophie asked hopefully. A magic sister! To play spells with, to have a forever best friend, a magic one of her own blood.

"No, only one girl magic girl, that certain. Kishka feed you both salt, see how you take it. Very scary moment. I here, in my workshop, I in deep trance, I inside baby you and your baby sister. Like how you go into hearts? Sad to do it to baby, baby so defenseless, feel very wrong. I light so many candle after, I do many spells to be pure, to align with the good. But, I do it for good, Sophie. I have your sister eat the salt. I have her eat so much she almost sicken. I try to take the toxin out of her, is complicated magic, like, like, surgery in operating room. I so scared I kill baby." Hennie shudders with the memory, her tears finally trickling from the corners of her eyes. "And all the while, I in you too. I stop you from eating salt. And you want so much salt! And your little baby will, so strong! No doubt you are the one, Sophia. Even in you as little baby, you like, like bucking bronco!" Hennie laughed, full of affection for her niece. Sophie was stunned. Hennie was inside her heart as a baby. Hennie knew her so well, and in a way Sophie could not understand. She could not understand what she meant to Hennie, and she was humbled by it.

"It work," Hennie said, her voice a mixture of sadness and relief, pride and regret. "It work well. Baby not die. I stay with baby long time. I keep purifying. Kishka believe she the one, Kishka take the baby. She tell Andrea baby wicked, evil, spelled. She tell Kishka baby sick from alcohol in the belly. Kishka tell Andrea all sort of thing but it doesn't matter, Andrea so broken now, Andrea has no fight. She let Kishka take baby. She never even ask what happen."

"She let Kishka take my sister." *My sister, my sister.* Sophie was shocked at how she had so recently had no one, no sister at all, and now an allegiance burned sharply inside her.

"Oh, Sophie. Try not to be mad at Andrea. This—all this so crazy, yah? What would you do? Try to understand Andrea."

"What would I do?" Sophie flared. "I'd fight Kishka! I wouldn't let her take my sister! I'd do anything! Anything I could, I'd make the biggest zagavory—"

"Sophie, Andrea not have magic. Andrea have nothing. Kishka hurt Andrea Andrea's whole life. Andrea, she was defenseless."

It could have been me, Sophie thought. Her mother just as easily would have let Kishka spirit her away, gone. Sophie felt cold at the thought, cold and small. She turned on Hennie.

"You let her?" she accused. "You had a part in this! You let Kishka take my sister!"

Hennie nodded, crying freely now. "Yes I did, child. It is what was meant to happen. One of you would go. One would stay. I did like Boginki, I make switch. So that you stay free. So that you grow powerful to do what you are meant to do."

"What am I meant to do, Hennie?"

"All the sadness upon the humans is like a deep spell from the bad, the source Kishka takes her power from. Over time it grow and grow and grow, you know. Humans not used to be so sad. Everyone on the sad pills or happy pills. Everyone scared inside and no one know why. People fighting, people so mean, not used to be so. You will take it all, child. You will take it all out of everyone. You will make the world so different it will be as if you had recreated it."

"Me?" Sophie was sickened with dread.

"Yes. There will be others, other girls. You will have help."

"Where are they?"

"You will find each other when time is right. You are all growing, all training, all magic. Part human, so you can feel the zagavory of sadness yourself, it is in your heart. But magic, too. Magic you can find it and take it away."

"Hennie," Sophie said. "Where is my sister?"

"She is with Kishka."

Sophie remembered the plants, the wall of plants in the trailer, a fortress of greenery. The tiny hello.

"In Kishka's trailer," Sophie said. "In the plants."

"Yes, child."

"Right there. She's just right there, right here in Chelsea, at the dump, and no one is helping her?"

"Sophia, the plants. They are so poison. Kishka raise her inside a poison garden, now the only air she know is air of poison flowers. Her air would kill anyone. She live inside it since two, three days old. She maybe poison now, herself."

"It wouldn't kill me," Sophie asserted, though she remembered the dizzying affect of being so close to the plants, the way her breath had turned leaden in her lungs. "I could do a zagavory, so could you— we—could take her—"

"Take her where, Sophie? She does not breathe air like we do. She cannot leave the plants. Our clean, healthy air is poison to her. She would die, love. And we would sicken from her closeness. She is a poison flower."

Sophie cried tears of frustration. "There's nothing we can do?" she wailed. "I'm able to save the world and swim with mermaids and talk to pigeons but I can't rescue my own sister?"

"Just because many things are possible does not mean all is possible, Sophie."

"She has no name," Sophie said.

"No one has named her. She is like, little flower creature. Like little animal girl."

"Is she... happy?"

"I do not know."

"Go inside her! See if she's happy!"

Hennie held a hand up in front of her. "No more go inside that child. That a promise I make to the good."

"Well I will, then."

"That fine, Sophie. You do as you will. But I ask you, you must focus on what is your duty here. It is bigger than you, than your sister, than me. You must not be distracted by this, this tragedy."

"Why did Kishka even want her?"

"Kishka for bad. She enjoy humans being sad, being angry. Sad people easy to control, yah? She have power, it feel good to her. She make many people do her will. She want to make sure no good magic girl come and mess it up for her. So she make this flower jail."

"Why is she controlling people, does she take their money?"

"Earthly wealth means nothing, any Odmieńce can make wealth, here—" Without even sounding her zawolanie, Hennie produced a giant bar of gold. She placed it on the table with a *thunk*, smooshing a stray grape.

"Oh my god," Sophie breathed. "That's real? It's not, like, counterfeit?"

"Is real," Hennie said.

"Could I do that? Could I make, like dollars, like a big wad of cash?"

"You do what you like, sure. Is not point of your power. Do as have to do. My point is, Kishka have such things, yah. Have own cave in Poland, full with jewels, with gold, what you say, wads of cash. Such things, who cares? You live so long with such power, you stop to care. But, Kishka care. Gives her much power over humans."

Sophie didn't know what felt more unreal, that her grandmother was a gazillionaire, or that she had the power to make *herself* a gazillionaire. Sophie had often daydreamed that maybe she was really the child of some *other* family, one with money, money like a key to unlock the door to the world. Sophie could go to school, travel, eat delicious food. Now she had the means to such a life, but it didn't seem like such a life was available to her. *When all this is over, I'm going to boarding school,* Sophie decided.

"Does Kishka know?" Sophie asked. "Does she know she has the wrong girl?"

"Yah." Hennie nodded. "Yah, I think she is figuring it out."

"Why is she so stupid?" Sophie asked snarkily. "How come she couldn't figure that out if she's such a big deal?"

"Kishka not stupid," Hennie warned. "Do not endanger yourself to think that. Witches powerful, but imperfect. All beings imperfect, all creatures. Only the good is perfect, perfect good. And the bad, too. The bad is perfect bad." Hennie sighed. "You could be Harvard professor now, child. You be philosopher. I know this all confusing for a small girl."

"I'm not small," Sophie challenged. Though she had felt tiny only moments ago, her anger, this injustice, it had filled her heart. She felt giant with feeling and with purpose.

"No, dear," Hennie agreed. "You not so very small. Your heart very, very big. You must care for it, keep pure. You must eat much salt. You go with Syrena, the mermaid, she live in the salt, she teach you very much."

"So, I guess I'm not going to high school," Sophie said.

"Oh, no, child. You will have to go to high school! Cannot be— what you say—drop-out! You spend summer with Syrena, you come back for school."

"Hennie," Sophie said. "That is the most ridiculous thing I have ever heard."

"No worry now," Hennie brushed the topic away. "You go, do what you must do right now."

"Can I take this?" Sophie's eyes had continued to catch on the gleaming bar of gold on the wooden table. It looked like a candy bar made to *look* like gold, a fat bar of chocolate wrapped in foil. "I want to give it to my mom."

"I think that would be fine." Hennie nodded. Sophie picked up the thing, which weighed as much as she thought it would, and slipped it into her magic pouch. The bag sagged with its heft.

"Okay, then," Sophie said.

Beside them, on the straw mattress, Laurie LeClair twitched in her sleep, coming awake slowly, then quickly. She felt the foreign room around her, the strange, rough bed she slept upon, and sat bolt upright, her eyes flashing like a cornered animal. Carl growled a low growl and moved closer to Hennie. Laurie looked the witch square in the face, her face alive with the absence of the Dola.

"Who the fuck are *you?*" she demanded, and Alize began to cry.

Chapter 19

Outside Hennie's, Sophie was greeted by the pigeons. They swooped down from the wire above, arranging themselves at Sophie's dusty feet. Roy spoke.

"We will escort you to the creek tonight," he told her. "And we will escort you home now, but at a distance, for there are people around." He looked nervously to Livia, who nodded warmly.

"Thank you, Roy," she said. Roy, relieved to be free of his messenger duties, dashed into the sky, his wings aflutter with nervous energy.

"Wait," Sophie said, something clicking. "Is Roy your son?"

Arthur stepped forward, his breast jutting out above his limping feet, bands of heather gray and charcoal ringing his throat like strands of kingly jewels, the whole feathered length of it gleaming green, then fuchsia. "Roy is our son." He stretched his wing around Livia, who relaxed into the curve of it, exulting, for a moment, in being beloved.

"How great," Sophie said, grinning at the little family, their pride and love and close work.

"He hatched a year ago this spring," Livia said.

"Wow," Sophie said. She looked at Livia and Arthur. "How old are you guys?"

"Birds," Arthur corrected. "We're not guys, we're not humans. 'How old are you *birds*?'"

"Okay, so." Sophie waited.

"We're five," Livia said. "Arthur and I are five years old."

How long do pigeons live for? Sophie wanted to ask, but it was a rude question, a cruel question, and one that Sophie wasn't sure she wanted answered.

The birds took off above her, and Sophie shuffled down Heard Street, toward home. It was only three blocks away, and the blocks were not long, but they could feel interminable. Sophie's belly clenched with dread as she spied the familiar heap of dirt bikes laid out across the sidewalk, their nubby black tires spinning, the sun shooting like lightning off their silver spokes. Sophie tried walking past the house with her eyes cast down. Maybe if she ignored them the boys would ignore her or, even better, not see her at all. But this never worked; all it ever did was make her look scared. Sophie knew that she didn't have the luxury of being scared of anything anymore. She couldn't afford to be scared of a bunch of stupid human boys when she was about to hop into the sea with a mermaid.

The taunts were a white noise of kissy squeaks and dog barks and facetious wolf-whistles. Sophie raised her head to face her harassers and found herself looking straight at Ella. Ella, with a cigarette in her hand, sitting on the lap of the smoking boy, who also held a cigarette in his hand. The two of them were encased in a fog of smoke, the boy's arm slung around Ella's middle, anchoring her to the slope of his lap. Ella looked away quickly. *Is she going to pretend she doesn't know me?* The boy she sat upon joined his friend in a braying howl, and Ella winced at how close the sound was to her ear.

Sophie stopped short before the mound of bikes, and took in the scene.

"That's the bitch who hissed at us!" the big one yelled, excited. "You gonna do that again? Hiss again, pussy!" The boys thought that was hilarious. Their guffaws filled the air, sounding to Sophie like donkeys, which made her think of Pinocchio, of so many fairy tales where boys were turned into animals. She could do that to them. She could make them a pack of mules, crammed onto a crumbling porch in Chelsea, looking ashamed, their long ears drooping. But Sophie thought of her grandfather. He didn't even know he was cursed, he was just a dog. Sophie wanted to hurt these boys. And Ella. She wanted to hurt Ella, too.

"Hi, Ella," she said to her friend. *Best friend,* Sophie thought.

"You know that freak?" the big boy asked, surprised.

"Yeah," Ella said blandly. She took a long drag from her cigarette, buying time.

"Yeah, she's my best friend," Sophie blurted possessively. The boys cracked up.

"That your bestie, Ella?" the boy whose lap she sat upon said, in that high, annoying voice certain boys used to imitate girls. He tickled Ella in the stomach, and she bent over, slapping his hands away, laughing.

"Ella." Sophie stared at her intensely.

"What, *Sophie*?" she snapped, suddenly mean. "You happy now, *Sophie*? I know you, okay? Sophie, Sophie, Sophie."

"You *know* me?" Sophie was outraged. "You more than *know* me."

The boys howled at this, warping it into an unintended innuendo.

"Oh, yeah?" a short boy in a low baseball cap asked. "You lez-be-friends?" The others sounded their approval.

"Cut it out!" Ella squealed, sounding like a fake girl too, like an imitation of her own self. "Gross!"

"Ella's my best friend," Sophie announced. "I'm her best friend." She looked deeply at Ella. "Do you even *know* these jerks?" she demanded. "What are you doing?"

"Junior's my boyfriend," she said with a stiff pride.

"Yeah, Junior's her boyfriend, not you, lez-be-friend!" Baseball Hat quipped, and was rewarded with claps and back slaps at his wit. Sophie rolled her eyes. She felt trapped, there on the sidewalk. If she was just her regular self, her *old* self, she'd be scared. Scared

Sophie. But she wasn't regular. She was a witch, a znakharka, she had just restarted time. If it wasn't for her, they would still be frozen, an arrangement of statuary on a porch.

She pushed into the boys, one by one. Their interiors were jungles, emotions growing upward and outward, restless leaves of feeling unfurling, poking Sophie in the face, and making it hard to see. The feeling of them was a wild energy, rising. But sunken beneath the branches of their bravado, Sophie could feel their tenderness. She seized on it like a bat to swing at their heads. The big one's father had left him, had said mean, drunken things on the way out the door, and the boy thought about it when he should be falling asleep. It kept him up, the mad, sad cruelty of it.

Baseball Hat was terrified. He felt so small and lost among the boys, he feared they would turn on him like a pack of dogs, he was powered by an anxious need to keep them laughing, if he kept them laughing they'd keep him around, their laughter was the sound of pure relief washing over him, but the moment it faded the anxiety returned: *make them laugh, do it again, again again again.* Baseball Hat was exhausted.

And Junior, who held Ella on her lap. The raw desire he felt for the girl took Sophie's breath away; he wanted to *eat* her. His heart was shaking with excitement, like he was sliding down the top peak of a roller coaster, like he had won the lotto. He had to work to keep his arm loose around her belly, he wanted to squeeze her, never let her go. And under this, fear. Junior had hardly even kissed a girl. He'd kissed a cousin, felt like a creep because of it, and had kissed no one else, ever. He'd kissed Ella but once, and he feared he did it wrong, that his mouth had moved incorrectly; he wasn't sure what to do with his tongue, and what about his nose, and what about his teeth?

Ella, Sophie could barely look into Ella. It was too painful to feel. As bad as it felt to be betrayed, Sophie discovered, it felt differently awful to betray someone. When you betrayed a person you betrayed yourself as well, and Sophie caught the edges of Ella's guilt and fear and hurt and confusion, anger, frustration, and among it, something bright and exciting, something meant for Junior. Sophie caught only the radiance of these emotions, like the last glow of a sunset, before pulling away from her friend.

Sophie knew what she wanted to do. *Your father hates you,* she would say to the biggest boy. She would repeat the parting words the man drunkenly spat, that the boy was weak, *maricón,* a shame; he would be left with his mother and aunts, with the women, where he belonged. She would say to Baseball Hat, *They're not going to laugh much longer. Your jokes are getting boring. They're not laughing with you, they're laughing at you, idiot.* And Junior, Junior would be the best. *Ella told me you kiss like a fish. Your mouth is disgusting; it's like you're sliming her face. You poke your tongue around like an eel. She hates making out with you, you cousin-kissing creep.* To Ella, her grand finale: *Your boyfriend's lap is filthy.* And a zagavory, the simplest, easiest one, to make Junior's legs swarming with every disgusting thing she could think of, maggots and excrement and rotting swill and creek filth, all of it running down his legs and Ella perched in the middle of it, soiled.

But the problem with feeling a person's feelings is, you feel their feelings. Sophie felt sad about the boy whose father had hurt him. *He was just drunk*, she wanted to say, *he didn't mean it, get some sleep.* She wanted to assure Baseball Hat that everyone liked him, that he was quite funny, that maybe one day he could be a comedian, even. To Junior she would tell the truth, that Ella loved his kisses, replayed them in her mind over and over just to feel a ghost of the warm thrill that flushed her body when their mouths had touched. How it had felt like a conversation, a puzzle or a dance, a wonderful game they both were winning. To have such information and to use it to wound was the deepest betrayal. And to betray anyone was to betray yourself. Sophie felt bad, but she had peeked in on Ella's feelings and found them even worse, a new kind of sadness Sophie was not interested in experiencing. She would stick with her own small sadness, the familiar feeling of being shut out from love. She realized she was crying. The boys realized it too, and Ella, and there was a split second when there was a hush upon the porch, where they wondered, *Did we go too far?* and the better parts of themselves buckled inside, softened at the face of someone vulnerable before them, but the feeling was too hard to hold. It hurt. *Why did it hurt?* Sophie wondered. Baseball Hat was the first to break, unable to hold it, to hear it harmonize with his own sad feelings. He began to fake cry, big, blubbering sounds like the biggest baby in the world, howling and rubbing his eyes, his lower lip stuck out in a parody of a pout, and the others joined in.

"Waaaaaaa, waaaaaaaa, waaaaaaaa!" the biggest boy wailed, burping dramatic hiccups between phony sobs.

"Booo hoooo," Junior sounded. "Boooo hooooooo."

Sophie looked at Ella, her head hung just enough for her hair to curtain her face. She remembered what Hennie had told her, how she didn't even have to speak if she didn't want to, how she could think her thoughts into someone's mind. She looked at Ella, her shoulders hunched around the bad feelings churning her up, and she beamed her thoughts into her friend. *I'm leaving tonight, I'm going far away, I don't know when I'll be back but I will find you again, I love you, you are my best friend, I'm sorry you had to do all of this, I hope you feel better.* And Ella's head shot up as the words entered her, her hair flipped away from her face and Sophie could see that she was crying, too.

Chapter 20

Sophie crept back into her house. She was not looking forward to the spectacle of her own mother on the floor. It was humiliating for Andrea to be knocked down by her very own daughter, and the guilt Sophie felt at her zagavory throbbed alongside a somber respect for her mother, as if the woman had died or something. *And she had,* Sophie thought. Part of her mother had died before she had ever come to know her.

As she walked through the house, Sophie smelled smoke. Cigarette smoke. And something else, the smell of a meal—an actual, cooked meal, the smell of meat and spices, a warm smell. A foreign smell in this house, where dinner was often a bowl of cereal. She headed for the kitchen.

Kishka was smoking a cigarette at the kitchen table, lazily ashing into a dish smeared with grease and gravy and sharp, charred bones. Little bones. Kishka looked at Sophie and smiled, a wide smile that

showed teeth stuck with meat.

"Nana," Sophie said dumbly. "You have something in your teeth."

"Do I?" Kishka smirked. She pushed the bones around her plate and came out with a single gray feather. Like it was a toothpick, she cleaned her teeth with it, the summer sun glinting off of it, shining an iridescent purple and green. A pigeon feather. Sophie looked frantically at the remains in the dish. *Who was it? Who was it?* Her heart sprung with panic and dread. Beside her, there was a whimper, a dry sound scratching at the edges of a throat.

On the floor was Andrea, right where Sophie had left her, though something about her was different, different and wrong. The zagavory had been a simple sleeping spell; Sophie had left her mother supernaturally pranked, but at peace. But Andrea was not peaceful. Her body was tensed in a rigor mortis clench, her fingers curling and uncurling, her legs kicking stiff little kicks, like a dog that dreams of running. Mostly it was Andrea's face that tore Sophie open. Her mother's face, so much like her own—more freckles and more wrinkles, the graffiti of time tagging her skin—her face was a twisted mask, a response to some terror that Sophie could neither see nor imagine.

It was a grotesque joke of a face, something a teenage boy throws over his head on Halloween night as he rushes out into the street to pummel children with eggs. Andrea's jaw was open in a scream that never came, or perhaps had come and gone. It appeared unhinged, and the strain of it had ripped the corners of her mouth; a few drops of blood, like tears, sprinkled her chin. Sophie's heart seized in fear for her and fear of her—what was this crazed statue, where was her mother? Oh god, her eyes, how they bulged, in pain or disbelief. When eyes bulge in shock it's just a tic, a moment, then they go back to normal. Andrea's eyes were frozen that way, horrible and blank, unblinking; how dry they looked, it hurt Sophie to behold. The flutter of an eyelid would be excruciating on an eye that bulged and dry. What had happened to her mother?

A cloud of smoke blew lazily from Kishka's chapped and lipsticked mouth, around Sophie's face, like a bank of clouds tumbling with the weather. It broke her mother's awful grip on her, and Sophie turned away, her own mouth hung nearly as wide. She could taste her grandmother's cigarettes on her tongue. "I didn't do this," Sophie said. "I didn't leave her like this. What's happening to her." It was not a question, but a demand of the old woman.

Kishka took a long, thoughtful drag on her turd-colored cigarette, arching an eyebrow, contemplating how much to share with her granddaughter. A smirk played at the edges of her mouth. So, it was going to be like *this*, then, Sophie fumed, furious. "Nana!" she screamed. Against the windows, a soft, insistent thud. Sophie looked up. Pigeons, flying into the glass, bouncing lightly off the pane. A rain of them, body after body, pillows of gray bouncing off the glass.

"I'm surprised you'd still call me that," the woman said dryly. "After all you've *learned*." The cool sarcasm left Kishka's lips on a bubble of smoke.

"Well, you're still my grandmother," Sophie said awkwardly. "Technically or legally or whatever."

"You have no idea what I am," Kishka said. And then she showed her. Never had Sophie been so forcefully yanked into a person's interior. Kishka grabbed onto Sophie with the paralyzing grip of a headlock and dragged the girl into her dark and fathomless heart. It was the records of a history of human despair and Sophie sensed all of it, feelings the color of the earth, muddy brown and dark, jagged black, streaked with clawed slashes of red. She plummeted through the despair. Despair at loneliness, despair at cruelty, despair at a torture that sees no earthly end. Despair at the death of a great beloved, oh, so many great beloveds, dying and dying and dying and Sophie felt every one, the impossible anguish of *no more not ever gone gone gone forever*. She felt terror at mortality, the terror of an eternity of mortals facing the great empty nothingness. Sophie tumbled as if down a well, each shade of tragedy shifting slightly in its flavor and hue as she plummeted through its next ring. She was in an outer space of agony, the pure agony of the human heart. She felt the sickening need of addictions like a rain of arrows in her gut—hopeless and spiraling, mad with repetition. As she entered what felt to be a sprawling, infinite chamber of war she wondered if perhaps *this* was where her mother lay, for surely Sophie's own face was as contorted, her body as rigid with resistance, saying *no no no no* to the psychic onslaught of impossible cruelty.

Sophie thought she might lose her mind from it. What had Hennie said, that some zagavory changed people forever? Sophie had always known that there were bad things upon the earth, and bad people, but to know it firsthand, to feel the terrible power of mania and cruelty upon you, how it alters your mind, the chemicals in your body, the magical passageways of thought and instinct within the brain, all of it forever damaged by this indescribable *sorrow* that evil brings. Sophie felt people herded together to die, she felt the sorrow of bodies worked to death, she felt the regret of capture, she felt the crush of living while around you everyone died, she felt degradations and humiliations too perverse for her to comprehend, and she felt the aftermath. The broken hearts. Sophie knew now that a broken heart was not the silly red cartoon of a jilted lover. Hearts were real, and they could be crushed. And all of this was alive inside her grandmother, all this raging ache, pulses of pain beating, a galaxy of broken hearts, all of it inside this old woman as she tottered around, acting normal.

As if she were an ant that had crawled up her pant leg at a picnic, Kishka flicked Sophie from her psyche. In an instant she was in the world again, in her kitchen with its soft, worn curtains hanging in the windows, their sweet Dutch print framing the glass against which the birds again and again hurled themselves, their bodies a feathered *thunk* that shook the pane again and again. Sophie didn't understand how everything was still standing. It was if a tornado had ripped through her, leaving everything perfectly perfect, unharmed. Sophie reeled. She reached for the salt shaker and dumped the entirety into her mouth, crunching on the delicious, healing paste of it.

To look at her mother was too much; Andrea still grimaced on the floor, trapped in her own private hell, unreachable, maybe even gone insane. But to look at Kishka was worse—the woman seemed to flicker now, like a television station with bad reception. She saw Kishka, her grandmother, in her lime green polyester pantsuit, bathed in her perpetual haze of cigarette smoke. But she saw other people, too: people or creatures, some elegantly, terrifyingly beautiful, like sexy villians in comic books, sleek and glossy black. She saw a young and haunted girl with holes where her eyes should be, her dress a tattered shroud. She saw what she thought was a dinosaur and realized was a dragon, a scaled and ugly thing with nostrils you could sink your fist into. She saw the terrible bird with its mouth full of worms. Sophie, dizzy already, from all that she'd felt, could not look at her flickering grandmother. And she could not close her eyes, because when she did she was overtaken by a horrible sensation of *falling*, an endless falling, as if some part of her was still trapped in Kishka's consciousness, and the emotions she'd experienced echoing, ricocheting between her brain and her heart.

"How'd you like that, kiddo?" Kishka stubbed her cigarette out in the corner of her dish. Thoughtfully regarding her plate, she lifted a wing unsullied by her ashing and snapped it in half, slurping at the marrow. "So light, so flavorful," she mused, dripping the torn bones back into her ashtray of a plate. "It's a pity we don't eat pigeons anymore in this country. You know, they were always good for food in the old country, in the olden days."

The pigeons beat a tattoo on the window pane.

"What have you done?" Sophie whispered. "What *are* you?"

"You've learned all about what *I* am, girl," Kishka sneered. There was a flash of something, a many-legged insect, and then the strange flickering subsided, and Kishka's form as the grandmotherly owner of the city dump stabilized. She undid the knot that bound her scarf to her throat and used the chiffon to daub pigeon grease from her lipsticked mouth. "You best be learning what *you* are. Part me, that is what you are. Everything you just saw in there, everything, you felt— you are of that, Sophia. It is inside you, too."

"I don't know what foolishness everyone has been filling your head with," Kishka said casually, oblivious to the horror around her. "Sadness is a natural part of life. Tears, pain—it's all as natural as— what? As happiness, as eating and breathing. It is a power for us Odmieńce, and for humans, it has always been their lot. What are you going to do about it? You felt that." Kishka motioned to the place where her heart should be. "What will you do? You will fight that? That is me. It's you as well. Fight that, you fight me, you fight yourself, and for what?" With disgust, Kishka lit another cigarette. The curl of her lip and the curl of the smoke. "Humans, their lives are so brief.

A snap." She snapped her brittle fingers. "So they cry. They feel some pain. It is all over soon enough. Me, I am here forever. You too, if you choose to be, my little Sophia." She pointed the smoldering cherry of her thin cigarette at her granddaughter. "I can show you more than these scabby birds and that wretch in the creek. Don't think I don't know what's going on. I might not be able to get inside you with your fancy shield and all that, but I can get inside everyone else." She gave a snort of triumph. "I'm already there. Inside most everyone. Where their sadness sits, their loneliness. Their cruelty. I'm right there. You can't hide from me, girl."

"What you showed me, what's in you—that's not regular sadness. That's evil."

"Well, it feels that way, all roped together like that." Kishka shrugged lightly. "That was millions of years of the stuff."

"It wasn't just—natural. It was war, it was torture, it—"

"All things that are totally natural for humans," Kishka said almost kindly.

Sophie grabbed the plate away from her grandmother as she went to ash again on the desiccated pigeon. "*Who was this?*" she thundered, shaking it.

"Oh, no one you know," Kishka snapped. "Calm down."

Sophie gazed down at the food congealing in the plate. She thought of all the pigeons she didn't know, the quieter ones who flew in Livia's flock, the others around the city, truly everywhere there were pigeons and now they were all precious to Sophie, every one a messenger, all of them related, somehow, to the ones who had her heart. Tears pricked at the corners of her eyes. She moved the dish to the counter, placing it somberly. There would be a burial, there would have to be. The rhythmic thudding of the birds outside had become a kind of rain against the windows.

"I'll let them in," she said to Kishka. "They will tear you apart."

"Oh, please. You think this is an Alfred Hitchcock movie?"

Sophie crouched down to her mother. She forced herself to behold her, and petted her head gently, hoping that it gave her some sort of comfort, somehow, wherever she was. "Where is she?" she whispered.

"It's a sort of nightmare," Kishka explained. "There's a pack of Naw I let play with her, ever since she was a girl. Violent men who died violently, hundreds of years ago. They're torturing her, basically."

Andrea's foot gave a little twitch, like a rabbit.

"Stop it," Sophie demanded. She felt her zawolanie at the back of her throat.

"Make me," Kishka taunted like a little girl, a schoolyard brat. "You're so big and powerful now, I hear. Why don't you do it yourself?"

It felt like Sophie's heart exploded inside her chest, creating a burst of flame, her zawolanie rocketing up through the core of her self. The sound of her heart was what it was, the power and beauty of her heart, the good vibes of it, its sweetness and its pains, all of it swarmed together into a sound that tore through her body and out her mouth. The sound was so loud Sophie couldn't even hear it. She had become it. Never yet had she allowed it to burst out of her so wild and harsh. It beat its way from her throat, bruising it, a living thing. It poured out of her, rupturing the kitchen window and filling the kitchen with birds. They funneled inside, a black swarm of feathers, and with their beaks and their claws they descended upon Kishka, who rose to greet their force. Her mouth clamped in a smirk around her cigarette, the woman spread her arms in a grand welcome, and her polyester body flickered, showing a gaping darkness inside her that the birds flew into, and were gone. And with a final smile at her granddaughter, Kishka was gone as well. And a rain of dead birds fell upon the kitchen floor.

. . .

ANDREA LAY FACEUP on the scuffed linoleum. She was relaxed. Her strained jaw was soft, her limbs limp. The Naw and their agonies had left, and she remained under her daughter's sleeping spell. Black and gray feathers wafted across the floor, skittering with the breeze that came in through the exploded kitchen windows. A heap of bodies, plump, their wings stretched into tatters and tangles, so many little bird-bones broken.

Sophie wept, sucking at the salt of her tears. She reached out to the terrible pile and stroked the chest of a bird gently, the feathers still warm.

A new clock had begun ticking inside her; she was due at the creek tonight, she would leave. She knew it. Her whole body wrapped around the knowledge with dull acceptance.

Sophie remembered how Hennie had cleaned up the mess of Sophie's graceless zawolanie with a simple magic. Sophie rummaged around in her magic, once a muscle dormant, now full of flex. Not very hard to clean up glass, to replace the windows with clean, shining panes. She barely sounded her zawolanie, allowing it to come out as a whisper, a blessing of sorts. The gritty sparkle and shards vanished. Sophie's kitchen had never seen such clean windows; she had to lay her hands upon the smoothness to know that they were there. She brought her face close and breathed upon the glass, gusting a small fog upon it. She traced a heart into the mist with her finger, then wiped it with her hand. The smudge made the window belong in the run-down apartment. *I made that,* Sophie marveled. What *was* glass? It was sand, wasn't it? Sophie regretted the time spent ignoring nuns when she could have been learning about the earth. Her planet! What was she thinking? Why did she think she wouldn't have to know such things, know everything? Sophie knew nothing. If this glass had once been sand, sand heated and melted and reconfigured into this hard, transparent substance, where had it all happened? How had Sophie done it? She backed away from her miracle. She had to take care of the birds, and her mother.

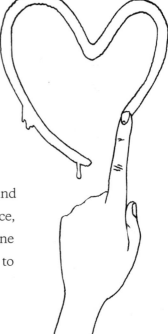

Sophie tenderly folded their outstretched wings, tucking them back into themselves, restoring their grace to them, sprinkling them with her tears as she worked. Sophie thought of fairy tales—were her salty tears magic? Could they bring the pigeons back to life? What about a kiss? She puckered her mouth and brought it down softly on the beaks of her friends. Nothing. Sophie cried harder. What kind of magic was this, then? To be able to build glass from nothing but the dead stayed dead. A stupid magic, a useless, troublesome magic. Sophie tidied the pile of the dead, collecting stray feathers and sticking them into her hair, now more ratted and snarled than ever before. Her face was fevered with fury and regret. She would send the pigeons' bodies back to their flocks. She did not know how to do it, but the birds knew, and they were in the air all around Sophie, guiding her as she dug into her bag and pulled forth a fistful of something silky. She threw it onto the pigeons and let a bubbling caw fly from her mouth, and there was a flash of pure blue fire, and the pigeons all were gone.

Now she had to awaken her mother.

At first Sophie struggled to lift Andrea, to bring her to her bed and break the zagavory there. It would be much nicer, Sophie thought, for her mother to come to in the comfort of her bed, the late afternoon light hazing through the edges of her window shades. Maybe she would just think she had fallen asleep. Maybe Sophie could hide from Andrea the fact that she'd been the victim of her own daughter's sorcery.

But Sophie was a weakling. Her efforts to heave her mother only made her more frightened of hurting the woman. Some part of Andrea's body was always lolling dangerously beyond the girl's grasp—her head, a leg twisting in a strange direction, an arm dragging along the linoleum. Sophie feared for her mother's neck, her spine. She laid her back down, gently. She reached back into the pouch dangling from her hip, heavy with the fat, golden bar. She set it on the kitchen table. It looked so out of place among the empty coffee cups, the coffee-stained unpaid bills, the old salt and pepper shakers, you barely noticed it. Your eyes skipped over the bar, unable to comprehend it. Sophie stuck her hand back in her pouch and felt around for the powder, milled by Hennie with her mortar and pestle. She pulled the dust into her fist.

Sophie let loose her call. She knew she needed one fuller than the mess-cleaning, window-replacing zawolanie, yet one softer than the call that had banished her grandmother, if that's what she had done. As she opened her mouth and sounded her howl she could feel the reins of her consciousness on it, like a harness on a wild beast. It sounded its fierce, feral noise, all the charged grace of a lightning storm but contained, crackling up and out from Sophie's wide mouth as she flung the powder onto her mom. Andrea's eyes opened to the spectacle of her daughter standing above her, her mouth cranked open, the last of her zawolanie curling up and away, gone. Her daughter, the witch.

Andrea scrambled up, unsteady on her feet. She seemed too tall, an ungainly giant. There were her legs bare in their shorts. Her hair was a disaster, her throat raw; she was still ill. She looked down at her daughter, as if for the first time. She could note the outline of the sea glass, a bulge beneath her shirt. "What is that?" she whispered, and Sophie removed it, could feel its warm light shine out toward Andrea. Andrea noted the pouch dangling from her daughter's waist, could see the bulk of things inside it. "And that?"

"That's private," Sophie said.

"I am still your mother," Andrea whispered. "You show me respect. You don't"—she motioned to the floor where she'd just been lying—"you don't *do* things like that to your mother. I don't care how special you are." Andrea spit the word *special* at her, and Sophie felt the echo of all the times Andrea had spat on Sophie's aspirations toward something special—a special outfit, a special school, a special thought. How Andrea had always come down hard on them, the lid of her wounded heart smothering it. *But it couldn't be smothered,* Sophie thought. *And I am so much more special than any of that.*

"I'm leaving," she told her mother. "You probably know. I mean, I know you're not magic"—it felt bad, not resisting the jab, but it was true, also, wasn't it?—"but I think you know everything. Who I am and how I have to go."

Andrea's face contorted with pride and shock and envy. "I *was* magic," she whispered. "Not magic enough for my mother, but I had a bit, I could feel it inside me. You are *my* child. Any magic I had, I held it for you. I gave it to you. It came to you from me. If I have none it is because you have it all, and if you have any, even a spark, it came from me." She did not stop the tears from sliding down her cheeks.

"Why didn't you tell me?" Sophie cried. "If you knew everything, why didn't you tell me?" *Why didn't you love me,* Sophie thought, *I was so special, why didn't you love me better?*

"I was protecting you," Andrea said. "That is what mothers do. I was protecting you."

"You let Nana take my sister. My twin sister."

"Sophie. Yes, yes I did. I didn't know what else to—"

"You could have fought!" Sophie raged. "You could have saved her!"

"Sophie." Andrea placed the heel of her hand to her sweaty brow. "You don't understand. Everything is a mess. It was supposed to be you Nana took. So much, so much—badness will happen now."

"I'm going to stop the badness, Ma. It's my work."

"Sophie, you have no idea what you are getting into. You could have been happy with Nana. Your sister—she's happy."

"You don't know that!"

"She's *fine,* Sophie! She's charmed. She doesn't know better. She loves the flowers. She's simple. She's simple, and happy. Look at you. You're already tormented. What will happen to you, Sophie? You want to spend the rest of your life fighting? You're just a girl!"

Don't listen to her, Sophie told herself. *Listen to Angel, listen to Livia and Arthur, to Hennie and the mermaid.*

"Your grandmother," Andrea said softly. "My mother. What would she have done if I had stopped her? Or if I had told you? Do you know what it's like to have no magic, and her so full of magic?" Andrea demanded. "She is in my head all the time. She's in me, I can feel her. I can hide nothing from her. Imagine it, Sophie. Imagine it."

MICHELLE TEA

Sophie didn't need to. The image of her mother, weakly kicking away the Naw in her nightmare, was seared into her. It felt wrong to know something so intimate about her mother, to know about a suffering she herself did not remember. She wrung her hands at the memory.

Sophie moved toward her mother, wrapping her arms around her waist. "I'm sorry, Ma." She knew she was apologizing for things she had no business apologizing for, for things that were and were not her fault, could not be placed on her shoulders, but there she was, alive and full of magic, about to run away with a mermaid, leaving her mother behind with Kishka. *Maybe,* Sophie thought. Maybe it was best that Kishka had deadened a piece of her mother's heart. Maybe it helped her not feel everything too much.

Andrea stroked Sophie's head, her fingers getting caught in the feathers and snarls. She lifted one with her finger, and watched her daughter's whole head of hair lift slightly, a mass of mats and tangles.

"Let's get you fixed up," Andrea said. "If you are going to do this thing, I can't stop you. But I can at least help you look presentable."

Andrea fetched a bottle of conditioner from the shower and sat her daughter between her legs, and with her nimble fingers unwove the balls of hair from themselves. She handed Sophie the feathers as she plucked them from her head, and Sophie clutched them, bundled in her hands like a bouquet. Andrea ran a comb through the locks, smoothing them, training them to lay flat. She plugged in the hair dryer and ran the warm air over Sophie's head. Through all of it, Sophie melted. She luxuriated in the sensation of her mother's hands

316

working around her scalp, her hair raised in a delicious chill. Even the pulls, the inevitable stings, were okay, because they were followed by such soothing pets. Sophie felt sleepy, and loved. *I feel loved*, she thought. *That doesn't mean you are*, came her next thought, and Sophie decided to stop thinking, just for a moment, and enjoy the feeling of it all, the feeling of there being so much time, this lazy, unhurried grooming, the tickle of her mother's hands and the slow, glowing sensation of love. When Andrea was finished she pulled Sophie to a mirror and Sophie regarded herself, her hair in twin braids that fell across her shoulders, a light fringe of hair wisping across her brow.

"Look," Andrea said, "at how pretty you are."

It was not a word Sophie ever would have used for herself. It was a word she would have batted away as a well-intentioned lie, but seeing herself in the mirror she thought, *Yes. Look how pretty.*

· · ·

ANDREA OPENED THE front door to a sidewalk full of pigeons. The pavement was alive with them, many shades and hues of gray, fat ones and malnourished ones, some standing solid on two good legs, many not, many standing stork-like, balanced on their one healthy claw, others shifting painfully on two twisted nubs, all of them silent, no coos or clucks. Many had traveled from distant cities to be there in Chelsea, at that moment, to escort Sophie to the creek. Andrea's dulled heart spasmed at the sight. She could not resist her revulsion, but there was a begrudging acceptance, too. The pigeons loved her daughter, and had helped her as she, the girl's own mother, had not been able to. *What is wrong with me?* She anguished inside, but she knew. She could feel her own mother sitting upon her heart, pecking away at it like a dark crow.

"I can't come with you," Andrea said. She held her hand over the place her heart hammered. Was it the beating of her heart, or Kishka beating upon her heart? She felt it always, and never knew.

"It's okay, Ma." Sophie stood on her tiptoes to whisper in her mother's ear. "There's a gold brick on the kitchen table, I brought it for you."

Andrea looked at her daughter, her face so raw; Sophie's face was always so raw, her need sitting right on top of it. Her earnestness, this face of her daughter, it had been so hard for Andrea to look at it, to feel someone needing so much from her. *She only needs love,* Andrea thought. Surely it did not have to be so hard. She wrapped her arms around Sophie, kissed her head, which smelled so good, the fruity bright stink of it obscured the heavy, bed-scented sick smell of Andrea's own hair.

"Thank you so much, Sophie," Andrea said. "I love you, baby."

She walked back into her house, her heart a thunder.

Chapter 21

Livia and Arthur stepped out from the mob of birds, holding in their beaks a ribbony garland, braided with tiny treasures—chestnuts, the green pods that fall from trees that Sophie played helicopter with as a kid, acorns, bottle caps, small dusty toys, twigs, strands of shredded plastic. All the things one might find brushed up against the curb on a Chelsea street. All of it braided together, strangely beautiful.

"We all made this for you," said Bix, as Livia's mouth was full and she could not speak. "We braided it together, with our beaks and with our feet, those who have good ones."

Livia and Arthur rose into the air with the wreath firmly in their beaks. The light clatter of the trinkets shaking together was a pleasant clatter.

"Could you bend, please," Bix directed. "At the waist."

Sophie did as she was asked, and the birds swooped beneath her, landing on her back. She enjoyed the scramble of claws, their sweet weight upon her. Her eyes stung with missing the pigeons in advance. Would there be pigeons in Poland? It didn't matter. Even if there were, there would not be Livia and Arthur and Giddy and Roy and Bix.

Livia and Arthur worked their tiny beaks expertly, tying the garland into a messy knot on the back of her neck. They lifted off with a scraping push, and Sophie righted herself.

"Ooooh," the birds hushed.

"Oh it's *very* pretty," Giddy cooed. Sophie rather liked the bustle of it, the unexpected sight of a plastic cowboy translucent from a decade in the sun, or a fragment of a rusted can looking fragile and lacy.

"This is really cool," Sophie said. "I can't believe you all made this for me."

"It was our pleasure," Arthur said. His melodic pigeon voice was taut with the swell of emotion butting up against his bluster. "We really love you, Sophie. We think of you as one of us, ours. Oh, crap—" Arthur's voice cracked, the sound of a violin trill slightly off key. "I said I wasn't going to do this." He pushed his face into Livia's feathers.

"Arthur hasn't cried since Roy hatched," Livia said.

"Well, I'm going to cry!" Sophie said to her audience of birds. Had her mother told her she loved her? Was it the first time Andrea had ever said such a thing? Sophie remembered hearing it as a little girl, but it had been a long time since Andrea had uttered that phrase. "I love you guys," she said to the birds, grateful to feel such an easy love inside her heart, uncontaminated by doubt or fear, no hurt there,

nothing worn away by time's passage, just a sweet and easy love for the birds. "I really love you."

Together they walked toward the creek. Sophie wished she could carry her closest friends upon her body, all of them, but she was too small for so many birds, so she let petite Giddy perch on one shoulder and still-growing Roy, eager and proud, on the other. Livia and Arthur led the dark cloud of pigeons in the sky above them, such a mass they blotted out the setting sun. Sophie watched people leave their houses to point up at the incredible swarm of them. Closer, hovering above Sophie, was Bix.

" 'How do I love thee?' " He said sadly. " 'Let me count the ways.' "

"Bix is in love with you," Giddy said, giggling.

"Giddy!" Roy chastised. "You weren't supposed to tell!"

"*You* weren't supposed to tell," Giddy corrected. "*You* made an oath. I was just eavesdropping."

Bix went on, quoting love poetry. " 'How will I be awake and aware / If the light of the beloved is absent?' " He asked mournfully. "The Muslim poet Rumi."

"Uh-oh," Sophie said.

"He wants to mate for life with you," Giddy said.

"I'm not a bird," Sophie said.

"I've told him that," Roy said. "I'm trying to get him to come to his senses."

. . .

THE SUNSET ON the creek almost made it look pretty. Hot reds and orange and neon pink, it looked like a stream of fire winding through the weedy earth. Sophie was delighted to see Angel and Dr. Chen standing side by side, watching Sophie pick carefully through the ripped chain-link. She wished she could run to them, but the weight of Giddy and Roy on her shoulders plus her massive garland of flora and trash forced her to walk slowly, with purpose. With dignity, even.

"Hi you guys," she said shyly. "I didn't know I would see you."

"I wouldn't miss this, are you kidding?" Angel said. "Hey, bird-brains." She held up her palm to Giddy and Roy, and they smacked their tiny claws upon it. "High five."

"Dr. Chen," Sophie said.

"The birds were so excited," the doctor said. "They had been making this necklace for you at the dovecote, and sending messages to other flocks. It has been quite an exciting time at our place." She paused. "And we all know about the tragedy, also. The birds from a flock in Lynn that your grandmother ate."

Sophie's hand flew to her face in sadness, causing Giddy and Roy to lift off in alarm.

"Oh, Dr. Chen! They will have—a burial? A service?" Sophie did not know the pigeon custom for such things.

"The flock will have their mourning. And their revenge." A wave of energy rippled through Dr. Chen, as if she were shaking something off her. Her perfect, shining bob tossed, glossy with the day's dying light. She put her hands on Sophie, gripping her by the arms and pulling her in for a tiny peck of a kiss on the top of her head. "What an adventure is before you. Try to enjoy yourself, okay? So many girls would *kill* to run away with a mermaid!"

"Well, you haven't seen this mermaid," Sophie said uneasily.

As if on cue, the oil-slicked waters rippled, and Syrena's gnarly head broke the surface. She pulled herself to the bank, stretching her arms onto the trash-strewn earth.

"Really," she spoke. "I look and look for some thing of worth in this creek, I find nothing. Terrible place. I not believe I trapped here so long. We go now, finally, yes?" She wiped at the water streaming down the sides of her face, leaving dark streaks of grime smeared across her skin, like war paint. "Hello, you people."

"Hello!" Dr. Chen said crisply, her excitement making the word sparkle.

"Hiiiiiiiiiii," Angel said, her greeting more of a dazed sigh. Her eyes upon the mermaid were wide. Sophie thought about Ella's declaration that all girls who looked like boys were lesbians. Angel was mesmerized by the creature.

"What they say here—What's matter, got staring problem?" Syrena shot Angel a dirty look, pulling the wild snarl of her hair around her shoulders. "No time for—big party, meet mermaid, oh, so magical, blah blah blah." With her strong, gnarled fingers she tied her impossible hair on the top of her head in a big knot. Fish sprung from it into the creek below, diving for their lives. "I been here for days, all alone, no one bring me party, no one see if I need anything." Syrena pouted. "Too late now. Time to go. Sophie, get in."

Sophie looked at the skanky creek. This was her grand exit, the climax to her braid of pigeon treasure, her skyfull of birds, her mother's gesture of love? She was going to climb into the lousy creek, Dr. Chen and Angel watching. She looked at the adults. Dr. Chen nodded encouragingly. "It's okay, Sophia."

Angel's eyes were still glued to the mermaid, in spite of her spiteful pronouncement. "If I had known you had needed for anything," she said, "I would have brought it for you."

"Get better magic, why don't you. I would have liked a fish to eat without, you know, the chemicals all inside. Maybe a crab, some oysters." She sighed. "Is fine. I am being, what you call, a snob. The

chemicals, they are interesting in their way. Get me drunk, I think."
Syrena smiled. Sophie's heart took on a new beat at the sight. She
hadn't seen the mermaid smile, ever, and it was a beautiful thing, like
shoots of sunlight cutting through water, illuminating beams. The
mermaid's smile changed everything.

Sophie ran to Angel and clutched her hard in a wordless goodbye. "Look inside," Angel said, and Sophie drew herself into Angel,
no wall to keep her out, and she felt the depth of Angel's love and concern, her hope and belief in her. She felt its purity and its strength.
"Remember that, okay?"

"Okay." Sophie nodded. She walked to the edge of the creek. She
would have liked it to be deep enough to just jump in. She was so
scared, scared and thrilled: to just hurl herself into the waters would
have felt right, but the creek was thin, shallow. She crouched to the
dirt awkwardly and looked at Syrena. To see the mermaid in person,
not beneath the waters, not in a dream. Her eyes were wide and circu-
lar as coins, and they flashed with a sort of silver human eyes didn't
have. Her face was smooth and rough at once, she had many wrinkles
in her face yet she was beautiful, somehow young. Something about
her made it seem like you weren't fully seeing her, and so you kept
staring, searching her face.

"What is the wait?" she asked Sophie.

"My sneakers," Sophie said. "Do I keep my sneakers on?"

"For creek, yah. Later, no. Come on, I tell you all you need to know."

"So, I can breathe under there?" Sophie checked.

"Come, come! Now not time to be ascared!" The mermaid's giant tail poked through the creekwater and slapped its surface. There was a gasp of awe from the crowd of birds and humans. Dirty water spattered Sophie's face. "Come now or I pull you in like Boginki."

Sophie stepped down into the creek. The water was warm, but creepily so. Stagnant water being baked by the sun, cooking the trash into a nasty stew. Syrena offered Sophie her hand, the chips of pearly seashell rings glinting in the last, orange light of the sky. "Come with me."

The mermaid dunked beneath the surface so that all Sophie saw of her was stray clumps of hair floating like seaweed. With her free hand Sophie waved goodbye, and disappeared beneath the creek.

. . .

SOPHIE WAS STILL trying to orient herself when Kishka broke through the water. Syrena had led her slowly down the narrow creek, warning her to dodge the various debris she had become intimate with during her stay. A car door, dismembered, wedged on its side in the sludge. A shopping cart, the weave of its metal dark with rust. There were hunks of car battery and chunks of random concrete, there was a refrigerator to maneuver around. Sophie picked her way around it all carefully, mimicking the ginger movements of the mermaid, whose hand she clutched. Syrena's hand, Sophie noted, was not wrinkled with her eternity in the water, the way Sophie's fingertips pruned when she stayed in the bathtub too long. The mermaid's hand was poreless and smooth, and the slick feel of it oddly familiar. What was it? *Dolphins!* Sophie's class had had a field trip to the aquarium in Boston, and Sophie had gotten to touch one of the smiling creatures. The feel of them was like a toy, just the way Syrena's hand felt inside her clutch, like it could slip away, some kind of rubber or plastic, something unalive yet alive, like the dolphins. Sophie's head swam with questions, and as if Syrena could feel them, a current in the water, she turned to her charge.

"We get to deeper water, we talk, yes? I tell you all. For now, you just stay close and walk careful. Soon you will learn to swim like mermaid. You learn to eat mermaid food, you understand water. Now, you are like human baby. You just follow me." Syrena paused and plucked a small dark fish from creek bed. She popped it in her mouth.

"My last chance to eat these!" she spoke around the fish as she chewed, then pulled the bones out intact, and stuck it into her hair like a comb. "Jewelry now, a snack later!" The mermaid hiccupped, and her eyes flashed silver beneath the dark water. "I maybe a little funny from the fish." Sophie couldn't be sure, but it seemed like Syrena was smiling. "Very bad for you, but I begin to like feeling." She giggled a little, giggles that rose toward the surface in little air bubbles. "Very glad we go now! Back to the sea! Back to my home, my river! Oh Neptune, let us get out of here!" She turned to Sophie, and yes, Sophie was sure of it, the mermaid was smiling! "So many people waiting to meet you, Sophia. My sisters, the Ogresses, so many animals! Let us begin."

Sophie felt calmed, momentarily by the mermaid's authority and sudden cheer.

And then her grandmother arrived.

Kishka's presence exploded the waters like a bomb. A wave rose above her. Like a bad magnet Kishka drew the waters toward her, and the waters, as if conscious, responded, came to do her bidding.

"Oh no." Syrena looked back at Sophie, her authority cut with fear, her cheer dead gone. Still disoriented by the little toxic fish but no longer giddy. For a terrible moment Syrena looked her age—ancient, withered, exhausted. In that glance Sophie knew that the mermaid had witnessed many, many things, bad things, and that those things had left some part of her sunken and resigned.

The wave rose like a tornado taking to the sky, carrying within it heaps of mud, layers of sediment embedded with decades of poisons. Toxins dumped and long settled were now stirred into this giant wet cloud arcing above them. Sophie thought of her friends on the creek bank, watching this liquid monster grow. The birds, at least the birds could fly. What about Angel, and Dr. Chen? Kishka's arms were stretched above her, her hands breaking the surface of the creek, and her face was contorted with her awesome power as she summoned the wave. Sophie looked to the mermaid, who shook her head in a sort of stuck panic.

"This will be bad, this will be very bad. She is making *rogue*." Her silver eyes flashed at Sophie, like the rhythmic flash of a lighthouse in the darkness. "Sophie, this is going to hurt."

But the hurt came before the rogue wave crashed upon them. It came when Kishka's hands plunged beneath the surface of the creek, clutching in their bony grip a drowning flutter of pigeon. Its wings churned the water, the struggle creating a tiny whirlpool. Fighting to free itself, all the bird could do was wrap the water around itself like a horrible cloak of drowning. Beneath the dark waters, the orange flash of a bird eye, tiny and desperate.

Sophie lurched toward the animal, the water both catching and stalling her, like in a slow-motion nightmare when you try to run away but you're stuck in molasses. Sophie's arms sunk thickly in the grimy creek bed as she pushed herself to where the bird lay thrashing in Kishka's hands. Too shocked to put up her shield, Sophie felt her grandmother enter her heart, a sickening swirl, like the poison of the dirty creek had slid right into her veins. Sophie realized that this was Kishka's terrain, too; this creek was part of her rotten heart, all the parts of the earth that had been ruined or killed were part of the vast, dark heart of her grandmother.

The rogue was descending. Sophie could feel it as a pressure change inside the water. Her ears did strange things, clogging and snapping; she grew dizzy. She made one last lunge toward the bird but it was too late. The creature was limp in Kishka's hands, which had taken on glamours and become goat hooves, chunky and cloven. Stilled by drowning waters, Sophie could finally see the pigeon—the thin stick of bamboo, the artfully carved whistle. The shine of the wire that held it to Livia's tailfeathers. Livia. Her tiny head turned to the side, her lovely eyes, that orange color, how nicely her eyes had matched the coral of her legs, Sophie realized, how beautiful Livia had been, how much like necklaces were the marking of her throat feathers. Livia was beautiful because Livia was *beautiful*, Sophie thought dumbly, realizing beauty to be a thing deeper than she had ever understood. In a sob she reached out to catch the bird as Kishka left the waters, grabbing for the precious body this thing called *Livia* had brought alive, this precious thing now empty of *Livia* but special for having held her.

And above Sophie's head, crashing through the creek's surface, were hundreds of pigeons, all working to save her, their claws piercing the water, their beaks and wings cutting through the waters and then retreating, because the pigeons were powerless before the creek. They dashed and retreated, dashed and retreated, stirring the water into a froth as above them the rogue wave curled against the sky like a fist and began its terrible topple. Catching Livia in her hands, Sophie flung herself out of the water as far as she could and lifted her arms high. She felt a flock of feathers scramble to meet her, she felt the scrape of claw and wing brush her skin as the birds received Livia. So many of them, Sophie could feel the wind they created, making the surface of the creek choppy with their tender efforts. They gathered their beloved friend, sweet Livia, and then Sophie's hands were empty of her. She couldn't cry, but it seemed that the creek itself was her tears, that she was swimming in her sorrow. When she brought her hands back beneath the waters she saw them scraped, scratched by bird feet, and stuck with a single feather from Livia's plume.

.

Syrena came toward Sophie, wrapping the length of her body around the girl, tightening her fish tail, bracing Sophie's back with its wide fin. She let down her hair and snared the girl within it, and with her hands she cupped Sophie's head, pulling it into her neck. *Like a dolphin,* Sophie thought once more, her face snug in the smooth hollow. Her hands clutching at Livia's wet feather like something magic, and perhaps it was. Sophie understood now that magic was everywhere, and there was no telling what held such power. Surely the feather grown from such a lovely creature as Livia held something in it still, even after her passing.

The feather in her fist, Sophie wrapped herself around the mermaid, clinging to her with all her might. The mermaid spoke into her ear as the water seemed to come apart around them. "Sophie," she said. "Prepare yourself."

The author would like to thank the San Francisco Arts Commission for its generous support of this project. Thanks to Beth Pickens, Ali Liebegott, and the Radar LAB, where much of this book was created, and to Eileen Myles for her feedback and support. Thanks to CEC ArtsLink, whose funding of my work in Poland allowed me to do research, and thanks to my Polish people for their assistance and enthusiasm: Anu Czerwinsx, Agnieszka Furla, Marta Konarzewska, Marta Wasik, and everyone at Ufa and Furia. To Daniel Handler and Marcus Ewert for being early readers and psychic cheerleaders. Much thanks to Lisa Brown for being pathologically kind and helpful. Thanks to Andi Mudd for being fantastic, and to Jason Polan for imagining the story so well, and to everyone at McSweeney's for their hard work and beautiful results. To Elizabeth Wales for her guidance. And to Chelsea, Massachusetts, for continuing to be such a surprising source of inspiration.

About the Author

Michelle Tea is the author of 4 ½ memoirs, 1 ½ novels, and a collection of poetry. Her memoir *Valencia* is an underground classic and is currently being made into a feature film by 21 different filmmakers. She is the founder and executive director of RADAR Productions, a literary non-profit which hosts the monthly RADAR Reading Series (voted Best Literary Series by *SF Bay Guardian* readers), the infamous Sister Spit Literary Performance tours, an annual poetry chapbook contest, and the Radar LAB Writers' Retreat in Akumal, Mexico. She is a former writer of horoscopes and a current reader of tarot cards.

COMING IN 2014
FROM McSWEENEY'S
McMULLENS

A GIRL
IN THE
RIVER
VISTULA

PART TWO IN
MICHELLE TEA'S
CHELSEA TRILOGY